The Last Prejudice

Bill Blodgett

Dear Mark & Sally,
It was great "seeing you this"
weekend. I hope we can "get
together" some time soon!
Bill 2022

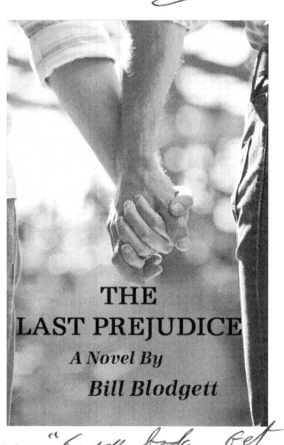

**THE
LAST PREJUDICE**
A Novel By
Bill Blodgett

The song "Everybody Get Together"
was a theme song for this
book. I spoke to Jesse Colin Young's
wife to see if I could use it
on my website while promoting the book.
she said he was flattered but didn't own
The rights to the song any longer,
but still, Everybody should Get Together in these
Troubled Times!.

The Last Prejudice

written by Bill Blodgett

Publisher's Note: This is a work of fiction. All characters, places, businesses, and incidents are from the author's imagination. Any resemblance to actual places, people, or events is purely coincidental. Any trademarks mentioned herein are not authorized by the trademark owners and do not in any way mean the work is sponsored by or associated with the trademark owners. Any trademarks used are specifically in a descriptive capacity.

Author's Note: This book does not represent any single person, either of my family or friends.

Cover by Bill Blodgett

Dedications and Acknowledgments

I'd like to dedicate this book to my wife, Janice, and my daughters, April and Lindsay, who have always encouraged me to keep writing even when I get disillusioned with this whole crazy process.

I'd also like to dedicate this book to my friends and family who have been misunderstood and misjudged because of their sexuality. I dedicate this book to their struggle, in hopes that society continues to mature in a way that recognizes that all people are created equal in every sense of the word, not just race, color, or creed.

I am not a part of any minority, so I can't honestly say that I truly understand the hurt inflicted by prejudice except in a very small way through my experiences as a young man when the hippie movement began. It was then that people like me were profiled by police, and attacked physically and verbally simply because of the length of our hair, our style of dress, and our belief in peace and love for all. Sounds silly now, doesn't it? It's my hope that someday the world will be able to look back at all of the prejudices inflicted upon so many people and think, "Sounds stupid now, doesn't it?"

I also want to thank Anthony Leo, Jr, Bill Goodman, Sharon Gordon, and Emma Jane Homes for sharing their thoughts about certain conflicts and concepts I have tried to convey. I believe their comments have helped make the situations in *The Last Prejudice* credible and true to reality.

Special thanks to Bill Goodman for his clear critique. His advice helped make *The Last Prejudice* a better book.

Thanks to Kate De Groot for copy-editing assistance

Bill Blodgett

Chapter One

July 18, 1 PM

The coffee cup shattered when it hit the white porcelain kitchen sink. She had just poured it and added a splash of half and half before she looked out the kitchen window to check on him. *Oh well, if it makes him happy. Some things I just can't change*, she thought. Then he slumped over the steering wheel of the lawn mower. Fortunately the mower's safety mechanism shut the mower down when he fell to the side and onto the newly mowed lawn.

The shattering of the cup had barely quieted before she was through the screen door and at his side. She pulled him the rest of the way off the mower and felt for a pulse. She found it. *Thank God.*

"Ed! Ed, can you hear me? Don't do this to me, you stubborn old fart. I told you not to be mowing this damn lawn."

His eyes opened when she cradled his head in her lap, and he mumbled something. She leaned closer. "… broken…" was all she heard.

"Broken? Ed, what's broken?"

When he didn't respond, she pulled back to look at him. His eyes went vacant and then slowly rolled back and closed.

"Help me, please… Anyone, please help me!"

She shrieked until someone heard her. Within minutes Beth, her neighbor, was at her side. "Jan, my God, what's happened?"

"Call 911."

*****

The Rock

When I became aware of my surroundings I didn't find myself on the mower or even in my own yard any longer. Instead, I found myself sitting on a large flat rock overlooking a lush green pasture at a sunrise equal to none I had ever seen. I took in a long, deep breath and exhaled slowly. That long release seemed to drain me of the anxiety I was so accustomed to. It was a relief to let it all go, and I wondered why I hadn't been able to do it until now.

My knees were pulled in close to me, and I hugged them tightly. As I enjoyed the scene before me, I felt the tight grip I had on them loosen. It was a breathtaking view. Again I wondered why I hadn't taken time to enjoy a sunrise like this. Was I always just too damn busy taking care of "things"?

When she slipped in next to me, it seemed as natural as if she had never been away. I unwrapped my arms from around my knees and stretched my legs out past the edge of the stone and leaned back on the palms of my hands. She slid her hand over mine and pulled me close, also as natural as if it had always been that way. "Where've you been?" I asked quietly, still a little confused.

"Oh, I've been here watching you finally trying to relax and enjoy the sunrise. I so wanted you to relax, even when we were dating and married." She pulled me in even more tightly and rested her head on my shoulder.

"Beautiful, isn't it?" she whispered ever so quietly, and it seemed to soothe my soul and quiet my questions.

I looked at her and enjoyed her beauty as the pink light bathed her face. "Not half as beautiful as you, Gracie O'Malley or should I say Grace Connor? I'm so happy we got married." I recoiled for a moment as a confused feeling raced across my heart, but it was gone as quickly as it came. I exhaled another releasing sigh and looked into her eyes. Her comforting smile quieted my nerves. I was comforted because it had been so difficult to smile when we were last together.

I had wanted to gaze into those eyes again for years. It was like life had again sprung into my heart. Why had cancer taken her from me before we could even begin our life together?

Grace must have sensed my feelings. She stroked the side of my face gently. "Are you okay?"

"Yeah, I'm fine. Just remembering… that's all," I told her.

She nodded with an all-knowing smile. "Good. I'm happy you're okay." She leaned into me.

"Seems like yesterday. Doesn't it?" I asked her.

"It was for me," she responded contentedly. Her smile convinced me she hadn't suffered the stretch of time like I had, and I was thankful for that.

"This doesn't make sense. Really, none of this does, but it doesn't seem to matter," I said. I still wasn't sure what was going on, but for some reason it didn't seem too important right now. I was with her and that's all I had really wanted for so many years now. Not that I don't love Jan and the beautiful family we've made together over the past fifty years, but Grace was my first love, and I never really settled up in my heart with losing her.

"Ah, now you're getting it," she comforted me.

"No. Not really. Sometimes I still wonder why it had to be. But tell me—why am I here with you now?"

*****

Hospital Room 321
4:21 PM

Slap, slap, slap. His red-and-green dino sneakers made the slapping noise, warning her of his fast approach. His footsteps echoed off the sterile white walls, violating the overwhelming quiet of the hospital. Tiny lights in the heels of the sneaks flashed on and off with each step.

"Gramma!" His little voice echoed even louder than his footfalls. She looked up to see the sandy-haired little scamp running toward her at full speed. She braced herself for what she knew would come next. She barely had time to hold out her arms to catch him before he landed on her lap.

"My Lord, Bennie, shhh. This is a hospital and you've got to be quiet." Even with the state of stress she was in, she couldn't hide her smile as she roughed up his hair. He wrapped his arms around her neck. "I'm so glad you're here," Jan said. She hugged him long and hard, maybe comforting herself more than him. She needed to be held. She needed comforting. Her heart was aching but she needed to be strong for herself and the family. She didn't let him go until he tried to squirm loose.

"Okay, okay, Gramma, I'll be quiet. I got new sneaks. They

flash!" he said with a proud smile, pointing to his sneakers just as the flashing in the heels stopped.

She smiled and roughed up his hair again. "I see. They're cool!"

"Gramma, nobody says cool anymore. They're awesome," he corrected her with a missing-front-tooth grin.

"I stand corrected," she said in an official-sounding voice. "They're awesome."

"Benjamin Tomás Perez," a voice said from the direction of the door. "You've got to slow down. You might hurt Gramma Jan someday jumping on her like that." She looked at Jan softly. "Sorry, Mom."

Jan looked up to see Kim. She lived close by, and Jan figured she must have just scooped Bennie up when she got the call. Kim gave Bennie a sharp look as she walked closer. "You can't run away from me, Benjamin. You might get lost." Her voice was stern but the sparkle in her eyes betrayed her.

"Okay, Mommy, I'll 'member," Bennie said as he scrambled down from Jan's lap and went to his mother.

"Good. Thank you, Bennie," she said. "I can't ever stay mad at him, Mom. Every day he looks more and more like Dad, and seeing the spitting image of Dad sitting on your lap just cracks me up." She patted his head but didn't pick him up. "How is Dad?" she asked, looking directly into her mother's eyes. Jan looked away and her smile disappeared instantly.

"No change, Kimmy." She slumped against the back of her chair and turned her attention to the hospital bed next to her. She watched as Ed's chest rose and fell silently. If it weren't for the incessant beeping from the monitor above the bed and the IV tubes in his arm, she could have believed he was just sleeping.

Kim dug some paper and crayons out of her shoulder bag and slid a straight-backed chair up to the oversize sill of a window that looked out over the parking lot. She arranged the paper and crayons on the sill and called, "Bennie, come on over here and draw us a picture."

Bennie eagerly took his place on the chair. "What should I draw, Mommy?"

"I don't know, Bennie. What do you think you should draw?"

4

"I dunno. But Uncle Steve always told me to draw what's in my heart. Do you know what that means, Mommy?"

Kim glanced at Jan. "Well, I think so, but what do you think it means?"

"Uncle Steve said it means to draw how I feel."

"And how do you feel right now, sweetie?"

"I think I feel a little sad because you cried after you got off the phone with Gramma Jan."

Kim looked helplessly at her mother, and Jan sent her a reassuring smile. "Well, your mommy isn't crying anymore, so you don't have to be sad anymore. Why don't you draw something that would make Papa happy?"

Bennie took a long moment to answer. In a different time and place, she would have busted out laughing at his deep look of concentration. She watched as he pondered what he could draw that would make Papa happy. Today, just watching him helped lighten the hurt she was feeling deep in her heart.

"I think I'm going to draw me and Papa fishing on the big rock. We always have a good time there. I think that's what's in my heart. I think Papa would like that too. Why is he here?"

He said it so innocently, it prompted Jan to give him a light but fairly honest answer. "He got sick and fell off the mower, and now he's here sleeping until he gets better."

"Will it be a long time?" He asked with the innocence only a child could have.

"We hope not. Why don't you get started on your picture so it will be finished when he wakes up?"

Jan turned to Kim as Bennie got started with his drawing. "Steve's been giving him art lessons?"

"Not really, but he has worked with him a couple of times on school projects when he's been over for a visit. Bennie said he had fun with him."

"Good then. I guess all isn't lost." She looked at Ed and took his hand.

*****

The Rock

5

I found myself sitting on that huge rock again, but the setting had changed. There were trees now close by and the sound of running water. Everything was vaguely familiar. There in all that peace and quiet, you'd think I'd just be able to relax, but the tranquility that had captured me was gone. Something was nagging at me, but I just couldn't get to it. It was a strange, repeating electronic tone. I'd heard it before many times, but where? It wouldn't go away, and I couldn't find where it was coming from.

I looked out over the pasture and listened to the wind rustling the branches of a nearby tree. A little bird jumped from branch to branch. That was the sound—or at least that's what the tone had transitioned to. It wasn't electronic at all. I remembered it now.

I sat back, resting against the rock while the beautiful tweets of a songbird filled the air. I'd heard it countless times but never taken the time to determine what bird was actually capable of such a sweet melody. Why hadn't I taken that time?

"It's a song thrush," she said.

I looked over and Grace was next to me again. "Song thrush?" I repeated.

"Yes. That song you've heard countless times but never taken the time to investigate. It's made by the song thrush."

Again, I was a little confused. I almost had to laugh at myself. Being confused seemed to be the only constant thing in this little adventure I was on.

"That's what you were asking yourself, wasn't it?" she said with that understanding look she had so often given me when I was doubting myself or having some other internal dilemma.

Her question was smooth and simple. I realized I had been thinking about the bird's song and what creature could make such a sweet melody. "How did you know?"

"From where I am, I know a lot of things, and I like bird songs too."

"No, I mean how did you know that's what I was thinking about?"

"I just knew, that's all."

"Why didn't I know that?"

"What? The bird's name?" she said with a coy smile.

"No, that you liked bird songs."

"I guess the subject never came up. You can't know everything about everyone in your life instantly."

"Yes, but we spent every minute together. I should have known that."

"Well, sometimes things just aren't discussed for any number of reasons. Maybe there just wasn't enough time."

"Yes, but I should know everything about the people I love, and they should know everything about me and how I feel about them."

"Sometimes you can't. Sometimes people just don't share their true feelings or just assume others know how they feel. It happens whether we intend to be closed up or not."

I knew what she was telling me. I had lived a closed life, especially when we got married. I was just a kid. I never put my true feelings out there, fearing… well… fearing someone would think I was silly. Maybe they'd even laugh. Later, I did learn to share with Jan, and I found great comfort in it. But there just hadn't been enough time with Grace to get to that point.

It all happened so quickly. First we met, and we were filled with all that excitement of dating. Then we were married, and we were filled with all that excitement of setting up a house. Busy making plans for the future.

And then the cancer. It seemed like it almost dared me to let my feelings out but I knew that it'd be the end of me if I did.

*****

Hospital Room 321

Without turning toward Kim, Jan began to speak. "The doctor said the next twelve to twenty-four hours will be crucial to his recovery. The MRI showed a clot in the right side—" she paused briefly and corrected herself "—the right hemisphere of his brain. He said they gave him the medicine in time to bust it up, but there's no telling how much damage has been done or even if he'll ever wake up." She stopped speaking, closed her eyes, and sat silently. The lump in her throat ached, but she'd be damned if she'd let it beat her down. No, not to her and not this day. She clenched her jaw and her lips trembled, but still she didn't cry.

Kim stepped close to her and squatted just enough to give her a hug. "Mom, it's okay. He'll pull through. He's a tough one, and a stroke isn't about to hold him down. Besides, it may just be one of those ministrokes and there won't be any lasting effects at all."

It was then the dam broke that held back Jan's tears. Try as she might, she just couldn't be stoic now. Not when the love of her life lay helplessly before her. There was nothing she could do about it. It made her mad and scared the hell out of her, knowing what she had to say next.

"It's not a ministroke, Kim. Dr. Mehra already told me that. If it had been a TIA, he'd be awake already. That's what I prayed for too. A TIA would be the least of all evils at this point, but the doctor was very clear and made sure I understood it. No, it's not a mini. This is the real thing, Kimmy. What am I going to do if he doesn't wake up? He's all I've got." Jan choked out the words between her heartbroken sobs.

"Mom, you've got us: me, Bennie, Mike, Peter, Laura, and Steve. We're always here for you. You know that." She looked into her mother's eyes and then gently pushed her hair back. She paid special attention to the few gray strands that clung to Jan's tear-drenched cheeks. "Shh," Kim said. "It'll be okay."

Jan felt Kim pull her close and let herself be comforted in the arms of the woman who used to be her own baby girl. She remembered when she'd had to do the same for Kim after a hard day. It was nice to be on the other side of that gift.

"I know you'll always be here for me, Kim… you all will. But you've got your own lives now, and rightfully so. Your father and I are on our own, and that's okay. We finally have time to enjoy our life together. Not that we didn't love having a house full of kids and the constant activity and all of the craziness that came along with it. It's just that that time has passed for us. It was the best part of our lives, but now there's just the two of us. It's kind of like when we were first married. Now, suddenly, we realize we're still lovers, not just best friends and parents. We're free to enjoy a late breakfast together, to watch our gardens grow, or just to sit and enjoy each

8

other's company, even if that means reading a book or watching TV. We were actually looking forward to growing old together. Now it's all gone. I feel so helpless."

Jan broke away from Kim's arms and buried her face in her hands. "Damn. I can't let this beat me. He needs me thinking straight."

"Mom, look at me," Kim insisted sternly. When Jan didn't respond, she repeated, "Mom, look at me. Mom…" Kim's voice turned from stern to demanding, and finally Jan lifted her head and looked at her daughter. "Never, ever say that again. We are not going to lose him. Daddy will pull through. I'm sure of it. And they do say that sometimes people in comas are aware of their surroundings and can hear. Do you want Daddy to hear you talking like that? I know I don't. You've got to be brave—not only for him, but for the rest of the family. They'll be looking to you for strength and direction regardless of how you feel. You're still the mother."

Jan straightened a bit in the chair. "You're right, of course, this is no time for a pity party. I'm back in mom mode, but you sound more like the mom than I do."

"I learned from the best," Kim said.

Jan stood and hugged her daughter. They embraced for a while, both in need of strength and support.

"Oh my God," Mike said as he walked through the doorway. "He isn't… I mean, he didn't…" He didn't finish either sentence but instead rushed toward Kim and Jan.

"Daddy!" Bennie yelled out and ran to Mike, scattering the crayons and paper on the floor. Mike scooped him up with one arm without missing a step.

"Mike, what's wrong? What are you talking about?" Kim asked as he wrapped a strong arm around her waist.

Mike looked down at Ed and sighed. "When I came in, I saw you two hugging and I was afraid Ed had… well, you know."

"Here now, there won't be any more talk like that. They say people can still hear when they're in a coma," Jan said. She smiled and winked at Kim and continued, "He's fine, Mike. From now on, he's just resting. No sick talk, okay?"

She moved to Ed's bedside and stroked his head. "It's okay, Ed. Just rest for now and wake up when you're ready. We'll be right

9

here." She continued to stroke his head a few more times and then returned to Kim and Mike.

"I'm with you on that one. No more sick talk," Mike agreed. "Why don't we all sit down and relax a bit? What do you say?" He motioned toward the chair that Jan had been sitting in. Jan sat while he pulled an extra chair from across the room for Kim to sit in. He sat on the windowsill, balancing Bennie on his knee.

"Have you heard from Peter yet?" Mike said without directing the question to anyone in particular.

"Uncle Peter is coming?" Bennie said with excitement. "I can't wait to see him. Is Aunt Laura coming and Sarah too? Are we going to have a party?" Bennie scrambled down his father's leg and crawled up on Jan's lap.

Jan smiled a distant smile and said, "From the mouths of babes." She glanced over to Kim. Jan pulled Bennie in tight and cradled him almost as if he were a baby. She kissed the top of his head and continued to speak directly to him. "Well, I don't know about a party, but yes, Uncle Peter is coming. I'm sure he can't wait to see you too."

She smiled gently at the boy and then answered Mike's question more directly. "I left him a message to come home as soon as possible. I said that his father was sick and in the hospital, but I didn't leave any details. While we were en route to the hospital, he left a message on my cell phone that he was boarding a plane at O'Hare Airport and would arrive five p.m. our time. When I called him back, I just got his voice mail again, so he's probably still in the air. I'm sure he'll be here soon. He doesn't really know anything more than Dad is sick." Jan shrugged her shoulders helplessly. "I didn't know what else to say."

"I think you said the right thing," Mike consoled her. "There is no need to get him all upset when we really don't have any answers."

"What about Uncle Steve? Is he coming too?" Bennie blurted out.

Jan stole a quick glance at Mike and Kim before answering. "Of course Uncle Steve is coming, and he's bringing his friend Greg with him. They're driving up right now." She ruffled Bennie's hair again.

Kim drew in a deep breath before she spoke. "When will they be here? We haven't even met Greg yet. Why now? Why drive?" Her frustration was evident.

"They'll be here by nine or so. He said it's a two-hour drive to JFK and the next plane here didn't leave until nine, so they'd be here just as quickly if they drove, maybe even quicker. I didn't ask about why Greg was coming. Maybe he has a client up here. You know your brother. He likes to help Greg with his medical equipment sales business whenever he can."

"Whatever. It's aggravating, that's all. It's his business too. Isn't it?"

"I suppose so, but Greg is the one who actually started it," Jan said.

"Nevertheless, I don't see the need for introductions right now," Kim insisted.

"Just let it go, honey. You know your brother," Mike said in a condescending tone.

"Yes. I know my brother." Kim shot him a "don't go there" look. "And I don't really care about all that other crap. Steve and I are fine about all that and you know it. It's just that there's so much to deal with right at this moment. That's all."

Mike's tone softened. "You're right. I'm sorry. We have bigger fish to fry right now than to let that start another family ruckus."

"Fish?" Bennie chirped.

Mike sighed, while Kim and Jan shot each other little grins. "Not now, Ben. I'll explain later, okay, buddy?" Mike moaned.

"Okay," Bennie relented.

"Right now Ed is the only thing we should concern ourselves with, and as far as we're concerned, Ed is just taking a nap. Right?" Jan reminded them.

"A nap?" Bennie crinkled up his forehead in confusion. "Papa's been sleeping since me and Mommy got here. How long does he have to take a nap for, anyway?"

"That, we don't know, sweetie. I guess he'll wake up when he's good and ready," Jan said. "We'll just have to be patient for now. I've learned over the years to be patient with your papa. It's always seemed to work before."

11

"What do you mean, Mom?" Mike asked.

"Well, it took him a long time to get over Grace, so I had to be patient. I knew it wouldn't be wise to rush him."

"You mean he was moping around thinking about Grace after you got married?"

"No, not at all. But sometimes there'd be a song on the radio or something else that'd stop him in his tracks, and I knew it reminded him of her. I never asked or even cared for that matter. He had a right to miss her. As time went on, those flashback moments came less often. I knew he loved me with all his heart, and those few moments he spent remembering her didn't take anything away from us." She smiled and shook her head. Her eyes looked off as she conjured up an old memory.

She was pulled back into the present when she heard a gentle knock at the door.

"Hello, Jan," Dr. Mehra said as he entered the room. "How's he doing?"

"That's what we're waiting for you to tell us, Karash," Jan responded. She and Ed had long ago dropped the formality of addressing him as Dr. Mehra. They had been seeing him for so long that he seemed like part of the family. He was the last of his kind, the last of the true family doctors, and Jan knew she could trust him without question.

"Well, right now, you know as much as I do. By the look of the monitor, his pulse rate and blood pressure seem to be good, and there's no fever. I wish I could give you more of a definitive answer, but I can't. If it were a broken leg, I could say twelve weeks in a cast. If it were an infection, I could give him antibiotics for ten days and he'd be fine. But strokes aren't like that. Basically he's on his own." He gave her a helpless smile and sideways apologetic nod of his head.

"That's where you're wrong, Karash. He's not on his own; we're here with him." With a gentle sweep of her hand, Jan gestured toward her family.

Dr. Mehra acknowledged them all with an approving smile. "You're right. If there's any medicine that can help Ed, it's you and the family being here with him. I firmly believe that at some level he's aware of you all being here, and your presence can only help him to recover. The unit is very quiet tonight. I'll make sure you all can stay as long as you want and are made comfortable."

"Thank you," Jan said as she got up and handed Bennie to Kim. She walked over to Dr. Mehra, and they turned toward Ed.

At that moment Ed's eyelids began to tremble. They could see his eyes moving under them. Jan covered her mouth with both hands and her eyes widened. "What's happening, Karash?"

The rest of the family came nearer and watched as Dr. Mehra examined Ed. He listened to Ed's breathing and then his heartbeat with a stethoscope.

"His pulse rate is up a bit, as well as his respiration, but other than that I don't see anything wrong except the obvious. Probably just an autonomic nerve response. Or maybe he's dreaming, considering the rapid eye movement. His condition doesn't seem to be worsening."

"Thank you…"

Chapter Two
The Rock

I was back atop the rock after what seemed to be some sort of absence. I didn't think I had gone anywhere, but still I felt there was a moment when I became aware of being back. Where I had been between when I had last spoken to her and now, I had no idea. Had I fallen asleep and was just now waking up?

She touched my hand again, bringing me back into our conversation. I looked at her and she was as beautiful as the day we married. I knew I was an old man of seventy-two, but what the hell. Nothing made sense here anyway.

"I remember being tired. You were just so damn sick from the chemo, you could hardly keep your head up, but you were brave for me. I spent endless days at the hospital, first hoping for a miracle and then just waiting for the… I had nothing left in me to care about except for you."

"I know those were hard times, but we had each other and you were like a rock for me." Grace's comforting tone stilled my anxiety. "It made me love you even more. It's okay. Everything is fine now."

"Why is everything fine?" I was confused by what she said. Things weren't okay. Everything was snarled and balled up in my mind. My thoughts and memories across the decades were enmeshed and inseparable, and I couldn't straighten them out.

"Because everything is okay with me in the here and now and then, and you've done well over the years," Grace reassured me.

"Have I?"

*****

Hospital Room 321

5 *PM*

"He seems to have quieted down now," Jan said as she turned from the bed to face Kim, Mike, and Bennie.

"That's good. Why don't we go down to the cafeteria and get something to eat?" Kim asked.

"Maybe in a little while, Kimmy. I'm not hungry right now. Let's just sit down and talk a bit and keep your father company."

Just then a nurse came through the door, pushing a recliner. "Hi, I'm Angie, the charge nurse. I grabbed this out of pediatrics. They're slow tonight too, so they won't miss it."

"Thank you, Angie," Jan said as she walked closer and took her hand. "I don't know what we'd do without the care and help from the nursing staff here."

"You're welcome. Dr. Mehra said you and some of the family would be staying late or maybe overnight. We have more of these if you need them. Okay?"

"Yes, and thank you again. We'll try to keep everything down to a dull roar," Jan said with a smile. Angie replied with a nod and a little approving wink, and left the room. "Now, Mike, why don't you and Bennie sit right down in that nice big chair. You've been sitting on the windowsill since you got here."

"No, really. You take it. I'm fine," Mike protested.

"I insist. Please take the chair and take that little fifty-pound sack of potatoes with you." She shot a quick glance toward Kim. Bennie had taken up residence on Kim's lap for the last half hour. They all smiled, except Bennie.

"What potatoes, Gramma?" He scrunched up his eyebrows in confusion.

"Nothing, Bennie. Just a little joke, that's all." And with that Mike lifted Bennie off of Kim's lap.

"Did you bring the Leap Frog, Kim?" Mike asked.

"Yes, it's in the bag. I brought along all of the accessories for you two boys to play with," she said with a playful smile. She knew Bennie wouldn't be able to sit still for any length of time, but she also knew her husband. He'd do anything for the family, and spending time with Bennie on the Leap Frog wasn't new to him.

"Thanks, love. I don't know what I would have done without

15

a couple of hours of Leap Frog today," he said playfully. It was friendly sarcasm. He let out a small chuckle, grabbed Bennie and the Leap Frog, and sat down in the chair.

"I'll tell you what," Jan suggested. "Why don't we all bring our chairs closer to Ed so that he's included?"

"Great idea, Mom," Kim said. They all pulled their chairs close to Ed's bed in a sort of horseshoe fashion. Ed completed the circle.

"Holy cow," Kim said. "It almost feels like one of the circles we made sitting around all those campfires Dad would build on our camping trips. All we need now is a fire here in the middle."

"Can we have marshmallows?" Bennie asked innocently.

That was it. The room's mood changed from one of dread and fear to a festive family gathering as they all laughed out loud. Even Bennie giggled in his childish voice, though it was apparent he didn't really know what he was laughing at.

When they finally stopped laughing, Kim cleared her throat and spoke up. "My God, do you know how many campfires Dad's made over all the years?" She shook her head in wistful memory. They were her favorite family memories: camping and singing and telling stories around a blazing campfire.

"Hundreds, I'm sure," Jan said. "I think that was my favorite part about camping. Just sitting around the fire, roasting marshmallows and making s'mores. There's nothing better. We'd all take turns with the story stick and tell some really whopping tales."

Mike interrupted, "Story stick? What is a story stick?"

"A story stick is just any stick you pick up and pass around the circle. When you have it, it is your turn to tell a story. Ed would tell ghost stories and Kim would always tell stories about school and things they did and I would tell stories about Kimmy, Steve, and Peter when they were younger. Things they did and didn't remember, but they loved to hear about themselves. I liked to pass down the family history."

"Well, I liked the trip to Yellowstone," Kim injected. "That was awesome—"

"Ahh, now I see who Bennie gets his expressions from. Oh, sorry to interrupt you, dear. Go ahead with the awesome trip tale," Jan said with a wink.

16

"As I was saying," Kim said in with mock insult, "the Yellowstone trip was cool. Better, Mom?" Jan nodded. "We saw Old Faithful and bears. We rode horses and then a stagecoach. Every day we did something new and exciting, and then in the evening… The campfire, on the open range with a vista of open sky and stars, was like nothing I'd ever seen before. It was fantastic. I'll never forget it."

She reached over and patted Ed's hand. "Mike, I hope we can bring Bennie there someday." Mike nodded his agreement.

"I agree. It was something I'll cherish forever," Jan said. She put her hand on top of Kim's, and they looked deeply into each other's eyes.

Mike took Kim's other hand and brought it over to Bennie's. Then with his free hand, he held Jan's. The circle was complete.

*****

The Rock

I thought for what seemed a lifetime about what Grace told me. Maybe I did do well in some things, like the trip to Yellowstone. It was a destination I'd always wanted to share with my kids. My parents had a coffee table book of the park, filled with glossy pictures, and I would leaf through it time after time, staring at the pictures of nature at its grandest. Mom and Dad teased me that I was going to wear out the pictures just by looking at them.

I always wanted to go there, but Mom and Dad couldn't afford it. Dad was just a working stiff at the mill, and we never really had much. We never starved nor did we lack any of the important things in life, but we couldn't travel across country like that. We did take trips to local places for fishing adventures, camping out, and amusement parks. Mom was always a good sport. I don't think she really cared much for camping, but she never let on.

Once when I was looking at the book, Dad said that maybe when I had my own family, I'd be well off enough to take them there. That was the day I decided to make that dream my reality.

*****

Hospital Room *321*
6 PM

"We love you, Ed. Thank you for giving us that special trip to Yellowstone. We're waiting right here for you to finish this little trip you're on." Jan touched his hand, wondering if she would ever really get him back. She tried to be strong for the family.

They fell into a comfortable silence. After some time, Kim said, "Mom, the mountains, fun parks, and camping were all great times, but why didn't we ever go to the ocean for vacation? It's something we always wanted, but Dad said that the salty air gave him headaches. I've never heard of that before or since from anyone. Is that right?" They all sat back in their chairs, waiting for a reply.

Not now. I can't answer that question now. Of all the bad times to ask. Your father can't jump in and help me with the answer. I don't know what to tell you, my dear. I begged him to share that part of his life with his children now that they were all grown up, but he was too private. He felt he had to keep up that manly exterior and not allow his children to see him as a mere mortal man. Too much of a superhero to show them his frailties and failures or even how much he really loved them. No, I won't be the one to tell them. Lie. I should lie. Just a half truth. That's not really lying, is it? I should still protect his wishes, no matter how misguided they are. No. If something is to happen here and now, they should know their father as the man he is. How full of feelings he really is. Maybe that'll help them understand how deeply he loves each of them too. No matter what they ever did, he gave them his love unconditionally. Oh, they'd get a lecture, but he would never forsake them. They should know just how deep his feelings go. No. I think it's okay now. I think maybe now is the time for them to really known the man they call Father.

She stole a look at Bennie, who was sitting on Mike's lap, to make sure he was fully engrossed in the Leap Frog. "Your father never really enjoyed the seashore after Grace died. When I spoke to him about it, he said he thought it would stir up old memories that he

18

didn't want to relive again. Then he'd leave the room. So I left it at that. I knew he had to keep that part of himself buried so deep that it'd never hurt him again. I could understand because when I thought about losing him and everything we had, I pushed that thought so far away that I'd never think it again. But here we are."

She leaned into the bed and took his hand. She felt the spirit drain from her but she refused to cry, for Ed's sake… for the kids… but more importantly for her sake. She knew if she let the darkness take control of her, she'd never recover.

*****

The Rock

I suppose it was selfish of me to keep the kids away from the ocean just because of my own personal feelings and memories, but I just couldn't do it. I was afraid. I was afraid of what seeing the ocean again might do to me. I was afraid it'd spoil everybody's trip, not just mine.

That's how all this anxiety took hold of me and never really left. During those last few days, I thought my heart would explode. That feeling never really went away. Whenever I got that foreboding feeling, like when the kids were sick or out later than curfew, it'd come rushing back over me with a vengeance. It had its own life that I couldn't control. It was a part of me that I wished I could lose. Instead I lost Grace and kept that as my internal scar that I knew would never go away.

Gracie and I started our life together there, near the sea. We had such high hopes and even grander dreams. There'd be a white house facing the open ocean, with a white picket fence and a swing set in the back. I thought if I took the kids and Jan to other places, it would make up for their loss of never seeing the glory of the ocean, but maybe not.

"You'll never really know, I guess."

I was startled by the voice that was now beside me. The voice brought me from a state of pure thought back atop the big rock I had been sitting on earlier. Its cold, hard surface didn't seem as comforting as it had when I was visiting with Gracie.

19

It was a man's voice. Not Grace's, like I'd become accustomed to, popping in and out of this—for lack of a better term—dream.

"Dad?" It could have been comical, the way people were popping in and out of this new-found existence of mine, if it weren't for the fact that this was my father—the young father I had grown up with. "What... How? Grace was just with me," I stammered out.

He chuckled the way he did when I'd get confused about something as a kid. "Was she?"

"Yes. We were talking about the old days before she..." I stopped mid-sentence. I still couldn't say it. I had been so heartbroken at the time, I couldn't bring myself to say she was dead. Later, I just never said it. I didn't need to relive that horrible episode of my life over again.

But there, I just said it—at least in my thoughts. I said she was dead and nothing happened. The earth didn't come crumbling down. Or was that what was happening? Was that why I was here? Was I learning to accept death?

"Hello. Earth to Eddie. Come in, Eddie." His voice brought me out of my trance-like state. Whenever I was daydreaming, he'd say it, and I'd spring back to the here and now.

"Huh?"

"You were saying..." he asked me.

"Yeah. I was talking with Grace and about how she died." There, I'd said it again. "And wondering if I stole something from my kids by not taking them to the seashore because of the horrible memories I have, and if they hate me because of it."

*****

Hospital Room 321

"Dad told me that he and Gracie loved it there, and he just couldn't go back without it bringing back sad memories," Jan explained to the closed circle around Ed's hospital bed. "Grace suffered for months in a hospital near the ocean. They'd look out toward the open sea, making plans for what they knew would probably never happen but always hoped and prayed for. He never wanted to burden you children with any of that gushy stuff. You know him, tough as nails! And that's all I know."

Jan crossed her legs and folded her arms across her chest. She hoped her body language would cut Kim off from asking more questions. But it wasn't to be.

"Why, Mom? We knew he was married before and we knew she died, so why wouldn't he talk about it?"

Mike said, "It's a guy thing, Kim. Some of us aren't very good at showing our emotions."

"Oh really, Mr. Macho Miguel Tomás Perez?" Kim teased him. "I guess they're right when they say some girls marry their fathers. You never share either!"

His eyes shifted away from hers. "Well, we men do show it in other ways," he said, sounding a little hurt.

She grabbed his hand. "Honey, you're doing just fine. I'm just teasing you. I could never doubt your devotion to me. Don't worry. You show it in many ways, and I love you for it."

Chapter Three

Hospital Room 321
6:30 *PM*

"Gramma, he's doing it again," Bennie said as he hopped off his father's lap and raced to the edge of Ed's bed.

Jan stood up and joined Bennie at Ed's bedside. Kim and Mike weren't far behind.

"Why's he doing that, Gramma?"

"Well, Dr. Mehra said that it might be some sort of an uncontrolled movement or Papa could be dreaming."

"I think he's dreaming. Don't you, Gramma?" Bennie said in his usual innocent way.

"Yes, I do, Bennie. Yes, I do." She smiled and almost hoped she could be so sure, because if she weren't, she would have this terrible, foreboding feeling gnawing at her all of the time. "I hope they're pleasant dreams." She put her arm around Bennie's shoulders and pulled him close. They stood watching Ed dream.

"What do you think he's dreaming about, Gramma?"

"I don't know. He seems to be smiling. Maybe he's thinking of the day you were born."

"Why? Was it funny the day I was born?"

"No, not funny at all, just a very happy one." She wrapped her arm around his shoulder and brought him close.

"I'm here. How is he? What's happened?" asked a man's voice from the doorway. He was tall and lean and dressed in an obviously expensive three-piece suit. He didn't resemble Ed like Bennie and Kim did, but he had a striking resemblance to Jan. They all turned.

"Thank God you're here. Slow down, Peter," Jan cautioned. "He's stable right now, so take a breath."

He took a deep breath, crossed the room to Jan, and hugged

her. "Okay. Let's have it," he said as he pulled back from her.

"Like I said, he's stable right now. But the bad news is that he's had a stroke and he's in a coma."

Peter froze for a minute when he heard the word *stroke*. "Will he pull through?" he asked.

Jan saw a look cross his face that she had rarely seen before: uncertainty. Even as a kid, he had been self-assured and confident. He always took control of any situation. She surmised that was why he had been so successful as a stockbroker. He kept those downturns and bull markets in perspective and always seemed to make the right decision.

Now he couldn't take control. She knew he felt helpless. It was in God's hands, and that was a concept he had never really embraced. He was a black or white sort of kid. He had never allowed the gray area to cloud his judgment, and he was no different now. Yes or no, buy or sell, good or evil.

"We're not sure," Jan explained. "The next twelve to twenty-four hours will be crucial to his recovery." She took his hand.

He just looked at her with the sad little boy eyes she remembered and hugged her hard again. His stockbroker persona was lost to the seriousness of the moment. "I'm here, Mom. Don't worry. Everything will be all right. We'll have the best doctors on this case by morning. I'll see to that."

"Peter, we do have a good doctor and he's already asked for a consult by a specialist. We're doing all that can be done."

"Okay, but if you don't mind, I'll make some inquiries in the morning."

Jan smiled at him sweetly and put her hand on his shoulder. "Okay, honey, we'll see what the morning light brings. But for now this is a 'no doom or gloom' area." She gave a grand, sweeping gesture around the room. "Only happy thoughts and good memories."

He looked past her to Ed's bed, catching first Mike's eye and then Kim's. He forced a smile, "Okay. Got it."

"Granny!" was the next thing everyone heard. They turned toward the door to see Laura and little Sarah standing there.

"Is it okay to come in?" Laura seemed hesitant to come into the room before she got the all clear sign.

"Yeah, sure. Dad's just sleeping," Peter said with an expression that said he was underplaying the diagnosis for Sarah's sake.

"No," Bennie said. "Dr. Mehra said he's in a coma and dreaming." His announcement was clear and concise in his best "little man" manner. His arms were crossed against his chest and his expression was very serious.

"That too," Peter said with a grin toward his younger sister. "Bennie's grown. Now, tell me what's happened?"

"Why don't you take your coat off and stay for a while?" Jan teased him. "We have plenty of time for the story. Let's just settle in and let me get a good look at the three of you. It's been too long." She held out her hands to Sarah, who came running to her.

"Granny, I missed you," Sarah said as soon as she fell into the warmth of her grandmother's hug.

"I missed you too, sweetie," Jan said. "Now let me see you. My, you've grown four inches!"

"About that, Mom. I'm sorry—"

Jan cut him off. "Remember our 'no doom or gloom' rule, Peter."

"Okay. And you're right; let's get settled in a bit before we get down to business— I mean, before you have to tell me the whole story. I'm sure you're sick of telling it by now anyway."

Jan just shrugged. "I'll ask the nurses for a few more chairs. Be right back." Before she left, she took time to give Laura a hug and squatted down to face Sarah again. "You get prettier every day, Sarah. Now where's that smile?" She tickled the child's ribs, which, of course, brought about the biggest smile she had seen in a while. "Ah, there it is. Perfect," Jan said. She gave Sarah a little hug and left the room to speak to Angie about getting the chairs. She was thankful Dr. Mehra had already given the nurse a head's up about that.

When she returned, Peter was standing at the foot of the bed alongside Kim. They were speaking softly while looking at Ed. "Mike," Jan said, "can you help the nurses bring in the chairs?"

"Sure thing," he said and left the room.

Jan walked over to Peter and hooked her arm around his. "He seems very peaceful most of the time. Not so much now though," she said. The three of them watched Ed going through one of his rapid eye movement episodes. "Dr. Mehra believes the eye movements are autonomic responses, or maybe Dad is dreaming. Either way, the doctor believes that people in comas may be able to hear and understand what those around them are saying. They might even feel the positive or negative energy that's going on in the room. That's why we have the 'no doom or gloom' rule in place." She pulled Peter a little closer and rested her head against his shoulder as they both looked down on Ed.

"Jesus, I feel rotten, Mom."

"Why?" She knew why he felt rotten, but she also knew that Peter needed to say what he was about to say, regardless of the rule.

"I should have been here more for him… for you both. He probably thinks I don't care," he confessed.

"I understand what you're saying, hon, but he wasn't mad at you. He understood the stressful job you have and that it's sometimes hard for you to get away. It's okay, Peter. I happen to know he knows that you love him. But enough of that for now. The 'no doom or gloom' rule is now officially back in force." She squeezed his hand.

"Here we go," Mike said as he rolled a chair in. "There's a couple more, Peter, want to help?"

"You got it," Peter said, and they both left the room. When they returned with the chairs, they arranged them near Ed's bedside. They all sat. Jan sat next to the bed, closest to Ed.

"Now where were we?" Jan asked.

"Before we get started with whatever you're doing, is anyone hungry?"

"Famished. Starving," were just a couple of the responses.

"All right then," Peter said. "Laura, why don't you take the kids to that Chuck E. Cheese we saw coming in and bring us all back a couple of pizzas? The kids can play while you wait. Does that sound okay with everyone?"

"Sounds great," Kim said. "The kids could use the break. Here, let me help out." She reached for her pocketbook.

That's my "take charge" boy at his best. Jan smiled to herself. *They're all so different.*

"Won't hear of it, sis. I got it. Just use the card, hon," Peter said. She nodded and left with Sarah and Bennie in tow. "Now, you were saying, Mom?"

"I was saying pull your chair up closer to our campfire circle and tell us what your favorite family adventure was."

Peter gave her a confused look that gave way to understanding. "Ah, so we're circling up the wagons, as Dad used to say after the campfire got going. Maybe I have a story or two still left in me." He reached over and took Kim's hand. She took Mike's, and Mike took Jan's.

"I seem to remember a time we were camping next to the big rock. And after a most successful day at catching those little brook trout, we all sat around our campfire much like we are now." He surveyed those sitting around the imaginary campfire until he got to Mike. "Except then Steve was sitting on a rock just about where Mike is now." They all looked at him as Peter fell silent.

"What?" Mike questioned the not-so-merry campers.

"Oh, nothing in particular. It's just that that little getaway was one of our best vacations," Peter said. "We had none of the creature comforts we later grew to enjoy with our big trailer. Just a couple of tents and a few sleeping bags. But God, it was fun. I think that's when we decided to expand our horizons and get the big RV."

"Maybe we should have just left everything as it was. Maybe we shouldn't have tried to stretch our horizons." The sullen tone of Kim's voice filled the heavy air.

Jan looked at Kim curiously as Mike slipped his hand away from Jan's. He turned to Kim and covered her hand with his. "Why?" he said after their eyes touched.

It took a while before she spoke. "You know the saying, 'you can never go home again'?"

"Sure."

"Well, it just seemed like we were always chasing that vacation. Don't get me wrong. We had tons of fun on our trips. But nothing seemed to equal that one time we spent along that quiet brook next to the big rock."

Jan broke in, "I never knew you felt that way. I always thought you loved our vacations."

"I did, Mom. Maybe it was my age or something else, but that one was always special for me."

26

"I understand what you're saying," Peter added. "Maybe we should have left well enough alone."

"Nonsense," Jan said. "We had plenty of good times. So that was Kim's favorite. What was your favorite family trip, Peter?"

"Oh, I think I've said enough. Let Kim go first."

"No way. Mom asked you, mister," Kim shot back.

"Come on, sis. I'm still suffering from jet lag here. You go and then I'll be next, I promise. Okay?"

"Oh, all right, you coward," Kim said with a wink. "You know I can't ever refuse your begging. Just like when we were kids. I'll go first then. I think my second favorite, and it was a close second, was the camping trip to Big Moose River in upstate New York."

Jan shot Peter a quick glance and saw him draw in a deep breath. He held it for a while and then exhaled. An icy cold stare claimed his expression.

Peter settled back in his chair. "Well, out with it, kid. Let's hear all about your second-favorite vacation."

Jan gave Peter an approving wink as Kim began her favorite tale.

"Well, let's see. The trip seemed to take forever, and the more we drove, the more I knew I'd just hate this vacation. In my mind, a million miles out in the 'Forever Wild' mountains of New York State was not the place for a fifteen-year-old girl to spend a vacation. And then we got there, Merry Moose Park." Kim said each word with a dreamy gleam in her eyes.

Jan laughed out loud. "Oh, Kim, it was not called the Merry Moose Park. Come on now, be serious."

"It was! It was called Merry Moose Park. We always called it the Merry Moose Park. It was Merry Moose, wasn't it, Peter?"

Peter smiled and then laughed a bit. "Yes, we did always call it Merry Moose Park. I'm sorry to burst your bubble, kid, but it was me who dubbed it Merry Moose Park. The real name was Ted and Mary's Moose River RV Park, and, well, I guess it just caught on with Mom and Dad. Sorry, did your bubble really burst?"

Kim sat still for a moment with a pensive look on her face, her arms folded across her chest. Finally she spoke up. "I don't care what you want to call it. To me, it is and always will be Merry

Moose Park. It's my story and I'll call it what I want. So if you want to hear the rest of the story, clam up. Anyway, I've already told Bennie that we were going to the Merry Moose Park, and we will!"

"Maybe I should have Laura make you a Merry Moose sign and you can hang it from the RV when you get there. She's very crafty and can do anything she puts her mind to, you know," Peter needled her playfully.

"Why not you? You and Dad used to make lots of neat things," Kim said.

"Let's not go there," Peter said in a suddenly distant tone. "I'm not sure he noticed. He was always too busy trying to get Steve interested in the woodworking. Maybe we should just let Dad make the sign when he wakes up."

Jan glanced over to Peter and watched him take in a slow, deep breath as he closed his eyes. His face turned controlled and expressionless.

Finally Kim broke the silence. "Am I missing something here?"

Jan and Peter exchanged looks. Jan spoke up. "No, everything is fine. It was a wonderful trip. Let's hear your story."

"Okay, but somebody's going to make a sign."

"Absolutely, sis, but first the story."

"Okay, then. We finally got there and set up camp. After dinner, we decided to explore a little, so off we went toward the heart of the park, Little Moose Lodge." She stopped suddenly and looked around the circle, pausing a brief second on each of them. "Now, nobody is going to try to tell me that it wasn't Little Moose Lodge, because I remember it as clearly as yesterday." She sat quietly, challenging anyone to make a comment.

"You got it, sis. No argument from me." Peter raised both hands in surrender.

"Okay, good. So all of us went into the store, and they had everything you can imagine in this little room-size store. Everything from fishing worms to bacon and eggs to soda, all in the same cooler. I remembered Dad whispering to us, 'I think we'll find another place to buy our eggs. Okay, kids?'

"Oh my God, you're right, Kimmy. I had forgotten all about the worms with the eggs." Peter laughed, and Jan saw the sparkle return to his eyes. "I thought Steve was going to barf at the thought." Pete and Kim laughed while Jan only smiled.

There you go, Peter. See? It wasn't all a catastrophe. Jan gave him an encouraging smile, but he put the wall back up as quickly as it had come down. "I remember that too, Kim," Jan said. "We all had a good laugh over that. Keep going. I want to hear more about our stay at Merry Moose Park."

"So then we passed an awesome pool." Kim smiled at Jan. "And then on to the rec room. Remember? It was a big, open building with arcade games, pool tables, pinball machines, foosball tables, and a jukebox that was blasting the music out. Oh, and did I mention *boys*? I remember Peter asking Dad if we could play a few games, and Dad gave him a five-dollar bill for us all to play. I almost dropped. All Dad said was, 'No later than nine o'clock and no excuses, got it?' And Peter just said, 'Yes, sir. I'll keep an eye on them.' And he grabbed the bill."

Jan saw Pete's eyes go distant for a moment. They came back to life quickly. "Yeah, I couldn't believe it. Dad had never shelled out five bucks for video games before. Then he and Mom went walking off toward the trailer…" He paused for a minute as if a picture was forming in his mind. "… holding hands! Mom, you and Dad *never* held hands."

Jan blushed and didn't let her eyes make contact with any of theirs. Finally she said, "You're not the only ones who needed a vacation, you know." She looked up with a foolish grin.

Peter held up his hand to signal her to stop, "Mom, I think that's way past our need to know." He cringed a little for effect.

"So you don't want to know the sordid details?" Jan teased.

"Eeew," Kim squeaked, throwing her hands over her ears. She began stomping her feet while repeating, "La la la la, I can't hear you. I can't hear you. La la la…"

Mike closed his eyes, lowered his head, and rubbed his forehead as if he had a headache. Peter grinned at all three of them. Finally Jan sat back in her chair and Kim uncovered her ears.

"Go on with your story, Kim, or I'll go on with mine," Jan threatened.

"All right, no argument there. So off you two went. We all spent the better part of two hours hanging out and playing video

29

games. Oh God, *Donkey Kong* and *Mario Brothers* were the new games out, and there was a line to play them. Remember the sign, Pete?"

"Sure do, 'One game per person at a time. Let others have a turn too.' So we had to take turns all night. Oh God, that was so much fun. Yeah, Kimmy, we did have some fun on that trip. I kind of forgot about that." He smiled softly for a moment but shot Jan a hard glance.

"I think he's dreaming again, Mom," Kim said, nodding toward Ed.

Jan looked over to Ed. She laid her hand over his and patted it and then rubbed it with a soothing caress. She continued to repeat the process, the way someone would soothe an upset child. "It's okay, Ed. We're all here," she comforted him.

Chapter Four

The Rock

"Don't you think you'd know if you'd ruined their lives by not taking them to the ocean?" Dad asked me in the straightforward manner I remembered so well. "Wouldn't that be a silly assumption?"

"I suppose so," I said gazing out across the field. I could hear the flow of the stream lapping against the bottom of the rock. It was rhythmic and relaxing and it made me want to sleep, maybe to escape the self-examination that Grace and my father were leading me through. At the moment it seemed pleasant and almost reassuring but I had a gut feeling the road would get bumpy and difficult to travel. "I did try my best to give them good times, but they weren't always perfect."

"Son, life isn't supposed to be fulfilled by expensive or luxurious vacations. It's made of the things we do as family, whether on those vacations or just being around the house together."

"I know. I tried hard to do that… like you taught us, Dad. But I could have done better. I made mistakes."

With my confession, my father leaned back, his hands flat against the rock, and waited patiently.

*****
Hospital Room 321
7:30 *PM*

"Well," Kim said. "We all hung out for a couple of hours, but not really Pete. In about two seconds he was talking up this blonde, and in fifteen he was on his way out of the rec hall with her, hand in hand. He stopped by and told Steve to make sure he and I were here at eight forty-five and not a minute later. Of course, Steve agreed,

31

and you, Mr. Peter 'Don Juan' Connor, took off."

"Peter!" Jan scolded. "You didn't stay with your brother and sister? Now this is news to me."

"He did for a little while," Kim said. "But when he met up with blondie, he delegated my babysitting to Steve and we had a good time. We met a lot of kids and had some laughs. But as time went on, Steve and I kind of… well… gravitated toward a guy and a girl we met, so we decided to take a walk to the beach. Steve even checked his watch so we wouldn't be late getting back. I mean, why not? Peter had ditched us soon enough. Not that he was trying to be irresponsible. That was just his way," She emphasized the word *irresponsible*, tying it to a teasing smile. "I'm sure he just figured we'd be okay, and we were. We were old enough to take care of ourselves." She glanced again at Peter.

He wasn't smiling. "Well, I did," Peter defended himself. "I mean, Steve was sixteen and you were fifteen. I figured, what trouble could you get into? It was a safe place."

Kim continued, "So we left. Steve was with this Nancy girl, who seemed to be taken by his boyish good looks. And I…" She looked at Mike. "Well, I forgot his name."

"Let me get this straight," Mike said. "You remember Pete's girl's name, but the guy's name you were about to suck face with just happens to have slipped your mind? It's okay, hon. I understand summer flings. Had a few myself."

Kim sat back, looking at him.

"Stories for another time, my dear," he said. "Just go ahead with your second-favorite vacation story."

She shook her head and let her hair fly a bit. "So *Randy* and I and Steve and Nancy left the rec hall to walk toward the beach." She paused. "There, happy now, Mr. Ya Gotta Know It All?"

Mike smiled. "Yep. Go on."

"Okay, so time got away from us, and before we knew it, it was quarter after nine. We were scared out of our wits when Mr. Subtle over there," she nodded toward Peter, "started screaming at Steve about if he knew how to tell time."

"What did you expect?" Pete's tone wasn't so playful. "I got back to the rec hall at quarter to nine and you two were nowhere to be found. It took me half an hour to find you, and when I did, the four of you were sucking faces like a couple of schoolkids. Which in retrospect doesn't make any sense to me at all. I mean, he's freakin' gay and…"

"Peter—" Jan was cut off before she could finish.

"So true, brother dearest."

Peter spun around to see Steve and Greg standing in the doorway.

"Wasn't making much sense to me either," Steve continued. "For years I went on trying to be 'normal' for Mom, Dad, you, Kimmy and the rest of the freakin' world, all the while feeling like a creep because I knew I wasn't the definition of normal. A feeling you haven't helped me much get over."

Peter stood. So did Jan. "Boys! This is not the time *or* the place!"

"You're right, Mom. Sorry," Steve said.

"Me too, Mom. Steve, I'm sorry." Peter sounded sincere. "Things have been a little tense today and I'm on edge."

Peter walked to his brother and reached out to shake his hand. Of course, Steve accepted the manly gesture of contrition and they shook hands.

Jan said, "Come on, you two. Let's sit down and relax. We're here for Dad's sake. Let's just drop the… whatever it is we're doing." They both agreed with a silent nod.

Steve walked toward his mother. "We'll take care of introductions later, but first, how's he doing, Mom?"

*****
The Rock

When I became aware again, it was gray and cloudy. I was still on that big rock but all alone. Lightning bolts streaked across the sky from one mountain and then back again, like the god Zeus was throwing bolts of lightning at the distant mountains only to have them thrust right back at him by an equally powerful force. It was a strange sight, accompanied by a continuous, low rumble of thunder.

I had no visitors. I was looking forward to seeing them again if it was to be. Those visits were more than just calming, and I wasn't feeling too calm. Dad's and Gracie's visits were healing for

33

my heart and soul. I supposed, by their absence, that I needed time to reflect on what we had spoken about.

"So did they hate you for not taking them to see the ocean?" Dad had asked me. I knew I had done my best. He was right.

As a father and husband, I had felt I needed to walk a thin line, one that was both of the heart and of reason and logic. I felt my decisions and actions could not be ruled by my heart. I had the responsibility to be strong. I felt as if I needed to always do the right thing—making the correct decision whether it hurt someone's feelings or not, whether they liked it or not, whether they liked *me* or not. It was a very thin line indeed.

Dad was right. It hadn't been a life-altering event that I didn't take them to the coast. Maybe I did the damage all by myself. Like when we went to the Moose River RV Park.

Kimmy always called it the Merry Moose Park, and we all thought it was so cute that we never corrected her. That was Peter's little nickname, and just in that little quip he brought tons of smiles into our family. Why hadn't I spent more time telling him how much fun he brought us with that comment rather than chewing his ass out royally when he was late bringing the kids back from the rec hall that night?

Boy, did I let him have it that night. I just got so damned worried and worked up that when I got to the rec hall at ten after and none of them were there, I couldn't help myself. It was like I was having an out-of-body experience, watching myself spinning out of control. The more I looked for them, the higher my anxiety rose. There could have been more than one creep lurking among those two hundred or more campers, just waiting to lure unsuspecting kids to their deaths or maybe a fate even worse than death.

It was 1999, the great year of the millennium and the Y2K bug that was expected to shut down countless computers at the stroke of midnight on New Year's Eve. But even more threatening was the ever-increasing rate of missing and abducted children. Their faces were on billboards, department store bulletin boards, and even milk cartons. When I was growing up, it had been unheard of, but now it was all too common.

When I saw the bunch of them walking merrily up the road from the beach, I almost lost it. But there were the other kids, the

34

new friends they had made, to think about, so I held my cool until we got back to our camper. I sent Steve and Kimmy in but asked Pete to stay back. Once they were inside, I let him have it. Even in my hushed tone, my words must have sounded like gunshots and been hurtful to Peter.

I guess I didn't have to be loud to be hurtful. Jesus, he was always such a good kid, but at that moment none of that mattered. My kids had been missing and I had left him in charge. I told him I was disappointed in him and he had to grow up and be responsible. That he was useless and a disappointment to me.

In a sense, that was the last time we were really friends. I just didn't realize it at that time. The next summer, during his senior year, he was busy getting ready for college and being with his friends. I was just Dad from that night till today. I think he did grow up that night, and I got what I asked for. I'm not too sure I liked it, especially the way it happened.

I mean, we still went fishing and stuff, but in my heart I felt it wasn't the same. I told him I was proud of him and all of his accomplishments as they came along, and he seemed to take it in, but I never spoke of that night. Maybe that's what I really should have been talking with him about. He was the firstborn, and I think the firstborn, boy or girl, always bears a heavy weight. I'm sure I added an unbearable weight to him that night.

*****
Hospital Room 321
8 *PM*

An uneasy silence settled over the room as Steve and Jan spoke quietly next to the bed. Steve was holding her hand. Greg stood at Steve's side.

Kim took Peter by the elbow and directed him out of the room. "Jesus Christ, Pete, what the hell were you thinking?" she said when they were out of earshot of the rest of the family.

"I don't know what the hell I was thinking. I just didn't expect him to show up right then. I was caught up in the anger of that moment. I felt like I was actually there again. Weren't you surprised by his entrance too?"

35

"Well, yeah, I guess so. But that was uncalled for at any time or level. I'm just happy the kids weren't here."

"I got carried away, I know, but I still have some hard feelings about that night."

"Oh yeah? How so?"

"Well, for beginners, I trusted him, and secondly—"

"Hey, you two. What's up?" Laura said as she walked toward them with Bennie and Sarah leading the charge. She had two big pizza boxes. Peter jumped to help her and took the boxes.

"Hi, Mommy," Bennie said. "Did Uncle Steve get here yet?"

Kim sighed. "As a matter of fact, yes, he did. He's in Grampa's room."

Laura looked at Peter. He just shrugged.

"Yippee! Is Papa still taking his nap?"

"Yes, he's still sleeping, Ben. Why don't you go in and say hello to Uncle Steve and his friend Greg?"

"Okay. Come on, Sarah. Let's see if Uncle Steve can still make that funny noise with his hands," Bennie said. He grabbed Sarah by the hand and pulled her into the room.

"Bennie, try to be quiet," Kim called after him as they disappeared into the room.

"What the hell was the long sigh about, Kim?" Laura asked.

Kim shifted her weight from one foot to the other. "It's not good, Laura. Steve overheard us—well, overheard Peter—talking about his... his lifestyle."

Laura glared at Peter. "You didn't."

Peter sheepishly admitted to his wrong. "I did," he said without explanation.

*****

"Hey, Uncle Steve!" Bennie yelled as he ran to him.

Steve scooped the boy up and gave him a big hug. "How you doin', buckaroo?"

"I'm good, Uncle Steve. You've been away for a long time. I missed you."

"I missed you too, Ben." Steve looked down to see Sarah standing patiently for her turn to say hello.

"Well, my Lord, Sarah Rose Connor. I think you must have grown a foot since I saw you last." He squatted down. "Now come on over here and give your Uncle Steve a big hug." When she came closer, he scooped her up too and hugged them both. They giggled with delight.

"Uncle Steve, you're the best," Bennie squeaked out between giggles.

Steve beamed at the comment and closed his eyes for a moment, seemingly letting all the unconditional love soak in. "I love you both sooo much, and I've missed you too."

"Hey, we brought pizza!" Laura announced.

Steve smacked his lips. "Mm-mm. I love pizza. I think I can smell it from here."

"Yeah, and it smelled up the car too. Aunt Laura said she's glad it was a rental!" They all got a little giggle out of that one.

Steve set the kids down and walked to Laura. "So nice to see you again. How long has it been?"

Laura smiled fondly. "Too long. Let's not let that happen again."

"Agreed."

"Grab some of this pizza, everybody, before it congeals into a solid mass of cheese and grease," Peter chimed in.

Jan pulled the bedside table away from the bed and cleared it to make room for the boxes. Peter set them down. He took napkins and paper plates from the brown paper bag that rested on the top box and put them on the table as well.

Everyone gathered around and took a piece. Peter and Laura moved to the low windowsill where Mike had originally sat. They set a few napkins down and pushed two straight-backed chairs up close to it. "Come over here, kids. You can have your pizza here," Peter said as he waved Bennie and Sarah over. They quickly took their places and scooped up the pizza from the paper plates Laura placed there.

Mike and Kim joined them. Steve and Greg stood near Ed's bed with Jan while they chatted and ate their pizza.

When they finished eating, Jan took Steve by the arm and walked him over to Pete. "Come on, you two. Let's sit down and relax. We're here for Dad's sake. The years are passing, and things aren't changing between you two."

"Okay, Mom. You're right. Okay with you, Steve?" Peter said.

"Sure. Of course. It's dropped."

Jan sat in a chair. Mike managed to scrounge up two more chairs for Steve and Greg, but Greg didn't sit.

"Ya know, why don't I check us in to the Holiday Inn, Steve?" Greg said. "When you're ready, I can swing over and pick you up. Or not, if you decide to stay all night."

Jan said, "Greg, you're more than welcome to stay. We haven't even had a moment to chat yet."

"I know, and I'm looking forward to getting to know everyone, but it seems to me that this is a time for family."

"But you *are* family now."

"Thank you, Mrs. Connor, but you're all reminiscing about the old days, and I don't have anything to share. I think it's best."

"I think I'll do the same," Laura said. "Sarah has to get to bed soon. Kim, do you want Bennie to stay with me? I'm going to book us a room at the Regency Grand."

"Nonsense! You'll stay at our house. We have plenty of room."

"Are you sure? It's last minute and all."

"Of course. If you won't mind the mess I left the house in when I rushed out, then we're fine."

Laura looked at Peter, and with his approving nod, she said yes.

"Okay, great." Kim turned to Mike. "Get fresh sheets and pillowcases out for the guest room and set up a fold-out in Ben's room. Bennie and Sarah can sleep there. Bennie can pick out his PJs himself."

"I like my dino PJs, Aunt Laura," Bennie chimed in. "I knew this was going to be a fun sleepover!"

Jan stepped closer to Bennie, squatted, and hugged him. "That's right, honey. You're going to have a blast." She stroked his hair.

"What's a blast, Gramma?"

"It's just an expression." She smiled and pulled him in closer, then reached out for Sarah and pulled her in too. "You two have a fun time tonight, but don't stay up too late."

Laura and Mike were beginning to leave with the kids when Greg spoke up. "Wait up. I'll walk you out." He gave Steve a little pat on the back, and the three left with the kids leading the way.

After they had gone, Jan, Pete, Steve, and Kim sat again in the semicircle around Ed's bed. Jan was the first to speak. "It wasn't all a disaster on our trip to Merry Moose Park, and we had plenty of other good times too." She glanced around. Steve smiled, knowing that's what she needed to see. He hoped Peter would play along. He was relieved when Peter also smiled and nodded agreeably.

Maybe it wasn't all bad, Steve thought. *There were some fun times. Peter wasn't such a big prick all the time.*

Chapter Five

Hospital Room 321

Without a warning of any sort, Ed's body tensed and his head rocked back and forth violently. The bells and whistles of the monitor attached to him screamed as the family watched in horror, waiting for what seemed to be the inevitable.

Steve, the only one with a medical background, rushed to Ed's side and tried to restrain him. The nurses arrived instantly, surrounding Ed and relieving Steve. They restrained Ed so he wouldn't hurt himself by thrashing about in the bed.

Then the seizure was over. The monitor went silent, other than the normal beeps and blips they were used to hearing.

Angie turned to Jan. "Dr. Mehra is in the hospital, doing his nightly rounds. I'll have him paged." In seconds Dr. Mehra's name echoed through the hospital halls.

Dr. Mehra and Angie came in the room a few minutes after the page. He went directly to Ed's bedside. He physically checked Ed's pulse even though the monitor had a constant readout. Then he listened to Ed's heart and lungs with his stethoscope. He took a chrome-handled rubber hammer from his coat pocket and checked Ed's reflexes. He gently tapped Ed's wrists, elbows, and knees. Ed responded to each bump of the hammer. Dr. Mehra uncovered Ed's feet and drew the end of a hammer across each instep, which resulted in Ed's foot arching downward.

Everyone in the room was absolutely silent while Dr. Mehra examined Ed. Finally Karash turned to Jan. "I spoke to Angie before I examined Ed. You saw the exam. I don't see any change in his condition. So that's a hopeful note."

"But what happened to him?"

"That I'm not too sure of, but it sounds like an NES seizure."

"NES?"

"Sorry. An NES is a non-epileptic seizure, meaning it's a seizure not associated with epilepsy. NESes can be brought on by stressful situations and may be an attempt by the mind to not deal with the stressors at work. As far as I know, they're normally not associated with people in the state Ed's in. It's a mental thing resulting in a physical reaction. Commonly, people with NES seizures are advised to seek a psychotherapist, but in Ed's case that doesn't make sense."

"This doesn't make any sense to me at all," Jan said. She sat down, covering her face with her hands.

"These are stressful times, Jan," Karash said. "But you're a strong woman, and you have your family here to help you through it. It doesn't seem his condition has changed at all. Even with that seizure, all of his vitals are great. I don't understand it. Of course, we'll know more in the morning after the neurologist examines him and they give him a brain scan. His reflexes seemed good, including the plantar response when I drew the handle of my reflex hammer across his feet. He arched his feet downward, which is a hopeful note. If he'd arched upward, it might have indicated brain damage. By all rights, he should be awake. I don't know what's keeping him down. Maybe tomorrow we'll know more."

He looked around the room to each of them. "This will be a long night for you all. I suggest you try to get rest whenever you can, even if it means taking shifts at Ed's bedside so the others can rest. And that includes you, Jan." He looked directly at her, and she nodded agreement.

"I'll see you all first thing in the morning. I'll be on call if he needs me." He turned to leave but stopped and turned back. "Jan, you did know he had a Do Not Resuscitate Order... a DNR on file in my office, didn't you?"

Shocked, Jan stepped back. "No. He never told me."

Karash shook his head. "I'm sorry he didn't tell you. I thought he did. I didn't see it noted on his chart, but I made the appropriate notation and informed the nursing staff accordingly."

Still in shock, Jan muttered, "Thank you, Karash." He nodded silently and left the room. Jan slumped in the chair. "Why would he do such a thing and not tell me?"

41

*****

The Rock

I was amazed as I watched the gray skies clear as quickly as they had appeared. I was still on my perch atop that big rock. Suddenly I realized I had been here before. *This is our fishin' rock*, I thought. I scrambled to the edge and saw our favorite fishing hole, where the kids and I would drop in our lines and wait to catch a brook trout or two.

Suddenly I spun around, looking for what I knew should be there. And it was. I could still see the faint trace of red, green, yellow, and blue crayons that Kimmy had left there one day so long ago.

I realized this place was my anchor. Whenever I saw Gracie or Dad, the rock was the only thing that was consistent. I looked over the edge for the jagged outcrop in the face of the stone, and it was there. We used it as a step when scrambling up the massive rock. It was bigger than any other rock I had ever seen in this area in all the time I lived here. The kids and I would walk to it often to throw in a line or just to hang out and maybe see a deer coming down to the creek to get a drink.

It was Kimmy's favorite spot to explore along the banks of the stream. She would catch a frog or two just to set them free again. She always had a heart bigger than most and wouldn't harm a fly. She would go out of her way to avoid doing harm to any of God's creatures.

We had so many fun times here. Maybe that's why it was my anchor. But an anchor to what? My past? My future? Was it my waiting place until I accepted that maybe I wasn't going back to the real world?

One thing was sure: I wasn't in a normal or real place at this moment. Was I in familiar and friendly territory to come to grips with my life, such as it was, before moving on? My mind was swirling so quickly I thought I'd slip off the edge of the rock and into the dark waters of our fishing hole.

But something drew me back. It was the colors on the rock. They caught my eye again and drew me back from my dark ponderings.

I didn't let Kim draw on the rock with her wide crayons intentionally. But while the boys and I were busy trying to hook an especially wily brookie, Kim had moved from her coloring book to the rock. Yes, she had a fishing line in, complete with its red-and-white bobber, but the minnows had probably stolen the worm quite some time ago, and she had lost interest even before that.

Long ago, I had learned to bring the crayons and a coloring book with me. First, it was for Pete. I always wanted to bring home a fresh fish dinner, so after he fished for a while and lost interest, I'd let him color until it was time to go. As he grew and began to have an interest in fishing, it was Steve who made use of the crayons and then Kimmy. It was almost like a rite of passage for my family of fishermen. The only thing Kimmy liked better than fishing at the rock was going to her dancing classes.

Though her scratchings were no longer distinct and almost obliterated by time and nature, I knew they were there. In my mind's eye, I could see the four of us in stick figures. Each one of us had our own color. I was red, Pete was blue, Steve was yellow, and Kimmy had drawn herself green.

If I hadn't known there was a yellow stick figure drawn there, I would never have caught the slightest trace left of Steve. He was almost invisible. How could I have let that happen? I should have brought the crayons back with me when we were there time after time, to preserve his image. But I didn't. He was almost entirely faded from our group portrait.

*****

Hospital Room 321
10 *PM*

"Well, I guess it's just us," Jan said.

Her children sat quietly, each waiting for someone else to break the ice.

Finally Peter broke the silence, "Boy, I'll tell you, that Bennie is a live wire, isn't he? Cute as a button, Kim."

Kim smiled but it was Steve who said, "Live wire? Are you

kidding me? That kid is so much like Kimmy, it's scary!"

"What do you mean, scary? I happen to know I was the most adorable kid around. Daddy told me all the time."

Jan laughed. "Of course he did. And you were adorable in every sense of the word, but you didn't sit still for a minute, honey."

"Well, okay, I remember being... busy. But aren't all kids at that age?" Kim held her ground. "Ya know, being the youngest isn't always the easiest thing."

"Waaah waah wah," Peter teased her. "Try being the oldest. Now that's a tough one. Parents make all the mistakes on the oldest, make sure they don't do it to the next one, and let the baby get away with everything." He sat back and waited for a rebuttal.

"Oh, you didn't have it so bad. You didn't want for anything," Jan said.

"True, but it's fun getting these two going! It's payback for when they were my constant companions."

"It wasn't so bad, was it? Really?" Kim's tone asked for an earnest reply.

Peter let his smile drop. He looked at Kim and then Steve. Kim's expression was still playful, but he couldn't read Steve at all. *Come on, Steve. Let it go. We were just kids*, Peter thought. Flashes of memories swirled through his mind. Even at that speed, he pushed some away without dwelling on them. It was called self-preservation by some, denial by others, but by whatever name, Peter preferred to wear rose-colored glasses when it came to his memories and actions.

"No," Kim answered her own question. "Not so bad at all. We had some good times, didn't we?"

That was the response Peter wanted from Kim. She smiled and leaned in just a little. Still nothing from Steve.

It appeared to Peter that Steve was examining the tile design of the floor. He was bent forward, forearms on his thighs, with his hands folded. *Is he praying or just being the quiet man he's grown to be whenever he's around me?* Peter wondered.

Jan caught the lack of an exchange from Steve and rested her hand on his arm. This too failed to bring a response.

"Come on, Daniel. We had fun," Peter said.

Almost begrudgingly, Steve let a smile form. Finally he

looked up at Peter from the corners of his eyes. The smile widened. "You asshole," he said playfully.

"There's my little bro," Peter teased back.

"Okay, we did have some fun," Steve said. "You did let us tag along almost everywhere you went. And if I wasn't hanging out with you, I was with Boone over here." He reached out and rubbed his father's arm. "Isn't that right, Boone?"

"Oh my God, I almost forgot about the names." Kim giggled. "You were Daniel, Dad was Boone, Pete was Davey, I was Crockett, and Mom was Laura Ingalls. She didn't have to share a name unless we brought the dog. Who came up with all that anyway?"

Steve shook his head. "Who do you think? Mr. Nickname over there. Mr. Merry Moose Park."

Peter grinned as widely as possible without hurting his cheeks. "Hey, I was born with the gift and it's served me well over the years. Anyway, we had fun with those names."

"I know it," Jan said. "We did indeed. It was always just a little extra to make our outings special."

"And you did always helped us catch our nightcrawlers the night before we went fishing," Kim added. "Either me or Steve would hold the flashlight while you went in for the catch. And you'd always bait our hooks for us."

Peter smiled. "Dad made me do it. It was punishment for being bad."

Jan broke in, "Not true. Not for one second."

Steve sat up slowly. "Mom's right. I distinctly remember you telling Dad you'd help us when he began to set up our poles." Steve's voice fell off and he looked pensively away at nothing. Peter watched him for a moment.

"Earth to Steve. Come in, Steve," Peter said, trying to break Steve from his musings. It was something his father had always said when trying to get someone's attention.

"I hear ya," Steve replied.

"Where were you, little bro?"

"Oh, just remembering the nightcrawlers."

"And…" Peter coaxed.

"That's it. Good times. Right?"

It didn't sound convincing to Peter. "Yep, you're right." *He knows there's more to it, just like I do. That doesn't mean those weren't good times in and of themselves.*

Kim exclaimed, "And the rock! Curly Rock, we called it. Did you name it, Pete?"

"No, Dad did because of the swirls in the texture of the rock. It was really cool. Wasn't it?"

"I don't remember the texture, but I remember how big it was and fishing and having picnic lunches on top. It was huge," Kim reminisced.

"Well, it wasn't really very big, kid," Steve told her. "You were just a little squirt."

"It… wasn't…" Kim tried to stammer out a sentence but was obviously shaken by what Peter had just said.

"Now stop that, Pete," Jan scolded. "Yes, Kimmy, it was very huge, and we did have picnic lunches on it. Your brother is teasing you again." Jan rolled her eyes at Peter.

"Sorry, sis. I just can't help myself sometimes."

"I pity your poor wife," Kim shot back with a smile. "I remember when we'd make a campfire on shore next to the rock and cook hotdogs and roast marshmallows. And then we'd sit in a circle around the fire and sing songs and tell stories."

Jan took Ed's hand. "They were the best of times," she said. She then took Steve's hand. Steve took Kim's and Kim took Pete's. Finally Peter reached out and touched Ed's leg.

"Yes, they were," Steve said. "When are you coming home, Boone?"

The room fell silent, other than a quiet sob from Kim and the beeping of the monitor.

Jan released her hand from Steve's and cupped Ed's hand in hers.

*****
Rock

Things were so much different now. People from my past were coming in and out. Events, memories, places seemed to meld together as a seamless stream. Yet I also felt like they were not continuous. It was like they were short filmstrips stitched together

46

between segments of black. I wasn't sure how long those black moments were, nor was I cognizant of the passage of time. Had I been here for minutes, days, years? I wasn't sure.

I began to become afraid that maybe this was my path to the hereafter. These memories, these thoughts could be the fleeting moments at the end of my life. After all, memories were only chemical reactions and electrical impulses racing across the brain.

I wasn't sure that death was an instantaneous event. Whether death came from old age or a violent accident, there must be time for the reactions to stop and for the electrical impulses to become too weak to spark that imagery.

I thought of the science project Kim and I had put together. It was no different from the ones put together by countless school-age kids over the years. It wasn't really about a volcano and lava coming out of it; it was about the chemical reaction of baking soda and vinegar. We poured the vinegar down the papier-mâché mountain and the "lava" bubbled up and out. It didn't stop instantly. At first the lava bubbled up ferociously. This was the point I likened to one's youth. The mind is quick and active, making memories and learning quickly. Slowly the reaction cooled. We watched as the lava flow slowed until the end, when the reaction was unable to support itself and came to a stop.

Was that where I was now? Were the chemical reactions— my memories—slowly coming to an end? Were these memories so engrained in my psyche that they were the last of the chemical reaction that was my life? Was I fading away just like that childhood experiment did so many years ago?

I sat there on the rock and studied the swirling texture of its surface, pondering my demise. I felt the anxiety take over my senses. What the hell was I doing and why the hell was I here?

"My, aren't we deep today." Her voice startled me. At first I thought it was Jan but then I became aware of Gracie sitting next to me. The roar of the ocean and the smell of salt filled my senses, replacing the babbling brook. It was like I was home again.

"You're back," I said. "I was hoping I'd see you one last time."

"One last time?"

"Well, yeah. You know, one last time before... well, you

47

know."

"No. I don't. Why should I?"

"Well, you are…" I swallowed the word back before I said it, but I knew I could. I could say anything to Gracie. "I mean you should know because you are"—I forced it out—"dead."

She laughed that same laugh that had always made my worst day brighten up. "So, I'm dead and that makes me all-knowing now?"

"You should know. You went through this, didn't you? That's why you're here, right?"

"I don't know if I went through something like this or not. I think you brought me here. What are you looking for, Eddie?"

"I don't really know. The scenes change. My visitors change. But the rock remains. It seems to be holding me here, immobile—unable to move forward or back."

"Forward or back? It seems to me you're moving around pretty good, visiting with your father and then me. Back and forth from good times to bad."

"Yes, remembering all the old times, but I mean back to my old life as I knew it or forward to what the next phase of my existence will be."

"Like I said, my, aren't we deep today. Did you ever take your family to an amusement park?"

"Of course. What self-respecting father never took their family to an amusement park?"

"Be that as it may." She smiled. "What was your favorite ride?"

"My favorite ride? I guess the roller coaster."

"Did you ride it all the time, or were there other rides?"

"No. Sometimes the boys would take off and ride the big kids' rides, but Kimmy was too young to go along. So I'd stay back with her, and we'd go on the rides she liked best."

"So it wasn't your choice? You'd go on rides that she enjoyed. Were you bored?"

"No, absolutely not. She'd have fun, and I enjoyed seeing her having fun. I guess I would just go along for the ride."

"So maybe that's what you should do now. Just go along for the ride and see where it leads. Don't worry so much about what it means. Relax. Maybe this isn't about life *or* death."

I felt her take my hand in hers and the anxiety melted away.

Chapter Six

Mike and Laura's House
11 *PM*

Mike was at the kitchen table with a cup of decaf when Laura walked in. "Well, Sarah's down for the count," she said with a sigh of relief.

Mike smiled. "Ben is getting his PJs on. He wants to show them to you, so he'll be here in a little bit."

"He's a handful, isn't he," Laura said. It was a statement, not a question.

"He sure is, and smart as a whip! Once when he was only three years old, he tried to figure out why the Easter Bunny appeared during the night. He explained it to Kim, 'The Easter Bunny is octurnal. All Easter Bunnies stay their eyes open at night and sleep in the day.' We didn't think it was necessary to correct him by telling him the correct word was *nocturnal*. We actually thought his assessment of the situation was just about as close as any three-year-old could ever get it all by himself. We don't really know where he picked up the word *nocturnal*—maybe day care or a show—but it didn't matter. He must have heard it somewhere and stored it away for future use at an appropriate time."

Laura laughed. "Oh my God, that's so cute. I love that story."

"Here I am. It's me, Bennie!" he said with his usual flair as he raised his hands over his head and raced into the room with his dino PJs on.

"He's been a big ham since he was a baby," Mike said to Laura. "Even when he was five months old, all we had to do was to say *yay!* and he'd clap his hands and bounce around in his Baby Bouncer seat. We called it the Baby Bennie Show."

"Well, don't you look great," Laura said, holding Bennie back at arm's length. "Let me take a look at you."

"Thanks, Aunt Laura. These are my favorite pair."

"You have more?"

"Sure do. I mostly have dino ones. I do have a pair with cars and two with just colors, but they're not my favorites."

"Yep, he's a dino man for sure. He has rubber replicas of all of the dinosaurs and knows their names by heart. Better than I do. When he's naming them off, he has me check the names stamped on the underside to make sure he's right. And he is." Mike beamed that proud-father smile, whether he knew he was doing it or not. He grabbed Bennie's hand and pulled him over and bent down to study his pajama top. "Now, let's see. What is this dino called?" he asked, pointing at one of the dinos on his PJs.

"*T. Rex*, Daddy. Even you know that one."

Mike looked up to Laura. "Like I said!"

Laura watched this proud man speak to his son and was happy to know Kim's family was well-adjusted and happy—much like hers, probably more so.

She knew Peter sometimes came off like a smooth-talking, superficial sort of guy, but she also knew that was his job persona. He had to be detached in his work. With the high stakes of being a stockbroker, he couldn't afford to be emotionally attached to his clients. Attachments might inhibit his decision-making process and ultimately cost them money. No, he had to be quick and clear-minded at all times.

Sometimes that persona spilled over into their home life. When she saw that happening, she'd pack their bags and plan a weekend getaway, and by Saturday night he'd be back to himself again.

She loved him with all of her heart, and without exception he treated her with the same love, respect, and tenderness. Peter always gave her all of his love and attention, which made her feel like she was the center of his world. Except, of course, for Sarah. She also existed as the center of his world—but it was a big world, and Laura was thrilled to be able to share it with her daughter.

From the day they met, she knew without doubt that he saw only her. He often told her that it was her smile, positive energy, and unwavering faith in him that saved him from becoming one of the heartless brokers that he worked with each day. She knew he never drifted away or faltered in his love and caring for her. They were equal partners in the relationship for sure.

Yet she wondered where Peter's comment about Steve had come from when they were at the hospital. It seemed out of character with the way he treated his own family. Though he never spoke about it, she knew there had been a falling out between the brothers. It was evident at every family outing.

"Now give Aunt Laura a big hug and good-night kisses," Mike told Bennie.

Laura pulled herself away from her thoughts. "That's right, Bennie. Come on over here and give me a hug." She pulled him in and gave him a big hug and a kiss. "You know, Bennie, I think those are just perfect PJs. I just might have to get Sarah a pair too."

"Really, Aunt Laura? That'd be awesome," Bennie said excitedly. "Then we'd be twins!"

Laura laughed. "I guess. Except that she has curly dark brown hair and brown eyes, and you have blond hair and blue eyes. Other than that, yes. I guess twins."

Bennie thought for a minute. "Well that's only because I look like my mommy and Sarah looks like you. That's the way God intends it."

Laura raised her eyebrows. "That's a big word for a little guy, Bennie."

"I know, but that's what Gramma said once when they were talking about how my hair and eyes look like my mommy's."

Laura smiled again peacefully. "That must be it then. Twins it is."

"Okay, champ. Time for bed," Mike said. "I'll read you a story."

Bennie ran over to Mike. As Mike picked him up, the boy turned to Laura. "Ya know why I like dinos so much, Aunt Laura?"

"I'm not sure, Bennie. I thought it was because of all the dino stuff on TV and at the movies."

"Nope, not really. I do like those shows. But it's because of Grampa."

"Grampa?"

"Yeah. Once when he was boy-sitting me, we were watching *Barney the Dinosaur*. He told me he was like an old dinosaur. That all the things he grew up with were changing, but he hoped he'd be a better dinosaur and change with them just like Barney. He said he'd learned he had to keep changing thanks to goin' on a fishing trip with Uncle Steve. So I'm going to be a changing dino just like Grampa."

"Uncle Steve?" She looked at Mike .

He just shrugged. "I don't know," Mike said, seeming a little baffled himself. "Ed and Bennie spend a lot of time together."

"Okay, my little dino friend. Tomorrow we'll go shopping with Sarah for some dino PJs while your dad goes to the hospital."

"Oh boy. I can't wait. Will Grampa be coming home tomorrow?"

"Well, maybe not tomorrow, but hopefully soon."

Mike said, "All right. Time for bed. What story tonight, Bennie?"

"I want... *Danny Dino Goes to Town.*"

Mike rolled his eyes at Laura with a wink. "Hmm, surprise, surprise, surprise." They walked off toward Bennie's bedroom.

Laura sat quietly, tracing the grain of the wooden tabletop with her finger. Sarah was a year younger and hadn't had the exposure to Ed the way Bennie had. Maybe it was a good thing in a way. She wouldn't be so devastated if Ed were to pass, but then again she wouldn't have dino memories about her grandfather to cherish for a lifetime the way Bennie would. Laura vowed that if Ed recovered, Sarah would make memories with him to have and to hold for the rest of her life too.

"He's out," Mike announced as he entered the room.

"That's good. He's had a long day," Laura said, looking up.

"Decaf?" Mike asked as he walked over to the coffee maker.

"Have any tea?"

Mike shuffled through the rack of plastic pods. "Yep, I've got green tea with spices, decaf green tea, Earl Grey, chamomile, herbal—"

"Thanks. I'll take the green decaf," she said.

"Sugar, half and half, honey?"

"Just a little honey, please."

When it was finished, he brewed himself a cup of coffee. He slid the tea and honey in front of her.

53

"Quite a day," he said flatly.

"Yes, it has been. Jan is holding up good though, I think."

"She's a trooper. She wasn't letting anything out when we first got there, but Kim coaxed her out of it."

"Kim's been her rock from what I've seen," Laura agreed.

"She has. We've been lucky living close by. She and Ed have always been there for us, and Bennie loves visiting them almost as much as they like having him over. But I think the rock she was waiting for was Peter. I could hear the relief in her voice when you guys came in the room. 'Thank God you're here,' I think I remember hearing."

Laura smiled. "Well, Pete has always been their voice of reason. He helped them with retirement planning for years before they were ready to retire, and he set them up pretty good. You know Ed. He was worried about not having enough to take care of Jan, and he wanted them to have the comfort of their own home for as long as they could be there."

"I know. Pete's given me some great financial advice too. He's been that level-headed guy everybody wants to rely on." Mike looked into his coffee cup and then took a swallow. "Except when it comes to Steve."

She wasn't shocked by what he said. It'd been that forbidden subject for years. At every Christmas, birthday, Fourth of July picnic—whenever the whole family got together, it'd been the unspoken dialogue. She knew Mike was trying to get the inside scoop that the family didn't talk about. He wasn't snooping; he just had the same questions she'd had.

"I wish I could enlighten you, but I can't. I've asked Pete several times. He just doesn't want to talk about it. He says, 'I doubt if he even really gets it anyway.'"

Mike sighed. "Kim insists she doesn't know, but thinks something happened in junior or early senior high school. She can't put a finger on an exact date."

"Well, you know more than I do. Thanks for that info."

"I was surprised to hear him being so cold-blooded when he mentioned about Steve... well, Steve being gay."

"Yeah. That wasn't so much of a surprise for me. He's never shown any love lost for gays. The whole thing seems to piss him

54

off."

Mike's forehead wrinkled with a questioning look. "That just baffles me."

"I know. Me too," Laura said.

Mike reached out and took her hand. "This is hard to say, but is he prejudiced about me? I mean me being Hispanic?"

She covered his hand with her free hand and held it tight. "Oh my God, no, Mike. He's not that way at all—except for the gays. That should be obvious. He's never treated you badly or disrespectfully, has he?"

"No, but after that, I wondered."

"Have you fully accepted the gay community?" The question was flat-out and clear. It demanded an honest answer.

Mike paused thoughtfully. "I have to admit that when I thought Kim was criticizing Steve's lifestyle, I was the first to chime in on it—and boy, did she shut me down. I was kind of embarrassed." Laura nodded encouragingly. He continued, "I don't know where it came from. It just roiled up inside me without thinking."

"Prejudice is a funny… rather, I guess, an odd thing. I don't think it comes from the higher brain functions but from fear. Fear of the unknown. Fear of something different. Fear of something upsetting our vision of what should be and how the world should turn. It seems to be this family's last prejudice."

"Mommy, I can't sleep. I had a bad dream," said a little voice from the doorway. They were startled from their deep conversation and looked up to see Sarah.

"It's okay, honey. You can sleep with me tonight. What was it about?"

"These dinosaurs were trying to get me," she whined sleepily.

Laura shot Mike a quick glance. "Maybe I need to rethink that shopping trip tomorrow." She grabbed Sarah up.

"Easier said than done, I think. Maybe she just needs to make friends with a few dinos before bed tomorrow," Mike said with a wink. "Good night."

"Good night, Mike. I'm happy we had this chance to talk."

Chapter Seven

The Rock

I'd been taking the kids fishing for years, and we all enjoyed it. The whole nickname thing and all that stuff made for good stories and memories.

Steve was the first to start pulling away. Yeah, he liked fishing, but he had other interests too. His painting, for one. It kind of made Pete angry, I think.

Pete wanted a fishing buddy close to his own age, and Kim... well, Kim was a squeamish little girl who was afraid to catch her own worms and bait her own hook. As Steve grew older, he wasn't afraid of worms, but he just wasn't into it. He'd rather paint a picture of the fish rather than catch it.

Once he brought his paints along in his tackle box. After his hook was baited and the bobber was floating in the center of the fishing hole, he unrolled a sheet of paper and began to paint the scene. Pete teased the heck out of him. Steve never brought them again, but he also didn't tag along on all of our fishing trips.

That seemed to me to be the beginning of them drifting apart. I would hear Pete practically begging Steve to come along because he didn't want to be alone with just Kimmy. Those two boys would take their poles and work their way upstream, dropping worms silently in each little fishing hole as they went along. Sometimes they would be gone for an hour or more and bring back a few little brook trout, but mostly I think it was like exploring for them. Maybe in their minds they really were Davy Crockett and Daniel Boone.

When Steve stopped coming along, I would see Pete looking upstream like he was wishing he could be there with Steve. Sometimes he'd go by himself, but he wouldn't be gone very long at all. When I asked him why he came back so soon, he'd just say that the fish weren't biting.

Once I suggested that maybe he missed his fishing partner. He said, "That little squirt? I don't need him to catch a fish."

Oh, he still enjoyed fishing with me, and I with him, but I knew it was never the same for Pete after that.

*****

Hospital Room 321

12 *AM*

After another check of Ed's vital signs and a few keystrokes at the bedside computer, the nurse turned to Jan. "Everything looks the same, Mrs. Connor. You all should try to get some rest." She dimmed the lights and left the room.

"She's right, Mom. Why don't you all go home and get some sleep? I'll stay here and call you if there's any change. I slept in this morning, and I'm not that tired," Steve said.

"I'm not leaving his side, Steve." Jan turned to Kim and Pete. "Why don't you two go? We'll call you at the first sign of any trouble."

"No way. I'm staying, Mom," Kim said. "The doctor said the first twelve to twenty-four hours are critical. I'm staying at least until we hear from the neurologist."

"Same with me, Mom. I'm staying too," Peter insisted.

"Well, all right. I don't have the energy to argue about it," Jan relented. "But we should rest here in shifts then. Why don't you and Kim kick back in the recliners, and Steve and I will sit with Dad?"

"I don't know…" Peter began.

"It's okay, Pete. You'll be in the same room, just seconds from Dad, and you need the sleep. You and Kim have kids to deal with tomorrow in addition to being here for Dad." She crossed to him and put her hand on his shoulder. "Peter, it's okay. Please get some rest."

Peter looked over to Kim, and she nodded in agreement. "Okay. A couple of hours, then you and Steve should rest. Deal?"

"Agreed. Now rest," Jan said.

Peter pushed the recliners to the far edge of the room, and

she drew the privacy curtain. "Nighty night, you two."

"Okay, okay. If you two keep it down out there, maybe we will get some rest," Peter answered in his gruffest, manliest voice.

Jan giggled. "Okay, we'll be quiet."

She sat next to Steve and Ed. She held a finger up to her lips, and they sat quietly until they heard Peter's smooth, rhythmic breathing from the other side of the curtain. Jan got up to steal a glance at the two sleeping beauties. She gave Steve the all-clear sign and returned to her chair.

"That's good," she said. "They need the rest. Now tell me, Steven, how are things?"

"Well, some things are great, some things are okay, and some things are not so good." He raised his eyebrows at her, wondering which she'd pick to hear more about. He figured she'd pick the good things first. She was never one to hang on to the bad things in life. She was unquestionably the optimist of the household. Whenever he or Peter or Kim had a bad moment in school or with each other, she'd put a good spin on it. "Well, if she doesn't want to go to the dance with you, Peter," he remembered her saying about Peter's eighth grade semiformal, "then it's her loss. I'm sure you'll find a date much better for you anyway."

And she'd been right. Peter did find a date for that dance, and they went on dating for a while afterward. "See? I told you it'd all work out," she'd reminded him a few weeks after the dance.

She always had the right words, as moms often did. Dads, more times than not, kind of grunted out a "buck up and bear it." Maybe if things were really bad, you'd get a "when the goin' gets tough, the tough get goin'" line. Guys just didn't pay attention to the details. It was a big picture sort of thing. Not a lot of touchy-feely stuff going on.

Each ideology had its good points and bad points, but Steve thought maybe his mom's way was a little more effective. At least it was for him.

"Is Greg part of the good?" Jan asked.

He already guessed she thought Greg was, or Steve wouldn't have brought him along on such an important event.

"Yes. Greg is part of the good." He smiled with his reply.

"Now there's my boy. I haven't seen a smile from you in a

long time."

"Mom, this isn't a time or place for many smiles," he countered.

"I'm not just talking about today. You haven't smiled much for some time now when you've been home. Want to talk about it?" she said. She leaned in toward him, taking his hand.

There she goes. It was the smoothest transition from a "good things" conversation to the "bad things" that he'd ever heard. A gentle approach, just to open the door a crack. He knew she wasn't prying or anything like that. She honestly wanted to know and help him with that whole sullen thing that happened when he was home.

"No, Mom, especially not now."

"Okay then, about Greg. You said he is one of the good things."

He was happy she let the subject go. "Yeah, he's a good thing. We get along great, and he understands me. I mean, not just the obvious way of loving me, but he understands me—my moods, my quirks, and all of those things that make me who I am."

"I'm not sure I'm following you, Stevie. You're perfect, aren't you?"

He knew he probably was perfect in her eyes. He always had been but he knew she was asking for more.

He lowered his head as he thought and then looked at her. "Remember when you were telling us about Dad and how he avoided going to the ocean?"

She nodded.

"Well, it's like that. You knew his history with Grace but never pushed him for more or asked him to give up his emotional ties with her because you were his wife now and Grace was gone. You knew in his heart he could love both you and Grace at the same time without it diminishing what you have with him. That's the way it is with Greg and me. Sometimes when I'm off in a distant world, he might ask if I want to talk, but if I don't want to, he understands.

"The few places? Your art and…?"

"Now's not the time," he said.

But she pushed on gently. "Peter?"

He studied her face. Maybe now she needed to have stability in one part of her life when the other was so out of control. Maybe she needed reassurance that her whole life wouldn't spin out of control and come to an abrupt end if something went terribly wrong here tonight.

"Well, yes. Peter and…" He paused and looked over to Ed. "Well, yeah, Peter," he repeated. He shrugged off the rest of his reply. "I need to stretch my legs. Will you be okay for a minute or two? Do you want a soda or something from the machine?"

"No, nothing now, and yes, I'll be fine." She patted his hand and he knew from that gentle pat she understood. He didn't want to dismiss the question like that, but he didn't want to deal with it either.

He stood and walked through the door and to the waiting room. He dug out a fistful of coins and inserted one after another into the vending machine. He allowed a moment for thought to elapse between each coin, as if trying to give himself time to collect himself. When a bottle rolled out of the machine, he opened it and took a sip. Then he reached for his phone.

"Hi, Greg. I'm sorry I woke you, but I needed to talk…"

*****

The Rock

I didn't remember feeling or seeing or experiencing one of those black moments that stitched my time here together, but here I was again—still atop the rock, with green pastures in front of me and the fishing hole at my feet.

"Sometimes we're too close to things to see things clearly," Dad said.

I looked over. "Hi, Dad. So what do you mean, too close?"

"Sometimes we're so close to something that we don't get the whole picture. It's like if you were in a dense forest, all you would see were the trees that surrounded you. You would know the color of their leaves, the texture of the bark, and all that close-up stuff, but you wouldn't know how to get out. On the other hand, if you could see from above, you'd know how big the forest was and the best way to walk out. It's the same with a family. Sometimes you kids would act out. I'd only deal with the actual event and never

60

really think about whether there was something more behind the problem."

"Yeah, I get that," I said. "So many times Peter and Steve argued about some meaningless thing, and I never gave a thought about if something else was afoot."

"That's right. Now take me, for example."

"You?" I asked. "What about you?"

"Well, what do you know about me?"

"I know everything." I was sure I knew everything about my father that there was to know. At least, everything of any importance.

"Everything? Really?"

"Well, practically everything."

"Okay then, tell me about me," my father challenged me.

"You were a good husband, a great father. You worked every day and came home like clockwork after work. You liked outdoor things, like camping and gardening and all that sort of stuff."

"That it?" he asked.

I knew I was getting set up. I could feel the apprehension growing in me—that feeling of doom you get when finding out something that maybe you didn't really want to know.

"Well, yeah, I guess that probably sums you up pretty good," I said confidently, trying to hide my building anxiety.

"Okay then. What's my favorite color?"

"That's silly. That doesn't count," I said, dismissing the question immediately. "Color preference doesn't make a man."

"All right. Why do I like the outdoors so much?" He pressed me for more answers.

"That's easy. You said it a million times when we were camping. You like the wide open expanses. You'd even get up sometimes and sleep under the stars rather than in the RV."

"I did say that, didn't I? And it was the truth. But why?"

"You just did. That's why. It's a part of you."

"Well, that's true, but it only became part of me because of the war. I spent days, weeks, in small trenches and foxholes and bombed-out buildings in France, just waiting for a German soldier to sneak up behind me and run a bayonet through my back or for a bomb or mortar shell to drop on me. It almost happened once. A guy by the name of Sam and I were in a foxhole, and the next thing I knew, there was an explosion and most of Sam wasn't there anymore."

I was speechless for a minute or two. He sat quietly next to me, waiting for my response. "I didn't know that. I knew you saw some horrible things, but you never shared any details before," I eked out.

"Exactly. Mom and I never spoke much about it, and I surely never shared it with you kids."

I looked at him speechlessly as images of my childhood began to click together and make a little more sense.

"Sound familiar?" my father asked.

"Familiar?"

"Yes. Your resistance to going to the ocean with the family."

"Well yes, but that was different," I insisted.

"Maybe, or maybe not. The point is that families have secrets. Some secrets are pretty much harmless, like yours and mine. But you and your family had another secret, didn't you?"

"I don't know what you're talking about." I rejected his statement flat out, all the while knowing he was right.

"Yes, you do. Be honest. Steven's secret?"

I blinked hard as my anxiety peaked. Yes, there was a secret, but it wasn't Steve's. It was mine.

Chapter Eight

Hospital Room 321
1 *AM*

When Steve came back to the room, he was carrying a couple of extra sodas and two bottles of water. Kim was sitting with Jan at Ed's bedside. Kim gave him a little silly wave and stood up and moved to another chair. She patted the chair she had been in, which was now between her and Jan.

He held out the sodas and water, but Jan and Kim both waved them off. He set them on the bedside table before he sat and whispered, "You didn't need to get up on my account."

"We want to have you where we can both get to you," Kim teased and rubbed his arm.

"Any changes?" Steve asked.

"No. Nothing," Jan said. "The nurse came in and checked him and then said there was no change." She drifted away for a minute and refocused. She felt her optimism starting to fade. "At first when they said that, it made me feel reassured that he wasn't getting any worse. Now I'm beginning to feel like it might mean he'll never get better."

Steve took her hand. "Don't talk like that, Mom. It still means he's not getting any worse, which is a good sign. Dr. Mehra said as much. And remember, there is a 'no doom or gloom' order in effect."

"You're right, honey. Thanks. Even I forget that sometimes."

They chatted for a while until the curtain behind them flew open. With a start they all turned to see Peter grinning his most devilish smile from ear to ear.

Jan instantly scolded him as if he were a bad little boy. "Peter. You scared the daylights out of us." She continued to be amazed by how little her children had changed since they were kids.

Peter was still the entertainer after all these years.

"Okay then, part one of the plan worked." Peter snickered.

"Part one?" Kim eyed him suspiciously.

"Yeah. What did you expect? Did you really think all that whispering wouldn't travel the extra two feet to where I was trying to sleep?" He emphasized the word *trying*. "I just felt it would be turnabout is fair play if I aggravated you three a little bit."

"Well, you succeeded. Part one accomplished in spades. What is part two of the plan?" Jan asked.

"I was hoping maybe it'd wake up Dad too."

Kim lowered her voice so it wouldn't travel to the hall. "You're officially a horse's ass. You know that, don't you?" She didn't try to hide her amusement.

"But you've got to admit a funny one."

"Okay, so a funny horse's ass. Now pull up a chair and join us."

He pushed a chair in closer, and once again the circle was full. "So what did I miss?"

"I thought you heard everything," Kim teased him.

"No. I could hear your annoying whispering, but I didn't understand most of the words. Fill me in. That's the least you can do."

"We were just talking about the old days. Like that one Christmas when Steve had to go pee and you wouldn't let him because you were afraid that if Santa was there, Steve would scare him off, and you wouldn't get the motorcycle you asked for."

"Yeah, and look what happened. He went to pee, and I didn't get my motorcycle."

"You always blamed me for that. It wasn't my fault, Peter," Steve complained.

Peter looked at him, shaking his head, and made an ugly face. "Duh. I know that now, Steven, but at the time…"

"Mom and Dad tried to explain to you that you were too young for a motorcycle and Santa couldn't bring you one."

"I know. But at the mall, Santa said he'd try, so I figured you screwed it up for me. How the hell was I supposed to know that the store Santa was probably an unemployed bum for most of the year? Crap, I was only eight—"

"Boys! Boys! Quiet down. Must we go through that again?" Jan didn't realize the boys were just acting out an old childhood argument.

Peter threw a smile and a wink toward Steve. Much to his surprise, he got a smile back. "You were always mad at me, you know," Steve said. The smile was gone.

"You were always being difficult," was Pete's response.

"Like what?"

"Well, for instance, you never let me be Boone if Dad wasn't around."

"That was his name. Why should you have it when he wasn't there? What was wrong with you being Davy and me being Daniel?"

"Because when we were out on our own, Dad put me in charge, and I figured I should be Boone."

"Boys," Jan interjected again.

Steve sat back. "You're right, Mom. That's just old crap and not worth fussing with anymore. I'm just overtired. I think I'll sack out for a while. Wake me if there's a change." He began to pull the curtain closed again.

"We will. Oh, and take the chair near the window. The road noise drowns out the whispers," Kim advised.

"Thanks. Will do." Steve pulled the curtain closed and disappeared behind it.

After some time, Jan peeked behind the curtain to see if Steve was asleep. Satisfied that he was, she sat back down. "Why must you two be fighting every second?"

"Mom, we don't fight every second. Hell, we barely speak most of the time."

"That's not fighting? Your lack of words is louder than your actual arguments."

"It's not my fault. This started years ago, and I doubt that it'll be ending anytime soon. He's too stubborn."

"You just need to be nice to him and he'll come around. I just know it. I see the hurt in his eyes when you two argue."

"Mom, you're always defending him. Believe it or not, I tried like hell to 'be nice to him,' but it never worked. Ever since we were kids, I tried to include him in a lot of the things I was doing, but he kept backing away. Ya know, I was just a kid too, and it hurt my feelings. For so long we did everything together, and then zip, nada, nothing. I don't know if it was the gay thing coming out or if he just didn't like me. Of course, none of us knew about the gay stuff then, so I figured it must be me."

"You were hard on him," Jan said.

"I was just trying to get him to do some of our fun things again with me. It made me mad." Peter sat back in his chair and folded his arms across his chest.

"But you did do some things together at that point. He still liked to fish occasionally. It was later that it became zip, nada, nothing. I recall that happening when you were in eleventh grade and he was in ninth. Everything you just said seems like smoke and mirrors to me." She stroked his back and then his hand.

Peter let out a long exhale and sank down in the chair. His arms dropped to his sides. He studied the monitor beeping away, measuring Ed's pulse rate and breathing and blood pressure. "That was our last trip to Merry Moose Park. That was the beginning of the end for Steve and me."

"The end?"

"Yeah. Dad put me in charge that night. We came home late, and he really chewed me out for not watching over Kim and Steve. I knew I had let him down. I could have lived with it if it had ended there but it didn't. I mean, hey, my little brother was being a lady-killer just like me. Hell, that babe he was with was hot. So I really tried to let it go. Dad told me to be more responsible, so was I was lurking around, keeping an eye on them both without them knowing I was."

"You were spying on us?" Kim moaned. A smile sneaked its way to her face.

"Well, I wouldn't actually call it spying. I thought of it as being on a mission for Dad. That guy... Todd. He was way too old and fast for you."

"What are you saying, Peter?" Her voice was firm. "What did you do?"

"Well, later I caught him putting on the moves with yet another chick when you went souvenir shopping with Mom, so I had a little chat with him."

"I don't like where this is going," Jan said playfully.

"Me neither, Mom," Kim said. "But keep going, Peter."

Peter swallowed. "Umm… After he came back from a little walk to the beach with her, I happened to meet up with him and asked him… well, kinda told him to stay away from you, or maybe we'd have another little talk which could end up being a bit painful for him." He looked at them sheepishly but still with a little twinkle in his eyes.

"You didn't!" Kim squeaked, trying not to be too loud.

"Yes… yes I did."

"How dare you?" Kim complained, but she couldn't hide her amusement. "So that's why he just about ran from me every day after that. I couldn't figure it out. You almost gave me a complex about boys not liking me."

"Yeah, well, that didn't last long, 'cause I saw you with that Jack kid not too long after."

"You were still spying?"

"Hell yes! The way Dad sounded, it wasn't just a one-time deal. I had a talk with Mike too. Then my job was done."

"What happened in between Merry Moose and marrying Mike?" Kim pressed.

"Well, for instance, I did let the word get out in high school that nobody misuses my baby sister."

Kim stared at him. "Did you put posters up in the male dormitories at my college too?"

"No. You were pretty much old enough then to take care of yourself on a day-to-day basis."

She punched him hard in the arm.

"Ouch! Stop it. That hurt!" His hushed tone and smirk didn't make his protest seem very convincing.

"Thanks for the vote of confidence, but I still don't see how being on Dad's mission would get between you and Steve. Even though Dad reamed you out, you still must have had lots of time for fun stuff."

"Well, that's just it. I was spying on Steve too, and I wasn't happy with what I heard."

"Why, Pete? What did you hear?" Jan coaxed.

Peter stood up and peeked behind the curtain, then sat back down. "It all seemed like good fun at first. He was hanging around with all of the guys at the arcade. Mind you now, I was just checking in on him occasionally. He was just a guy looking for a summer fling. What could be better? It was tops in my book, but—"

"Back up," Kim broke in. "A summer fling is tops, but only for the guys? Not me? Am I hearing you correctly?"

"Kim, yes, it was different. I know it doesn't make a lot of sense, but given a room full of guys and girls the same age, it's okay for the guys but not the girls. In my mind."

"I pity poor Sarah when she gets old enough to date."

"You and me both," Peter said, rubbing his forehead. He glanced back toward the curtain. "So anyway, it seemed like all good fun. But one day a guy my age came up to me and said, 'Keep your queer brother away from my brother and the rest of them, or he'll have me to answer to. I told him already, but I'm giving you fair warning.' And that was the real beginning of the end. I was sure the guy was a jerk and Stevie wasn't being queer. But he did stay close to the camper after that and only went to the arcade when we all went together. I didn't really believe the guy, but still I got a bad gut feeling about it."

"Why didn't you tell me or Dad?" Jan asked.

"What? Tell you that I thought Steve might be queer? I'd rather set myself on fire."

Jan nodded. "I guess we put you in a tough situation."

"You don't know how tough, Mom. I—"

"Queer is so disrespectful, Pete." Kim's tone was harsh and reprimanding.

"They didn't use the word 'gay' much at the time. It wasn't the days of political correctness. It was more like freakin' queer." Peter countered.

"Okay, but maybe refrain from it now."

"Yeah, whatever. I do now anyway."

"Well, most of the time, I guess. Except when it comes to your brother."

"Okay, okay. I get it."

"Do you?" Kim said, not giving an inch.

"Yes, I do. Can I go on with the story now?"

"I'm sorry for jumping in with all that tough love, but that kind of talk is hurtful to Steve and his friends. Please go on."

Peter nodded and continued, "That's the story, anyway, but I never said anything about it. I didn't want to believe it. I figured if I asked him and I was wrong, he'd hate me for thinking it about him. A double-edged sword there, I guess."

"So that's why Steve was hanging so close to me for the rest of the trip. I thought he was keeping tabs on me or using me as a pick-up partner. Oh God, I never knew."

"But it seemed like you all were having fun," Jan said.

"Yeah, we were," Kim said. "At least I was, and it seemed like Steve was too. He liked all the girls we met."

"Yep, best of friends, I'm sure," Peter interjected.

Kim gave him a look that could kill. "You just can't help yourself, can you?"

"She's right, Peter," Jan warned him.

"I'll try harder. Sorry," he said.

Jan doubted if anything would really change. She had seen Steve grow more and more distant from his brother since that time. The damage seemed irreparable.

"Everybody else had a great time that year," Peter said. "You and Dad hand in hand. Kim and Steve, surrounded by guys and girls, laughing and joking and dancing to the jukebox. Me? I was just thankful when we picked up stakes, packed up the camper, and got the hell out of there."

*****

The Rock

I didn't know it'd turn out to be my secret but it did. I didn't intend it to be my secret… it just turned out that way.

It all started out as a miscommunication. Peter's problem with the spring dance seemed to work out okay, thanks to Jan's encouragement. So why shouldn't it work for Steve's, and why couldn't it be me who helped him see the light? I was tired of being just the breadwinner. The guy who came home every night too exhausted to think, let alone solve the romantic problems of our teenagers.

Steve and I were doing some woodworking when he

broached the subject. I was sanding off the picnic bench I had made, and he was making a frame for a painting he had just finished. I asked him if he was going to the spring dance and, if so, who was he taking.

All he said was, "I don't know if I'm going or not."

"Don't be silly," I said. "Of course you're going. Don't worry about asking the girl. She'll say yes. Don't be shy, Stevie."

"It's not that, Dad," he began to say, but I cut him off. I knew better... I thought. Of course he was just shy. He was a big, handsome kid. What girl wouldn't want to go to the dance with him? I told him so.

"Dad, I want to talk to you about that," he said, and all I heard was my boy asking me about advice for dating girls. He hadn't had many dates yet. So I jumped right in. What a privilege it was for me to have my son seeking my advice! I wasn't about to let him down. He needed a push and I'd give it to him. I was happy to share a moment with him the way Jan had a couple of years earlier with Pete. She wasn't the only one capable of communicating with the kids and making things better.

Yeah, sure, I'd made things better before, but it was more like fixing broken bicycles or finding lost dolls. Whatever the kids needed growing up, I was able to find it, fix it, or buy it. They knew it, and I was proud of it.

But now that they were bigger, they needed that emotional rescuing, and Jan was so much better at it than me. I wasn't jealous of Jan's relationship with the kids. I knew I did my best whenever they came to me. But those times were becoming fewer and further apart. I was determined to change that here and now.

I put my sandpaper down. "Come on over here," I said to Steve. He stopped working on his picture frame and came over closer to me.

"Now, son, listen to me," I began. "You don't have to marry the girl. It's just a date and a dance. Your brother didn't stop talking about his Spring Fling for a couple of weeks afterward. He and his friends and their dates had a blast. It's one of those moments you won't ever forget or regret doing."

"But, Dad—" He tried again to make me hear him, but I forged on.

How the hell was I to know? I wasn't expecting any earth-shattering announcements. I hadn't planned on him trying to bare his soul to me. Especially not what he was attempting to tell me. Unfortunately, I only realized it years later, in hindsight. What father would? That wasn't part of the plan.

I know now it was part of neither his plan nor mine. John Lennon once said, "Life is what happens to you while you're busy making plans." Boy, how true is that?

"Son," I said, "we all get a little nervous asking a girl out. Yes, sometimes they'll say no. After all, girls will be girls and unpredictable."

"That's just it, Dad. I'm not sure if I… like the girls."

Zoom. It went right over my head. I forged on. "Nonsense, Stevie. Don't ever let them see you sweat. Just dig in and ask the question."

"But Dad," he said softly.

Poor damn kid. He was trying his best, but I couldn't hear him. I was too pigheaded to hear him. I was on a mission to get him to that dance. Nothing else mattered. So I cut him off again. I was going to get this kid on a date if it killed me. That's what dads do— or at least that's what I thought at the time. I realize now that it's a dad's job to listen too.

"No buts, Steve," I said. "There's nothing to worry about. You'll find a great date for the dance. All you've got to do is ask. How about that girl Peggy? The one you studied with a few times and did that school project with? She seemed real sweet and nice."

I remember him looking at me square in my eyes. I remember it seemed odd at the time. It wasn't a look I was expecting. I expected a look that said how much he appreciated my advice and help. It wasn't that. I wasn't sure what it was. None of the kids had given me that look before.

I know now it was disappointment, plain and simple and deep. I hadn't disappointed one of them before. I think I broke Steve's heart. Boone had let him down. I didn't know. I thought I'd saved the day. I'm sure it was easier for him to let it go than to tell me at that point. It was probably the hardest thing he had ever attempted to do, and I shut him down.

After that, we spoke for a while about taking Peggy to the

dance. Then we went into the house. Steve went to clean up, and I remember bragging to Jan that I had single-handedly solved Steve's spring dance problem. Jan asked me if I thought Steve would actually ask a girl to go, and I proudly announced that yes, he was going to ask Peggy to the dance, and he was pretty sure she'd say yes.

"So that's how it happened?" Dad asked me.

It startled me. I'd forgotten he was with me. I'd felt like I was alone with my thoughts. "I forgot you were here with me all this time and listening."

"Everybody needs someone to talk to from time to time. Someone to confide in."

"But that's just it," I said. "Steve tried to confide in me, and I totally blew it. I was too busy trying to be the hero one last time."

"That's not a sin. Your heart was in the right place. Your intentions were good," Dad said, trying to ease my guilt.

Another saying came to my mind: "The road to hell is paved with good intentions." I couldn't shake the horrible feeling. I pointed out, "But I didn't help him. As a matter of fact, I probably made things worse for him."

"That's not a sin either. It was only a mistake."

"You're right. Not catching what he was trying to tell me was a mistake. The sin is, my secret is… when I suspected what he was trying to say a few years later, I kept it to myself and never told Jan how badly I had managed that day. I never went to Steve to ask him if he wanted to talk. I never said I was sorry and that maybe, if I had listened just a little bit more, our son's life would have been a whole lot easier. I think I broke Steve's heart that day."

Chapter Nine

Hospital Room 321
2 AM

Steve slid the curtain open quietly and saw Pete, Kim, and Jan had all dozed off. The beeping monitor maintained its constant vigil over Ed. Steve stepped silently to the door and headed directly for the nurses' desk. "Any changes?" he asked.

"No, nothing other than your family dozing off a while ago. We didn't want to wake them," the nurse informed him.

"Good on both accounts. Thank you," he said. "I'll be close by I just need to stretch my legs a bit."

"Good idea. You know the cafeteria is open all night with light fare and hot coffee if you need something. Just take the elevator down to the ground floor and you'll be there."

"Thanks. Not now but maybe later," he said. He headed down the hall to the vending area. He slipped two singles into the soda machine and then a buck and a half into the candy machine for what would normally be a seventy-five cent bag of M&Ms. After retrieving both, he sat in one of the slightly cushioned, straight-backed chairs and quietly had his well-past-midnight snack.

No one was in the waiting room; he had the space and the TV to himself. He sat in the farthest row of chairs from the TV. He pushed his chair back as far as it could go so he could rest his head against the wall. After a few minutes he sat up, popped an M&M or two in his mouth, and washed them down with Coke. It wasn't the best flavor combo he'd ever had, but the M&Ms were sweet and the Coke was cold… and caffeinated. All served to help rejuvenate his dulled mind.

The audio was set so low, it was impossible for him to hear the words of the TV evangelist unless he moved up closer. It didn't

73

seem important enough to change. He glanced at the end table next to him and noticed a flyer left behind by the state, informing people about the low-cost medical insurance available to them. He set the Coke and M&Ms on the table next to the fliers.

I don't think either the evangelist or the state can help Dad or any of us at this moment, he thought. He leaned forward, his elbows on his knees, cradling his chin in his hands. He stared at the worn carpet under his feet and sank into deep thought.

Wish I believed in God. Maybe it'd make these times easier. But even with a belief in God, so many of the religious and nonreligious people call us a blight. I thought having religion would make people more tolerant, not less. I thought God loved all of his children. So many people see us as a scourge against the very existence of man. People talk about us like we're not people at all but a disease. Speak of us like we don't have feelings. As if we are a bad sack of flour on the shelf that needs to be thrown away, discarded, destroyed, so the others around it won't become contaminated. It's almost laughable. If we, the gay community, were able to contaminate the rest of the world just by association, then wouldn't the opposite be true? Wouldn't their heterosexuality, according to their own thought process, "cure" us?

Shakespeare seemed to be fighting a similar battle four hundred years ago. Was that the first prejudice? Wasn't he musing about the same bigoted hatreds then that are being delivered upon us now? Aren't we in the same place as they were then? Was Shakespeare centuries ahead of his time when he wrote, "Are we not... fed with the same food, hurt with the same weapons, subject to the same diseases, healed by the same means, warmed and cooled by the same winter and summer...? If you prick us, do we not bleed? if you tickle us, do we not laugh? if you poison us, do we not die?"

Steve mulled the words he had learned so long ago in a high school English class, until finally he murmured them aloud in an almost inaudible whisper: "'If you prick us, do we not bleed?' Oh God, I'm tired of this fight, of bleeding. Tired of having to justifying my very existence. Why must I carry it out in my own home, with my own family?"

"I thought I'd find you here." Kim's voice brought him back to the moment. When he looked up, the concern in her face was clear. "Are you okay?"

"Hi, sis. Yeah, sure. Come on in. There's plenty of room." He patted the seat next to him. He heard a distant chime. A quiet voice paged Dr. Tomowski to the delivery room.

She sat. "So what are you doing?"

"Oh, nothing. Just having a little snack. You three were dozed off, and Dad seemed to be doing the same, so I took a walk."

"Yeah, those two were still cutting some *Zs* when my neck screamed out in pain and woke me up. God, those chairs are uncomfortable."

"They're no better here. Actually a little worse. The backs are so short you can't even rest your head except against the wall. Believe me, those chair headrests are better than this wall." He smiled and winked.

"Yeah, I'll bet. But I asked what are you doing here?"

"I told you, just having a snack."

"Steve, I stood there for almost five minutes watching you, listening to you. You weren't just having a snack. I couldn't really hear what you were mumbling, but if your eyes were laser beams, you would have burned a hole through the carpeting and the concrete below it. A couple of times you even made the ugly face."

"Get out of here. The ugly face?"

"Yep, the face of disgust you'd make when I was teasing you or something when we were kids. When you had no other way to express your outrage. Want me to show you?"

"No, no, oh God, no." He smiled at her. "I know the ugly face. You were the champ at getting it out of me, but was I really doing the ugly face?"

"'Fraid so, kiddo. What was going on in there?"

He nodded toward the TV and she turned to it.

"A Veg-O-Mastic?" Her voice was confused.

Steve looked up at the TV. An infomercial for a vegetable chopping, slicing, and dicing device had taken the place of the evangelist while he was in his trance.

He gave her the ugly face again. "No." He let the word slide out in feigned contempt. "There was an evangelist on, and even though I couldn't hear his words, I imagined the words I've heard so often that he and people like him say about me."

"About you? People talk about you?"

"No, not necessarily me, even though I'm sure they do. My own brother is testament to that. I mean what people say about the gay community. How they think we all should be damned or all put on an island and bombed."

"Oh, that you. I see," she said slowly. After a quiet moment, she said, "Pete doesn't hate you for being gay."

"Really? Could have fooled me when he was referring to me as being, and I quote, 'freakin' gay.' He'll never change."

"He didn't really mean anything by it, Steve." She wrapped her arm around his shoulders.

"It hurts, Kim. I can take it from the rest of the world but not family. Not Pete."

It was then that the long hours of little sleep and even longer hours of waiting for Ed to wake up hit them both. When she touched her head to his, he turned and held her too, and they cried in each other's arms. Brother and sister, son and daughter, both helpless. Both crying over the torment Steve was feeling and their concern for their father. Both hurting. Both awaiting the worst. Steve was unable to ask for help from a God he felt had forsaken him.

*****

Peter woke himself up with a loud snort and saw Jan holding back a smile. "Good morning, sunshine," she said.

"How long have I been out?"

"Not long. It's about two thirty."

"God, I feel like a train hit me."

"Well, hold on there for a few more hours. The neurologist will be in this morning, and then we'll have a better picture of what to expect. Maybe we'll feel comfortable enough to go home."

"I'm not going anywhere, Mom."

"I understand. But maybe we'll feel comfortable enough to take shifts sitting with him."

"Maybe that'll work. We'll see," Peter agreed reluctantly. "There, he's dreaming again." He gestured toward Ed.

Jan looked and noticed the slight eye movement. She leaned into him. "We're here, honey, and we'll be here when you wake up."

The eye movements continued. After a few minutes, they stopped.

Jan turned to Peter. "So how are you holding up?" she asked. It was a pointed question, and he knew it. They were alone and he could talk freely. That's the way it always worked. She never picked a time to have one of her heart-to-hearts when anyone else was around to break the moment. This was about as private as they would get. So he decided to cut right to the chase.

"I feel like shit. To tell you the truth."

Jan seemed surprised and sat back in her chair. "Well, okay. I guess I'm not going to have to coax that out of you. About what?"

"I just feel out of control. I am so used to being in control, but here I have nothing in control. I feel like I'm letting everybody down."

"Honey, you can't control this situation."

"I know, but usually I can throw some money at whatever the issue is and make it better. Or make it go away."

"Money won't buy Dad's recovery. It's out of our hands no matter what. You can't change that."

"No, I guess not. I can't help Dad right now, and I can't change how I feel about Steve and his…friend either."

"Ah-ha. So that's the problem. Steve doesn't have to know everything about how you feel, does he? Can't you just keep it to yourself? Have a friendly little chat about something superfluous? A no-stress subject? Or maybe even apologize for your comment?"

"I wish I could. But after last night, when he heard me talking about him being gay he won't believe I really want to chat."

"Just talk to him. I'm sure he'll understand that you didn't mean anything by it and you were just stressed out."

"I don't think he will…" Peter's voice trailed off.

"What? You don't think he'll forgive you? Sure he will."

"No, Mom, he won't. He won't believe me. Ever."

"Peter, how can you say such a thing?"

"You don't understand. There's no use in me pretending. When we were kids, I was a lot worse to him about all that gay crap than I was yesterday. He'll never believe I've changed."

"You see, Pete? I think you hit the issue right on the head."

Peter looked at her for an explanation. "What is it then?" he asked.

"You said 'all that gay crap.' Maybe it's you who really needs to change. Be more understanding. My God, Pete. He's your brother."

"I know, and that is where the problem lies."

*****

The Rock

"Stuff happens in families, son," Dad told me as we sat on the big rock, dangling our hooks and worms over the edge into the fishing hole.

"What?" I said as I became aware that he was with me again. "Were you here all the time?" Had he just appeared out of nowhere, or was I the one who just showed up?

"Son, I've always been here. Where were you?"

"I'm not sure," I told him. I drifted off, trying to remember where I actually was while in that dark place.

"Like I said, stuff happens in families. Family doesn't desert family. Family conflicts aren't uncommon, ya know." He said it to me as if schooling me in understanding the subject of family crap. "We're not the first dysfunctional family."

That made me laugh. Where had he gotten that word? I would have expected him to say something like, "We're not the first screwed-up family." He sounded more like Jan now than himself. Whatever. I suspected nothing here was what it appeared to be anyway.

"Yeah, I know," I said. "But I hoped we'd have the perfect family. It started out so good."

"Ha," he laughed. "Most of the time it does start out great. The marriage, the little baby that is just so adorable that you can't believe you managed to be happy without it. But stuff happens to the best of families. Often, though, they don't speak of it. Somehow they manage to muddle along without it totally unhinging the whole process. Other times, though, they don't speak of it and it grows like a cancer. It strangles them. Though they try to manage it, they sit and watch as the heart of the family wastes away."

78

I looked at him. How had he known that? He wasn't speaking about our family when I was a kid—his family when I was growing up. Maybe he had been the lucky one. His family had had something to hide that didn't destroy them. But why would it? He suffered from war fatigue, or maybe what they called shell shock back then. Later, after the Vietnam War, they began to call it post-traumatic stress syndrome. Certainly nothing to be ashamed of.

My family today was different. We never spoke about… it. About Steve's… well, Steve's "problem." It was embarrassing to talk about. We never told our friends. If they wondered about Steve, well, then, let them wonder. I couldn't give two shits.

"Do you think that's what's happening to my family, Dad?" I asked. I was afraid to hear his answer. He was a straight shooter and always told it like it was. I could trust in him in much the same way I'd always wanted Steve to trust me.

But I let Steve down. In all honesty, I tried to make it right, but it had been too late.

"Yes, son. That is exactly what's happening to your family."

It crushed me. What could I do about it? I was in no-man's-land, visiting with the dead. I was probably dead myself, or at least not in the living world.

But why had it been so embarrassing to talk to Steve about it? Or, at least, recognize it? My God, it wasn't like he was a murderer or some jailbird. He was just a man. Plain and simple. Just a man. It's not like we had to talk about what went on behind the doors of his bedroom. I never asked Pete or any other straight person about that. It wasn't any of my business. I only had to ask Steve how he and his boyfriend were doing. All I really needed to know was if he was happy.

I'd asked Pete that every time he was home and dating someone. Most times he'd tell me that he was fine, but she wasn't the one. There was no shame involved in the conversation. Even when he was dating Laura, I'd ask and he'd say good and then I'd be happy for him.

When he said he thought she was the one, it made my day. There was no shame there either. Why should there be? I was happy that he would soon start that remarkable journey from just being responsible for himself to being responsible for someone other than himself and maybe more. I didn't shy away from wanting to hear more about her, even though we had already met several times while they were dating. When I engaged him in a conversation about her, I could see in his eyes that she was the one. I almost envied him the journey he was about to begin.

But Steve wouldn't take me on that journey. He didn't bring home dates, with the exception of Peggy one or two times after the spring dance.

Later on, after we knew about him being gay, he didn't bring home his boyfriends. I'm ashamed to say I was very okay with that. I didn't want to meet the man who was my son's lover. I wanted Steve to marry and bring me home grandsons and granddaughters. That was my plan. Not that I had the right to make a plan for Steve's life, but I think parents do. I'm sure I was not alone on that one.

Of course, I had Bennie and Sarah, and they made me happier than anything else. But there probably wouldn't be any more from Kim or Peter.

I had been so looking forward to Steve's kids. For whatever reason, I seemed to be closer to Steve. Maybe it was because we had spent time together in the woodshop when he was younger. Or maybe because he took after me like the way I looked like my father. I don't know. We had a bond until he started to drift away from me. I had hoped that when he had kids, we'd find common ground again and start up where we'd left off. I guess I felt cheated out of my dream.

But that was only my dream, not Steve's. What should have mattered was Steve's reality, not my selfish dreams.

Chapter Ten

Hospital Room 321
3 AM

Kim peeked around the corner of the door to see Jan and Peter sitting quietly at Ed's side. "Knock, knock," she whispered. When they looked up, she smiled and said, "Is it still visiting hours?"

Jan smiled too and was happy they were back. She felt like she needed all of her children around. "Have they ever ended?" she said cheerfully. "Come on in. We were just sitting around solving the world's problems."

Kim and Steve were already through the door before she finished the sentence. They took the remaining chairs. Kim quickly sat in the chair toward the bottom of the bed, leaving Steve the one next to Peter. Steve gave her the ugly face before he sat.

Peter broached the subject they had all been avoiding. "We should talk about the DNR Dad asked Dr. Mehra for."

"Why? What is there for us to talk about?" Steve confronted him quickly.

"Why? Because maybe we don't agree with it. I think it's time for us to take control of this situation and make our own decisions."

Steve looked Peter squarely in the eyes. "Us to take control? Why is it up to us to take control?"

"Because Dad's in a coma and can't speak for himself. That's why."

Peter's tone was trending toward condescending, but Steve ignored it. "I think Dad has made his decision, and I think we should abide by it."

"He never even spoke to Mom about it. What kind of decision is that?" Peter shot back.

"It's his decision. That's what kind. He's not dead yet, so you're not the boss, big brother. Dad made his decision when he put Dr. Mehra in charge of the DNR."

Jan felt Steve's temper was on the edge of flashing. The long hours and lack of sleep were affecting them all.

"That's it," Peter declared. "End of discussion." They were both trying to keep their voices low, but it was a losing battle. "I'll sue the bastard."

Jan broke in, "Pete, that's no way to speak about Dr. Mehra. He's your father's oldest friend."

"Don't care," Peter insisted. "It shouldn't be Mehra's decision to make."

"It's not your decision to make either," Steve retaliated.

"Okay, we'll let Mom decide. She told me she already has power of attorney for him and he has it for her. I think we can change the DNR with that. What do you think, Mom?"

Jan was already taken aback by their argument. Now she was being asked to decide whether to abide by Ed's DNR or try to change it, knowing her decision could save him—or commit him to a lifetime of low quality of life. He might end up resenting her for the rest of their time together.

"I don't know, boys. It's hard for me to make up my mind. If I make the wrong decision, he could die or he could hate me forever. Karash has the medical background. Maybe that's why Dad asked him to take it on."

Steve jumped in to rescue Jan from this torture. "See? This is what Dad was probably trying to avoid. He knew Dr. Mehra could make the decision based on medical knowledge and not get all confused by emotion. I think we should let it stand."

"No, we won't. I'll have my lawyers file an injunction by tomorrow."

"Boys! Stop it!" Jan was beside herself.

"Excuse me," the nurse said. They turned to face her and fell silent. "Your voices are carrying and disturbing other patients. You'll have to keep your voices low. What seems to be the problem?"

Jan said, "We're discussing the DNR, and we seem to be having a difference of opinion."

"Dr. Mehra has already given us instructions concerning the DNR. He's the sole person named as the decision maker in the DNR."

Peter said, "Yes, but he was given that without our knowledge. We are Mr. Connor's immediate family, and we feel we know Dad better than Dr. Mehra. Therefore, we are better equipped to make that decision."

Steve spoke up quickly, "There you go. Now you know more than a doctor about medical care? And furthermore—"

The nurse cut him off, "I won't ask again to lower your voices. If you can't control it, you'll have to take this to a conference room downstairs or out of the building."

"She's right." Kim stepped in as the voice of reason. "We'll respect your request and the other patients. Won't we, guys?"

Steve and Peter nodded.

"All right then," the nurse said. "I know these are hard times. Most families have a difficult time dealing with the issue you're dealing with now. I don't have a magic answer for you or how to make that decision."

"That's just it," Peter said in a controlled tone. "We don't have a say in it."

"Unfortunately, I can't change that either. I hope no one will have to make that decision. Now please try to get some rest, all of you. This has been a long, hard day and night for you all."

She left the room. Almost instantly, Peter was at it again. "I'm going to change this thing."

"Pete," Kim began. "Let's just let it go for now. Dr. Mehra will be making rounds in a few hours, and we'll talk to him then."

"Nope. The time for talking is done. I sent an email from my phone to my lawyers this afternoon after we heard about this craziness. They'll have an injunction here before we even see Mehra."

Steve looked at Peter and shook his head. "Why must you always be like that?"

"Like what?" Peter said, in a way that made Steve certain he knew exactly what Steve was implying.

"Like that. Like taking over everything."

"Because I know what's best. I'm the only level-headed one

here right now. You're being such a drama queen. Don't confuse the issue. Bottom line is that this should be our decision."

"There you go *again*. I'm *not* a drama queen just because I disagree with you. Stop trying to bully all of us. This will be a family decision, not a Pete decision."

"Think what you may. I'm going to use my own judgment because I know what's best."

"That's right. You always know what's best. What's right or wrong. You're the judge and jury. Just like in high school. Right?" Steve's words hung heavy in the room as he turned and left them all speechless.

Kim followed him out. Rather than turning to the right, as he did, toward the waiting room, she turned left toward the elevators.

*****

The Rock

It was the worst day of my life. It had crystallized in my memory as if it happened yesterday, even though it was forty-two years ago. It was the day I had to tell the doctors and nurses not to try to bring Grace back. It made a wound so deep in my heart that it would never heal.

Grace and I had had many talks about the inevitable. I knew she didn't want to linger on forever just because medical science had the ability to keep her here. It would be up to me to make that call if things went differently than we hoped—and, of course, they did.

We were in the hospital after a treatment when she collapsed. I caught her and… I think our eyes touched before hers closed. I want to believe we did touch each other in that last gaze, that final goodbye, but I don't really know. She never woke to tell me. Many more times than I could imagine, I wondered about that moment. Did we say goodbye?

I remember the nurses running to us and lifting her to a bed or gurney or something like it and compressing her chest.

I heard someone call out, "Crash cart, room 101. Code blue." There were frantic movements by the two or three nurses around Grace. In another second, a doctor came in and began to examine

84

her. Then the crash cart was brought in.

It was all a blur, but I wasn't a dummy. I knew what "code blue" meant. I knew what a crash cart was for.

Then everything stopped, and all eyes were on me.

The doctor looked at me for what seemed an eternity. I knew what he was waiting for. Thoughts rushed through my head. Grace and I had known she was going to die from the cancer, but that wasn't expected for a few more months. We wanted to spend the last few days close, and I wanted to care for her. To have just a little more time.

Now this. It wasn't in our plan book. Other than the fact that I had to make the call.

I turned to the doctor, looking for help.

"Her pupils are fixed and dilated, and her heart has stopped," he told me. "She's had some sort of stroke. I can't be sure what her prognosis will be if we resuscitate her. We can try to bring her back, but it's up to you, Mr. Connor."

I froze. Yet still they all stared at me. Waiting.

This was not in our plan. I didn't know what to do. I wanted to bring her back so we could play this thing out the way we'd planned. But I also knew she wouldn't want to be so disabled that she would be restricted to bed, suffering and just waiting for the end to come.

Selfishly, I wanted to bring her back. Even the few months we thought we still had were like gold to us. Every second, every day was a blessing.

I never forgot those few seconds of making that decision. The doctor was still looking at me for my call and I shook my head. But he spoke to me. "Mr. Connor. Do you want us to perform CPR on your wife?"

I was confused. Hadn't I just told him?

I looked at him and shook my head again. And again he asked me, adding, "You must say it, Mr. Connor. Do you want us to perform CPR on your wife?

Then I understood. I needed to say it. "No."

Everything stopped. It seemed like my heart stopped too. I went into a dazed state.

I felt the energy level in the room drop. The doctor said,

"Time of death, six twenty-three." They covered her body with a sheet and asked if I wanted a few minutes alone with her.

A few minutes alone? What the hell were they asking? I wanted a lifetime with her. We had planned on a lifetime. No, a few minutes wouldn't do.

I don't know how long I was there with her before a priest came in and sat with me. I felt as if I couldn't go on without her. She was the love of my life and now she was gone. So, it seemed, was my life. I went numb all over until the priest took my hand. Then I remember becoming aware of my surroundings once again.

He gave her last rites and again sat with me quietly. Sometime later, my parents and brother, John, arrived. Dad stood next to me, looking at Grace. Then he took me by the shoulders and directed me out the door.

I don't remember anything other than Grace's cold body lying under that sterile sheet. I wouldn't wish that day on anyone. I wouldn't inflict those moments I labored to make that decision on my worst enemy. No one deserves that.

They all stayed with me that night at my house. As I regained my wits, we discussed making the funeral arrangements and all that stuff. I don't know how I would've have made it through those days without my family by my side. They were my united front against the depression that was beginning to force its way into my mind.

*****

Mike and Kim's House

Mike reached instantly for his phone on the nightstand when it rang. He held his breath before he answered it.

It was a sound he had been hoping not to hear this evening. He knew how much Kim adored her father. He was dreading the thought of her losing him, and Bennie would be devastated too. Of course, that time would come someday, but he was hoping that day would not be this soon.

He saw how much Kim enjoyed the way he played with

Bennie. She would smile as she watched from a distance as the two of them played some silly dino game on the living room floor or under the card table covered with a sheet. She often said it reminded her of her childhood.

Mike was happy she could enjoy watching this playtime with Bennie, but he didn't have too many of that sort of memories himself. As an immigrant from Mexico, his father had had to work long, hard days in the fields to bring home barely enough money each week to pay the rent and feed his family. The man often said that a little hard work never hurt anyone, but it probably killed him. All the pesticides and dust in the fields. He developed lung cancer when Mike was in college, and died when Mike was in his junior year.

Before he died, he told Mike to never give up on his dreams and that he was proud of him. After the funeral, his mother moved back to her hometown to be with family. Mike and Maria stayed on in the United States to finish their college educations.

Mike never did give up on his dreams. He felt as if he was living his dream every day with his beautiful wife and his son Bennie. As far as he was concerned, life was good. He didn't want it to change.

Life had been hard when he was Bennie's age, but he remembered his mother and father being cheerful and thankful for what they did have. His father began each meal by giving thanks to God for the food they were about to eat and making a request to keep his family safe. As they ate, his mother and father would ask him and Maria what they had learned in school that day. Mike remembered how delighted his mother and father were as their stories unfolded. When they were finished, his parents would tell the children how proud they were of them. Eventually his father would tell them both that they would be the first in their family to go to college. Whenever Mike relived these memories, he smiled, knowing his mother and father had been right.

But he had no time for fond memories now. He answered the phone with his heart in his throat. "Hello… Hi, hon. What's wrong? No, don't worry. I'm glad you called. Is Ed okay? … I'm glad he's still all right, but what's wrong? I can hear it in your voice. Out with it, kid." He took a deep breath and listened to Kim.

When she had finished, he tried to console her. "Well, the good news is Ed's condition hasn't worsened , but I'm sorry Pete and Steve are having such troubles. I was afraid this might happen, especially because you're all so tired and stressed."

He listened some more. "Hon, this doesn't really change anything. Those two haven't been on good terms since I've been in the family."

He listened again for a few minutes. "I don't know if now would be the best time to demand an explanation from them. Talk to your mother about it before you say anything. Remember, she's got a lot on her plate right now. You all do… Yeah, okay. Call me if you want. I'm here for you. Remember, no family is perfect… Okay, love you too. Bye."

Chapter Eleven

Hospital Room 321
4 *AM*

Kim walked into the room and right up to Steve and Peter, who were standing next to Ed's bed. "All right, you two. I want to know exactly what the heck is going on here and what happened in high school that ruined your friendship. Nothing could be—"

Peter held a figure to his mouth and shushed her. "Dr. Mehra is talking with Mom behind the curtain." He pointed with his thumb over his shoulder toward the curtain behind him.

"What?" she whispered.

Steve pointed to the hallway, and they all moved to just outside the door.

"Dr. Mehra left instructions with the nurses to call him if there were any problems with Ed or the family," Steve said. "I guess our little outburst qualified as a reason to call, or so he said when he came in. Mom's talking to him about the DNR now."

Peter didn't waste any time. "As soon as he came, I told him if he didn't lift that DNR, we were going to sue him."

"You didn't! Oh my God. What did Mom say?"

Steve chuckled. "You should have seen her, sis! If looks could kill. I thought she was going to swat him in the back of the head. She always said she would do it when he was being a little brat when we were kids. I think this time he actually deserved it." He smiled a devilish smile.

"Just shut up, *Stevie*," Peter said.

"You shut up," Steve shot back.

"Boys! Or should I say *children*? Please behave yourselves. Back to the real world, please. What did Dr. Mehra say to Mom?"

Steve said, "Well, first of all, and the best part so far, is Dr. Mehra totally ignored Peter and asked Mom if they could speak privately. Mom said of course and mumbled some sort of apology about Peter's comment. They disappeared behind the curtain. That's when you came in. That's it. You know as much as we do now." He leaned against the door frame and folded his arms across his chest, looking at Peter. Peter turned to ignore him.

"Guys, please. We don't have time for this. Can't we just bury the hatchet for now?"

"I'm willing," Peter offered.

"Sure you are. You're the guy with the hatchet. Stop pretending you care."

"I do care, Steve. I really do care about you. I just don't care for what you're doing with your life."

Steve rolled his eyes. "See, Kimmy? He just doesn't get it and never will. He's always gotta be the last-word boss."

Steve's voice was beginning to escalate. Kim noticed a nurse look up at them. "Quiet down, Steven. Do you want to get us kicked out of here?"

Before he could answer, Kim saw Dr. Mehra and her mother emerge from behind the curtain. "Okay, guys. Shape up. Time to go back in and talk to Mom and Dr. Mehra and see if anything can be resolved."

They started into the room but Kim stopped abruptly and turned to Peter. "Pete, don't insult this man again. Maybe you're forgetting that this just isn't Dad's doctor. They're also friends." She gave him the look. "Got it?"

"Yeah, okay. I'll lay off for now," Peter said.

Kim led the delegation into the room. "Hi, Dr. Mehra. How are you? I'm sorry if the nurses got you out of bed just because of us," she said apologetically.

Karash smiled. "Not to worry, Kim. The only other option was to ask you to leave, and they knew I wouldn't want that. I'm happy they called."

Kim glared at her brothers.

"I start rounds at six anyway, and it was about to be getting up," the doctor added. Jan knew he was trying to make light of the situation for their sake and appreciated it.

Karash continued, "I've known this family for years. I've treated you all. I've played golf with Ed and broken bread with you at your house. What kind of friend would I be if I didn't come to your aid in a time of need like this? Why don't we all go to the conference room down the hall and talk about this?"

Jan responded, "Thank you, Karash. Yes, that sounds like a good idea. Isn't it?" She scanned each of her children's faces. It was clear that her statement was understood by everyone.

"Good," Karash said. "I'll ask the nurses to keep an eye on Ed while we're in there."

As they left the room Karash stopped at the nurses' station and spoke to the head nurse while the family waited a short distance away. When he finished, they followed him to the conference room. He took a seat at the table, and they all followed suit.

Karash spoke first. "I know this is a hard time for you all and you're all exhausted, so let me make this brief. It was obvious he was speaking directly to Kim, Pete and Steve. "Your father asked me to be the health care proxy because he didn't want to put your mother through the anguish of making that decision. This is how I understand his wishes to be. I thought it would be best if I—"

Peter interrupted, "I don't think it's your call. We are his—"

Jan sat forward, but before she said anything, Karash spoke over him. "If you let me finish, Peter." It wasn't a request. Peter sat back. "Thank you. Now, as I was saying, this is how I understand your father's wishes to be. But in all good faith, I don't feel I can make this decision knowing it is breaking this family apart. I'm saying if I relinquish my role as health care proxy and pass it on to your mother, it might still break this family apart, but at least it will be the family's decision. Maybe at some time in the future, you'll be able to reconcile your differences."

Peter nodded approvingly with just a hint of triumph.

Karash went on, "Your father told me how much he suffered when making this type of call for his first wife, Grace. He didn't want to put your mother through that. The fact is, he didn't even want to discuss it with her, knowing she would insist on taking it on. I tried to tell him that most couples go through this sort of the thing, and it's something they can eventually accept and deal with. But he insisted that I take on the role."

He stopped and surveyed each of them. Even Peter was keeping his mouth shut.

"You see, your father sank into a deep depression after Grace died. He always wondered if he had made the right decision. He, of course, had known she was going to pass away soon. But he wondered if he had stolen her last few days on earth away from her—away from them both.

"Unfortunately, however much we try, we just can't avoid the hardships that go along with this type of situation. I don't think his decision to spare you the grief is a viable one. If it were quick, without this long, arduous process we are all going through—well, then, maybe so. Not now.

"He said his family was a source of strength for him, and I'm giving that opportunity to you: an opportunity for you to be a source of strength for your mother and for him. She may have a hard decision coming up. She will need you to be there for her."

"Thank you, Karash," Jan said. "We deeply appreciate your efforts on Ed's behalf and on ours too. Please tell us what to expect."

"Well, in Ed's case in dealing with Grace, the doctor indicated there may have been brain damage after his examination. Certain signs were present that indicated Grace had suffered irreparable brain damage. If something happens to Ed, I hope an examination will give us some indication of how you should proceed. I will do my best to give you as much information as I can to base your decision on."

Steve said, "But Doctor, hasn't he already made that decision? Didn't he asked you to place a DNR order on his chart if something like this happened? Shouldn't we respect his wishes?"

"It's not that simple. His real wishes were to keep you all from suffering by having to make a decision not fully based on a prognosis."

"But didn't you make the medical decision that he was at the point where a DNR was appropriate?" Steve continued to push for what he felt was his father's dying wish.

"Yes, but I also thought there would come an event that would validate that decision earlier last night. It didn't happen."

"In other words?" Kim asked.

"I thought he would either wake up or have a seizure that would tell us that a full recovery would not be possible."

"So with that in mind, does that negate your decision about

the DNR?" Steve forged on.

"Not necessarily. There aren't any indicators at this moment either way. No man, including me, is infallible. I'm sorry that I can't make it any easier for you all, but that is where we are at this moment. A decision will have to be made when the time comes. If no one is here to make it, the nurses will have to do what is directed. So it will be the DNR or, if you rescind that, they will try their best to recover him."

"Thank you for understanding, Doctor," Kim said. "I guess it's up to us now. Let's hope that it won't even come to that point."

"That's true. We'll know more after the neurological examination and tests. After we get those results, we'll meet back here in this conference room, at which time you may be able to make an informed decision. However, the results may not be conclusive, and that will put us back to where we are now."

"In that case, Karash, I think if we are in this for the long haul, I'll make it that any of us can make the call. It's obvious that we all can't be here all the time. There may come a time when a decision will have to be made at the moment. If none of us are here then, I think I will keep the DNR in place." Jan looked at each of her children. No one spoke.

"All right," Karash said. "I think we're finished here. I'm going to get a cup of coffee and start my rounds. I'll check in with you later."

They all stood when Karash pushed back from the table and stood.. Karash took Jan's hand. "The next few days may be difficult, but you'll find the strength to make it through them with the help of your family." He shook Kim's, Steve's, and Peter's hands and left the room.

*****

The Rock

"Our fishing lines have been in for what seems like forever, but we haven't caught anything," I told Dad as we sat on the rock. Our lines hung gently from the tips of our poles into the cold water of the fishing hole, just as they always had when I brought my family there so many years ago. I had never come here with him. Why was he here with me now?

"Is that what we are doing?" he asked.

It seemed like a silly question. *Of course that's what we've been doing*, I thought. *Everything that's taken place has been on this old rock. I've spent enough time here to be sure of where I've been and what I've been doing.*

Of course, Gracie and I hadn't been fishing when she was here with me. But the kids and I had been fishing here not that long ago, and now Dad and I were.

"Yes, of course we're fishing," I told him. "What do you think?"

"Oh, I don't know. I thought we were just talking. Talking about family and this old rock. This old friend of yours."

"The rock? A friend?" I asked. I was confused by his statement.

"Sure, this rock. It's been here for years. Withstood the test of time. Wind, rain, the icy cold of winter, and the blistering heat of summer. Don't you remember how hot the surface would get when the sun had been beating on it for hours?"

"Yes, I do, now that you mention it. It would get so hot sometimes that I'd throw a bucket of water on it so the kids wouldn't hurt their hands or bare feet. It's odd that I forgot that."

"Not really so odd. There's a lot of things we do in life that we forget. We can't remember all things. But the rock you remember."

"Sure. We loved this place."

"And you remember the texture? The swirls of different colors?"

"Sure. The swirls are the prettiest thing about the rock. Sometimes it seemed like I could almost distinguish images or pictures in the swirls. Kind of like you can see shapes in the passing clouds."

He nodded knowingly. "And the rock has been like that since the beginning of time, hasn't it?"

"I guess," I said, "but what does this have to do with fishing?"

"It's not about fishing, son," he said. I felt the tenderness in his voice when he said it, but still I was confused. "It's about the rock," he said and then fell silent. Waiting.

"Dad, please tell me. What about the rock?"

He smiled that understanding smile he used to give me when I was a kid and he was helping me figure out a math problem I didn't understand. He never told me the answer. He asked me questions and helped me figure out the problem by myself.

"Look at the swirls, son."

I looked and saw exactly what I'd always seen for years: the bumpy surface of darker and lighter swirls of stone. The dark swirls were always the higher part of the surface, and the lighter ones—the white, pink, and blue—were slightly recessed. Each achieved its own level as it withstood the elements and time. Each layer had been created in the days when the earth was a swirling ball of molten rock and these were pushed together. As this giant ball began to cool, the different types and colors of rock were left joined together.

But still I was confused. "I see the swirls, but what else should I be seeing?"

"Well, say for instance, what if that layer of white rock was much softer than the rest? What would happen?"

I thought about it for a moment before I spoke. "It would erode much quicker than the rest. That groove in the rock would be deeper than the rest."

He stroked his chin and looked at me approvingly, as he did when he realized I was about to understand the problem we were working on. "Okay then. What if the white rock was so soft that it would be washed away by the harsh elements one hundred times faster than the others?"

It was such an elemental question, I found it almost laughable. All this time in questions and answers just to find out that the rock would eventually break down and become a pile of smaller, dissimilar rocks, just like the countless other ones in the stream bed now.

So I told him, "It would become a simple pile of rocks. So what?"

"So..." he repeated. "Isn't that what this is all about?"

"About a rock breaking down?"

"It's not really just a rock, is it, Ed? Isn't this rock an

important thing in your life? Isn't this rock your world? Isn't this rock where you and your family spent happy times? Isn't this rock your family? Aren't you afraid that your family is being broken down by time and harshness? Aren't you afraid that your family will soon become just a pile of unassociated rocks in the stream bed?"

*****

Hospital Room 321
4:30 *AM*

The assemblage of bells and alarms went off when the steady beeping of the heart monitor went silent. "Code blue, room 321" sounded over the intercom. Jan, Peter, Kim, and Steve stood helplessly at Ed's side.

"What should we do?" Kim choked out.

"Nothing," Peter instructed her in a calm, dispassionate voice. He knew the nurses would be there in a second or two with the crash cart. They would try to jump-start Ed's heart, and that's what Peter wanted. "The nurses will be here in a second," he added.

"That's what I mean. Do we have them do it, or do we follow Dad's instructions to Dr. Mehra?" Kim's voice sounded desperate.

"Don't be silly. Even Mehra said he wasn't sure of the outcome if Dad were to be brought back. We should just let them do their thing. We can't 'what if' this whole thing." Peter sounded convincing.

"It's not right," Steve objected. "Dad would be so God damn mad at us if we allowed them to bring him back and he ended up severely disabled. Mom? Tell him."

Jan stepped back as if frightened by the discussion. Then all hell broke loose. The nurses and a doctor on call charged through the door. One brought up the rear, pushing the crash cart with the possibly life-restoring defibrillator on board.

Immediately one nurse started chest compressions until the doctor instructed her to stop. He examined Ed and shook his head. He backed away while the nurse continued with the compressions. Periodically she would stop and another nurse would use a manual resuscitator to pump life-giving air into his lungs.

The doctor turned to Jan. "What would you like us to do, Mrs. Connor?"

She froze and the nurses continued their routine. Jan looked to her children for help or support or approval, but she didn't get a consensus. Peter told her, "Use all measures, Mom."

Steve jumped in immediately. "Don't do it. If he comes back paralyzed or maybe worse, it would be his hell on earth. He was always too vital to finish his days lying helplessly in a bed or wheelchair."

The seconds flew by. "Mrs. Connor, I need an answer."

Jan looked to Kim. "I don't know, Mom. They're both right. It's got to be your call, but I'll support any decision you make." She walked to Jan and took her hands.

All eyes were on Jan when she stammered out, "D-do whatever you can. I can't lose him."

At that moment, the heart monitor began to beep, and a nurse reported that Ed had established a normal sinus rhythm.

"It seems like he's made that decision for you. He's back... for now," the on-call doctor said.

"For now?" Jan questioned.

"I can't guarantee that this won't happen again in ten more minutes or ten more years. Each time something like this happens, there's a higher probability that more damage has been done. For now, he's stable."

"Thank God," Jan whispered and sat on the bed next to Ed.

The doctor said, "But it appears you all should come to some sort of agreement, or it could be a worse fate for this family than what Mr. Connor is suffering right now." He and the nurses left the room.

Steve walked up to Peter. "What the hell is wrong with you? We all know Dad didn't want these extraordinary efforts to keep him alive."

"I don't care. He was making it easy for Mom without thinking how much it would hurt us all. It was selfish."

"Selfish?" Steve repeated. The harshness in his voice left no doubt that this would be a battle to the end with his brother.

"Yeah. Did he even think how it would hurt the kids? My Sarah hasn't even gotten to know him yet."

"That's not his fault, Pete, and you know it."

"Maybe, but regardless of that, Sarah still has time to get to know him."

"Now you're the selfish one. Maybe Dad was thinking about the kids. Maybe he didn't want to have the kids trotted in to visit some drooling vegetable in a wheelchair."

"Never mind. You'll never understand because you'll never have kids."

Steve's jaw clenched at the comment. "That's bullshit and almost the lowest blow you've ever thrown at me. Almost. You three figure it out. You know my opinion. I respect Dad's wishes. You're just thinking of yourself, Pete. Just like you always did. You don't give a shit about the others who might really get hurt. Just as long as you don't get your hands dirty. Just like in high school." Steve fisted his hands at chest height and closed his eyes as if trying to hold back years of rage. "Judas!" he spit out in a deep, primal, guttural voice and walked from the room.

"What are we going to do, Mom?" Kim asked.

"I don't know. I think I was being the selfish one a few seconds ago. I'm afraid I wanted to save him for my sake. But that's past now. What I want to know is what happened between you and Steve in high school, Peter?" She folded her arms across her chest. It was a stance she had taken countless times in his life when she wanted to get to the bottom of something that had happened.

It usually worked, but Peter knew he couldn't let it work today. Those days would remain buried forever if he had anything to say about it. "Oh, he's just overreacting again, Mom. You know Steve. He's just a drama queen."

Jan sprang up from the bedside, stepped forward, and pointed her finger right in his face. "Don't ever talk about your brother like that again. I won't have it. Do you understand?"

Peter's jaw tightened, "Yeah, sure. Sorry, I got carried away."

"So what are you going to do about this… this falling out between you and Steve?" Jan's tone demanded an answer.

Peter's mind traveled back in time. He knew he could never forgive Steve any more than Steve would forgive him.

In those days he had been the big man on campus. President

of the class, girls chasing after him like bees to honey. He never had to wonder if he would have a date for a dance or a party. His biggest problem was figuring out which among the beautiful bevy of young ladies chasing him he'd go out with.

He never let himself get tied down to just one of them. Oh no, he had the world by the tail and he wasn't going to let it go. He liked to play the field.

And on the field, he was always the best too. Baseball, basketball, and captain of the football team. Oh yeah, life was good and he was enjoying its benefits.

But in twelfth grade, things began to change. There were parties he heard about that he didn't get invited to. Usually they were the backwoods drinking parties set up by the other guys on the football team.

At first he shrugged it off as an oversight. What the hell, it didn't really matter. He had been at the movies, making out with Patty that night anyway. But then other things started to catch him off guard. By the time football season was over and basketball had begun, he noticed the other guys clamming up when he came in the room and even on the court when they were practicing. He was getting fewer and fewer passes from his teammates, even when he was obviously in the clear for a shot. Once, the coach called a time out during a game just to chew the other guys out because they were missing passes to Peter, who could have easily made the basket. They lost that game despite being heavily favored.

When the spring baseball practices began, he was practically a loner. He was confused and lonely. No matter how he tried to placate them—even after he offered to snatch some booze from his parents' liquor cabinet—they continued to avoid him with flimsy excuses.

After one practice session, he stayed behind with the coach to get a little help on his curveball and was the last into the locker room. When he turned the corner of a row of lockers, the guys quickly stopped talking and turned away from him. He finally lost it.

"What the hell is going on around here lately? What's wrong with you guys? Shit, we've done almost everything together for the past four years, and now you shut up when I come into the room. You won't even look me in the eyes? What's up?"

When no one spoke, he called out, "Joe? What's up? Did I do something wrong? Hit on somebody's girlfriend? Jesus, Joe, we've been friends since grade school. Clue me in, will ya?"

Joe turned slowly and gave him a half-crooked, poor excuse of an apologetic look, "The word came up from the JV team that… well… Steve's had a little trouble with wandering eyes in the locker room after practice in the showers."

"What?" Peter demanded vehemently. But he knew damn well what Joe was getting at. "That's bullshit," he said, trying to hold back the shakiness in his voice.

"Sorry, Pete, but there's more. It's just… we know he's queer and… well… you're his brother. He's making us feel a little creepy when he comes in here, waiting for you to catch his ride home."

Peter's outrage crushed the momentary shakiness in his voice. "Who's telling you all this crap?" But what difference did it make? He already had evidence of the fact.

"Jimmy from the JV team. He says Steve came on to him and he had to shut him down."

"Well, don't worry about little Stevie. I'll take care of his bullshit. If you don't see him again, will that make everybody feel better? Will that be enough proof that I'm one of the guys?"

Joe looked around at the other guys and they nodded their agreement. "I suppose so. It'd be a start. Maybe then we'll get back to normal, as long as we know you're with us and not his queer ways."

"All right then, I'll take care of it. Are we okay now?" They again nodded in silence.

Peter didn't shower or even change out of his baseball uniform. He was ready and waiting outside for Steve when Steve showed up from his practice.

When Steve was in the car, Peter let him have it. "You asshole. The guys are sick of you coming around the locker room. They told me you're queer and they don't want you there."

Steve started to deny it, "No way, Pete. They got it all wrong. They—"

"Shit. Don't deny it. I've known since our last Merry Moose Park vacation."

"No. Never. What do you mean?" It was a weak protest.

"Don't act stupid, Steve. A guy came up to me when we were there and told me he set you straight. He said he told you to stay away from his brother. Please don't deny it. I know. I saw how you hung around the camper after that."

"Okay, there was a little problem at Merry Moose. What's that got to do with now?"

"Because Jimmy from the JV team told my guys that you came on to him."

Steve let out a defeated sigh. "Shit. That's not what happened. Jim came on to me and I shut him down because I didn't want to take any chances of people finding out so close to home. I was afraid things could get ugly—just like they are now. He's lying to save himself in case I said anything. Please believe me. I didn't do—"

"Spare me the lame excuses." Peter pulled into their driveway and slammed the car into park. "I don't give a rat's ass about what you say you did or didn't do, or any of that bullshit. I know the truth. This is what I'm telling you." He turned in his seat and pointed his finger directly in Steve's face. It was so close and violent that Steve backed his head away from his raging brother's hand. "You're a fucking embarrassment to me. You've lost me most of my friends because of your queer shit, and I don't want to hear it again. Quit the baseball team and stay the fuck out of my life. I'll stay out of yours. Got it? Go be queer, but not around me, and by that I mean not in this town."

Peter opened the car door, got out, and slammed it shut, leaving Steve alone to think about it. He knew things would never be the same with them, but then again they hadn't been the same for years. This wasn't the first time Steve had turned on him, and he'd be damned if he let him do it again.

Steve quit the JV team the next day and buried himself in his artwork. He never spoke to Peter much after that except when family times mandated it, and then just enough to keep up appearances. Steve vowed never to care about his brother again or be an embarrassment to his family for the rest of his life.

As far as Peter's return to his status as big man on campus—well, that never happened either.

Chapter Twelve

Hospital Room 321

"Peter, I asked you a question. What are you going to do about this falling out between you and Steve?"

Jan's voice brought him back from the past. He gratefully shook off the cold chills the memories gave him. "I don't know. What can I do?"

"I can't tell you what to do, but you'd better do something. I can't stand you two arguing every minute when your father's life hangs in the balance." She sat back down on the bed and held Ed's hand. "I'm sorry, honey. I've tried my best."

Peter turned toward the door and Kim followed him out. "Pete. Where are you going?"

He turned back slowly. "I guess to talk to that flaming—"

"Don't even go there. End this now. Do you hear me? Mom doesn't need this crap. Hell, none of us do."

"All right. I'll talk to him, but there's no guarantee that he'll listen."

"Fair enough, but try to be sincere, please. Will you?"

He nodded and headed toward the waiting room. He found Steve staring at the floor. "Okay, little brother," he announced. "It's time to drop this shit."

Steve looked up. "Sure easy for you to say, isn't it?"

Peter smirked. "I'm not saying get over it. I'm just saying drop it. Mom and Kim are beside themselves, and this crap isn't making it any easier on them."

"Sure, Pete. That'd be real convenient for you, wouldn't it? Spare everybody's feelings. Do this one for the Gipper. Hide myself away for the good of the family. Quit the team so you can be king of the hill again. Nope, sorry. Been there, done that. Took me years to recover."

"I'm not asking for me. For all I care, you can go on hating me to the grave. But it's not fair to Mom—or Dad, if he recovers."

Steve stood and faced his brother. "So what are you saying? Go on pretending forever?"

Peter shrugged. "Well, it's worked since high school. Why stop now? When Mom and Dad are gone, we can go our separate ways. Okay?"

"Okay. We'll put the act back on. But that doesn't mean I'm changing my opinion about the DNR. That will have to be Mom's decision, and I plan on helping her see it clearly enough to follow Dad's wishes. Dad had the right to make his own choices, to live and die the way he wanted to. That's a God-given right, not a Pete-given right."

"Whatever, Steve. Think what you want as long as you don't stress her out in doing so. I don't care what you say, just say it nicely. It seems like we've been on the opposite sides of the coin since high school. If I said black, you would inevitably say white just so you wouldn't have to agree with me. Are you sure that's not what's happening now?"

"That's ludicrous and even more insulting. You just can't help yourself, can you? Do you really think that I would risk Dad's life just to win an argument with you?"

"No, not really. Even I wouldn't think that badly of you. But we've been at odds so long, maybe it's just our way and we don't realize it."

"I'll keep it in mind." Steve pushed past him and headed toward the room.

*****

The Rock

"So, you had a secret and failed to share it with Jan. Is that such a crime?"

I was a little startled by Gracie's sudden appearance and her frankness, but was relieved to hear her voice once again.

"Were you purposely trying to deceive her?" she asked

gently. I looked deeply into her eyes, hoping to find answers to her questions.

Of course I didn't. Those answers were mine to find within myself. The question helped me focus. No, I hadn't been trying to deceive Jan. I didn't like to keep anything from her. But there was a time when I had my suspicions and failed to act on them, and I didn't share those suspicions with her.

Between the time Steve tried to tell me and the time he finally did tell me, I wondered if I should have said something… anything to him or Jan. I think I was disappointed. I didn't plan on my boy being gay. Who could? I wasn't ashamed, just confused. But still, what was I to do?

There were signs, flags, that kept making me wonder, and I'd have flashbacks to that day. I started to put things together, but I didn't know what to think. What if I were wrong? If I asked him if he was gay, wouldn't it be devastating for him to realize that's how I thought of him? And what if I said something to Jan? Would she have to wonder in silence too? I was between a rock and a hard place. Trapped. Maybe the bottom line was I was afraid to know the truth.

"You can't 'what if' yourself forever, Ed," Gracie said in the compassionate voice that always calmed me, and I became aware of her once again.

"I know, but I can't help myself," I finally said.

"It's okay. You did the best you could with the information you had. You meant no harm, nor did you cause any real damage. Things turned out okay between you and him, didn't they?"

"Yes, things between him and Jan, Kim, and I were fine, but not between him and Pete. I could feel it going bad between them. I even invented reasons for the three of us to go fishing again like the old days. It didn't work. I thought if we got back here—to this old rock—it would bring back memories and help them reconnect. But they never came back together. Maybe if I had said something to Steve or forced an answer from one of them about what was wrong, I could have fixed it."

"No man can do everything or fix everything that gets broken in life, Eddie."

Her calming tones soothed me. I drifted away as she held my

hand.

*****

Hospital Room 321
5 *AM*

When Steve and Peter came back in the room, Jan was still sitting next to Ed on the bed. Kim sat in the nearby chair. Kim jumped up quickly but Jan remained seated. She looked at her boys, wondering if anything had been resolved—really resolved.

"Hi, guys," Kim said. "How's it going? Were you finally able to straighten things out?"

"Sure. All's good," Peter replied, putting his arm around Steve's shoulder.

Steve smiled the obligatory smile. "Yep, all's good. It's about time we had that talk." He broke the hold Peter had on his shoulder and moved to Kim and hugged her. "Thanks, sis. How's Dad doing?"

Kim hugged him back. "No change. Hopefully that's good. At least there's not been another episode." They both turned to look at Ed. Kim kept her arm around Steve's waist.

Peter walked up and took her other hand. "Yeah, thanks, Kimmy."

Jan wasn't fully convinced that the boys had really settled things. A mother knew when her kids were holding something back, whether they were just little ones or grown-ups like these two lugheads.

She looked at the three of them. Other images flashed through her mind: Peter taking the blame for a broken window, even though she was later to find out it was Steve whose slingshot went astray. Kim hoisting up peanut butter and jelly sandwiches to the two boys in the treehouse, by way of a pail attached to a rope. Three innocent kids spending summer afternoons together in complete harmony.

Now look at them, she thought. *Still covering up for each other, but not so innocent any longer.*

Jan knew they were putting up a good front of togetherness

for her and, for that matter, Ed. That in itself was a gift, but what could she do with the peaceful truce? She feared it wouldn't last long after this ordeal ended. Maybe if she got the boys talking now while the truce was on, the dialogue would rekindle their boyhood friendship. Something good could come out of this after all.

She lifted her hand from Ed's, letting his rest on the bed at his side. She got up and walked to the kids. "Group hug," she announced. She allowed her kids to wrap her in a much-needed hug.

"Sorry to interrupt this Kodak moment, but coffee anyone?"

Jan was the first to see Greg walk through the door with a tray full of coffee cups and a box of doughnuts. "Oh God, yes," Jan moaned. She broke the hug, and the others turned toward him. "Thank you, Greg. It is so nice of you to think of us. You shouldn't have. We could have—"

"I wouldn't hear of it," Greg said. "It's the least I can do. I figured you've been up on and off all night." He gave them a big grin. Jan noticed him linger a bit, with a barely discernible wink, when his eyes met Steve's.

Greg placed the coffee and doughnuts on the wide windowsill, and they all gathered around to grab the hot caffeine.

Peter was the first to sit back in a chair with his cup of black coffee while the others added cream or sugar to theirs. He took a sip and leaned back with a deep sigh. "Oh yeah, just what I needed to start my engine."

Jan smiled. That had been one of his favorite sayings when he was a kid, especially when he and Steve were building their soap box racer. They'd worked together, using old carriage wheels and scrap lumber. She took a chair next to the bed and decided to exploit the situation. "Does that ring a bell, Steve?"

Steve turned, obviously unaware of what Jan was talking about. "Does what ring a bell?" He finished stirring his coffee, pushed another chair next to the bed for Greg, and sat in his own. Jan was pleased that Greg was finally able to join the circle at Ed's bedside.

She took a few sips of coffee as she waited for them all to get situated. When they were, she continued, "Start my engine. Do you remember Pete always saying that?"

Steve stifled a smile. "Of course I do. I *was* the engine!"

106

Kim laughed out loud. "Oh, God, even I remember that. Every time Pete got in that silly soap box, he'd say, 'Steve, start my engine!' And Steve would make a race car noise and push him up and down the driveway."

Steve halfheartedly objected, "Hell, it almost killed me. I think I must have pushed him a hundred miles in the fifty-foot segments of our driveway."

"If you pushed me a hundred miles, I must have pushed you a thousand," Peter retorted.

Steve stopped his coffee cup midway to his mouth and looked at Peter. The room fell silent except for the constant beeping of Ed's monitor.

Finally Steve spoke. "Ya know," he said, then paused to stroke the fresh growth of whiskers on his cheek. Jan swallowed hard. "You're probably right. Maybe two thousand. I remember getting a sore ass sitting on that plywood seat we had."

Peter laughed abruptly in mid-bite. A few crumbs went flying. "Talk about sore asses. It was so humiliating having Dad pull out the splinters I got from that damn thing. Next day he gave us a pillow to use."

They all laughed. If there were such a thing as a tension meter attached to Ed's monitoring station, it probably would have dropped off to nothing at that moment.

Thank God, Jan thought. She glanced at Kim. *Maybe this is why cease-fires work in wars. They give both sides a chance to cool off and reflect on what is really happening.*

"That soap box kept you two busy and out of trouble for the whole summer, I think," Kim chimed in. She turned to Greg. "It was quite a project, Greg. Did you ever have a soap box racer?"

He looked up from his coffee cup. "No, never. My neighborhood was more into skateboarding. I think maybe a soap box would have disappeared overnight if it wasn't locked up."

Hmm, humble beginnings, Jan thought. *Maybe that's where his generosity comes from. I think Steve could have done a lot worse. Greg seems like a good man.*

Steve glanced at Peter before he spoke. "It was truly amazing how well that thing came out, just using scraps of wood we found lying around."

"Yes, truly amazing," Kim said with a touch of sarcasm.

Steve ignored it and continued, "It all started when we walked by an old baby carriage in a junk pile on the curb and decided we could make a soap box out of it." "Pete saw the National Soap Box Derby on the *Wide World of Sports* that weekend and figured he would make one himself. The show talked about how they were made, and he figured he could do it if those kids could. It was supposed to be built without adult help, so it was simple enough. Worked pretty good too. I think you missed your calling, Pete old boy," he teased. "You would have made a better engineer."

Jan was amazed at the lightheartedness of the conversation. Were the good old days erasing the bad new days? She could only hope.

"Well yeah, it rolled pretty good until the front wheel came off and I crashed into the side of the house. I knew then my building days were over."

"But you did have fun," Jan said.

"Yeah, probably more fun building it than riding it," Peter said. "It was crazy how we kept finding these stacks of scrap wood all over."

"You probably won't believe it, Greg, but these two were inseparable." Kim stopped suddenly. "What I mean is these two worked day and night on that thing. I was there most of the time too. I was named the junior pit crew mechanic. Meaning I ran to the house for snacks," she said with twinkle in her eyes.

Greg looked at Steve and Steve nodded. "I know. Hard to believe," he said with a glance at Pete.

"Not so hard," Jan added.

Peter remained silent, only offering a slight nod.

"So anyways," Jan said, "they drew up a plan and had Dad look at it. He made a few necessary remarks about the design and had them break it down into steps so they wouldn't get ahead of themselves."

"According to the rules, we couldn't have help building it from an adult, but they could give us advice," Peter explained. "So before he let us use his tools, he wanted to see several sheets about the design: axles, steering, floor, seat, everything we needed to know."

"Wow, that's a lot for a couple of kids to do." Greg seemed truly amazed.

"Well he was—" Peter stopped suddenly. "—*is* a man of details. We'd seen the plans he drew up on graph paper whenever he built something. He always said, 'The first step of any project is making a good plan.'"

Jan sat back. *I just hope this plan continues to work, for everyone's sake.*

Steve jumped in. "So after three days of drawing and redrawing, with comments from Dad, we were ready to build. He laid out the hand tools and told us to use the wood out back of the garage, behind the garbage cans. We hammered, sawed, chiseled, and drilled until we had the baby carriage axles mounted in a trench down the middle of two-by-fours.

"We asked Dad to take a look. He was happy with the whole thing, but unfortunately we were out of wood. When we asked him if there was any more, he just asked us if we'd looked behind the shed. There we found another small pile of scraps, which happened to include a piece of plywood that we could use as the floor. So on we went, building the floor and attaching the wheels and axles. The pieces were falling together like parts of a puzzle."

"You must have had fun," Greg observed. Jan thought he said it with just a tinge of envy. Maybe he was wishing his childhood could have been so memorable.

"We did," Peter said. "The third week we had to build the cover where our feet would go, and the back of the seat. But our pile of wood was again depleted. We asked Dad, and he asked us if we had checked in the basement. Lo... and..."

He stopped and looked at Jan.

She grinned a devilish grin. "You're just now figuring that out?"

"What'd he do?" Peter asked between laughs.

Steve leaned forward in his chair too. "Come on, Mom, 'fess up!" he demanded.

"Daddy didn't want you two—" Kim began...

Jan cleared her throat. "Dad didn't want you *three* to be pounding that thing together and riding downhill on a bunch of boards held together with bent-over nails and duct tape. He made sure you completed one step at a time, and he didn't supply any more lumber until each phase was done right and according to the plan. He wasn't breaking the rules. You all still built it yourselves."

Peter looked at Steve. "Haven't really thought about that in years," Peter said.

"Yeah, me neither," Steve said. "I haven't thought about building it since we actually built it. Wow, that's strange. Did you have any idea, Kim?"

"Yeah. Mom told me a few years ago." She giggled her answer.

"What? She told you?" Peter sputtered. "Why did you get to hear about it and not us?"

"Because I was the baby of the family and not really expected to remember how we built that thing."

"It ain't fair," Steve teased.

"Fair or not, we were wondering if you two would ever figure it out. Dad told us not to tell you. It was part of his plan for you two to figure it out together."

Peter and Steve just shook their heads but Kim saw a reminiscent tear or two well up in each of their eyes.

Steve reached over and rubbed Ed's shoulder. "Thanks, Dad. You've taught us a lot. Where are ya, Boone? Comin' home soon?"

*****

The Rock

"Hey, I think you've got a bite," I heard Dad say, and I came out of my blackness. I looked down, but the bobber had stopped moving.

"Probably just the minnows playing with the worm," I guessed.

"You've got to pay attention if you plan on catching anything, son."

I guessed he was as much about plans as I was. I probably picked that up from him. And, yes, I made plans for everything. Buying the right house with room for a growing family. The right car to carry that growing family. It was a 1975 Dodge station wagon with imitation wood grain inside and out. It came complete with a third rear-facing seat, just in case the family grew more than even I had planned. It was very sleek looking. The outside of the car had a full-length wood-grain decal. It was a little faded but it still shined up with a good coat of wax.

It reminded me of a picture of a car Dad showed me once—one of his old cars when he was younger. It was called a woody. I have to admit his looked cooler than mine, but the Dodge was the best I could do.

Yes, I've made lots of plans. Some worked out good and others not so good. I never knew which ones would work or not, though.

"I want to share something with you I once heard that really stuck with me, Eddie," Dad said. 'We climb to heaven most often on the ruins of our cherished plans, finding our failures were successes.'" He then fell silent waiting, for it to sink in.

I was confused. "What do you mean?" I asked.

He smiled softly and took my shoulder. "It took me years to fully understand it, so maybe I should help you out a bit. After all, we don't have forever here, do we?"

I looked at his expressionless face and saw nothing to give me a hint if I was indeed here forever or not. "I guess not," I finally said.

"We can't plan for everything," he began. "It's fine to make plans. I must say you've made your share. But not every chair you build or car you buy will turn out exactly like you planned. Sometimes there might be a knot in the wood you bought, and you wish it weren't there. You didn't plan for it, but you work with it anyway. Then suddenly, after you apply the stain and varnish, that gnarly old knot turns out to be the most distinctive thing about the chair. You didn't plan it but it's still good. Understand?"

"I planned on the boys and Kim getting married and having kids and carrying on our family traditions after I was gone. But I'm afraid that won't happen now. They seem too far apart."

"You have grandkids," he reminded me.

"Yes, I know. But the boys are too far apart now to carry on."

"Carry on what?"

"Carry on our family ways. We were always so close while

they were growing up, and that's all gone now. I could have handled it better. If I had shared my thoughts with Jan earlier. If I had spoken to Steve about it. If I had tried to help Peter understand it better. But I didn't. I kept my secret too long."

"Son, listen to me," he said. "Life is full of 'what ifs' and 'if onlys.' But those things are for a perfect world, and the world we live in isn't perfect. No, things aren't as you planned, but you didn't change that plan. Life did. It's up to the boys to work it out. Not you. Your job is to appreciate that grain in the wood that you didn't plan for and appreciate it for what it is. Remember, you can lead two jackasses to water, but you can't make them drink. Sometimes they need to be pushed in chin deep before they give it a try." Then that damn all-knowing smile of his.

I looked off into the sky, pondering what he had just told me. I wondered who those jackasses were. Were they Jan and I for thinking we could get our old family ways back again? Or Pete and Steve for not wanting or even caring enough to get those ways back again? Maybe I should have been concentrating on Jan and I, so we could enjoy our last few years together and let the boys go their own separate ways.

As the black of night began to engulf my thoughts again, I wondered if I was just being a stubborn jackass myself. Maybe I should just let things take their natural course, no matter the outcome.

Chapter Thirteen

Hospital Room *321*
6 AM

Greg tossed his coffee cup into the wastebasket and turned to Steve. "You never told me about the soap box racer. Why not?"

Steve looked slightly puzzled and shrugged. "Ya know, I'm not sure. I guess I just put it out of my mind. There are a lot of things I haven't told you about my younger days. Not that I'm hiding anything. It's just that those subjects haven't come up."

Kim stepped closer. "Oh, well, then, has he told you about Merry Moose Park?"

"Let's not go there," Peter said from a few feet away. His voice was cold as steel.

It made Kim take a step back. "What's going on? Did I miss something?"

"Just forget it, sis. We're not going there right now," Peter insisted.

"I agree. I'll tell you later, Greg." Steve said. He looked over Greg's shoulder to give Peter an ice-cold stare.

Jan's voice was a little shaky when she broke in. "I agree. We covered that old tale a few hours ago—or was it days? God, it seems like we've been here forever. Doesn't it?"

"Forever," Kim moaned. "Okay then, if not Merry Moose, then what?" No one made any suggestions. "How about when they tried to make an ice skating rink in the backyard and froze up the driveway? It took two days for the salt that Daddy spread to finally melted it." No response. "Okay, then, how about when Pete thought he could fly and jumped off the porch railing with a Halloween Superman cape on and sprained his ankle?"

"Now that was funny." Steve laughed. Peter only scowled at him.

"Now wait one just darned minute here. You weren't perfect, you know," Peter taunted her.

"I most certainly was. Wasn't I, Mom?"

Jan sat back and waved off the question. "You started it, and you're not the baby any longer. You'll have to fight your own battles. Especially the ones you start." She clenched her teeth, holding back a smile.

Kim tilted her chin up and shook her head, letting her hair fly loosely over her shoulders. "I most certainly was perfect. I never gave Mom or Dad any reason for concern—unlike you two wild animals."

"Perfect? How about the time you cut up Dad's best thirty-dollar paisley tie to make a headband for your Judy doll? I don't remember him thinking that you were so perfect then."

"That was a misunderstanding. I thought that tie was out of style."

Peter grinned. "True. It was out of style. Nevertheless, Dad didn't think so and wasn't very happy about it."

"He got over it quickly. After all, I was his favorite," she teased.

Before Peter could offer his rebuttal, they heard a knock at the door and Dr. Mehra's voice. "May I come in? Am I interrupting anything?"

Jan replied quickly, "No, Karash, please come in. We were just talking about the good old days."

"Well the good old days for some of us." Peter gave Kim a wink.

"I see Ed had one episode after I left that resolved itself. I'm not sure if that's a good thing or a bad thing. I was hoping he'd be out of this by now. Most patients come out in twelve to twenty-four hours, and he's only seven hours from the twenty-four-hour mark. I'd rather have nothing happening than him being on the verge of having to be resuscitated." He paused as he looked around at the blank stares of the family. "I'm sorry to be so blunt, but I don't want to paint a rosy picture that isn't accurate."

"So what are you saying, Karash?" Jan finally asked.

"What I'm saying is there's been no sign of improvement and maybe a slight sign of deterioration. I understand from the chart that you gave the directive to use all means to resuscitate before he came around."

"Are you saying we shouldn't even allow CPR next time?"

"Well, by the accepted general definition of CPR—chest compressions and manual resuscitation bag—I can say I think Ed would allow that. It's the electronic means of defibrillation, breathing tubes, and feeding he would object to."

"Did the episode hurt his chances of recovery?" Jan was visibly shaken by what Mehra had just told them.

"I can't tell you any more than the on-call physician could last night, but it seems you made that call, according to the chart."

"Well, I did, but in light of what you just said, I find myself doubting that decision."

Peter spoke up. "Nevertheless, Mom. We… you made that call, and I think we should stick with it."

"Pete," Steve said, "things are changing. We should be able to change with them."

"You don't give up. Do you, Steve?" Peter chided him.

"If I saw more hope rather than less, maybe I would. But Dr. Mehra isn't saying that. What about you in the stock market? Don't you have to make changes in strategy when the market moves?"

"Of course I do, but this is Dad we're talking about, not a stock portfolio. Even I can see that. This isn't an issue of buy or sell. This is Dad. I'm not willing to sell him out, but apparently you are."

Steve clenched his teeth, but his response was calm. "I'm not selling Dad out. You should have been on the debate team rather than the football team. You're good at confusing the issue."

"Thanks. You almost took care of that for me, didn't you?"

Steve stepped forward, but Jan's steady tone stopped him in his tracks. "Boys," was all she said. It was enough to cut this old argument off before it got started again.

She had hoped that reminiscing would help them see good times rather than bad. Remind them of the love and friendship they had enjoyed as kids. But she knew at this moment it wasn't the case. She had prayed to God that Ed's situation would help mend the past. Instead it seemed their exhaustion was a far bigger adversary to their reconciliation than fond memories were to helping them to forgive and forget. Now everything; Ed's recovery, and the boys mending their rift, seemed so bleak again.

Karash closed his eyes and massaged his forehead. He finally spoke. "Yes… yes, let's just take a step back and wait for Dr. Chang to examine Ed and give us his opinion."

"Is this Chang good? I mean, is he the best?" Peter questioned.

"Yes, he's good. If it makes you feel any better, I would have him treat my own family member if I were in your situation."

Peter seemed to take that to heart, "Okay, then I guess he's all right for Dad."

"You guess?" Steve repeatcd.

"What?" Peter asked.

Jan broke in. "Thank you, Karash. Will Dr. Chang contact you when he arrives?"

"Yes, I've asked him to have me paged as soon as he arrives. We'll meet here after the tests are done and we've had a chance to review the results. They'll be taking Ed soon and it will be a few hours before we know anything. He'll be in good hands, and you won't be able to be with him, so take advantage of this opportunity to freshen up and rest." He looked at Jan, and she knew he was asking for her support.

"Maybe we should," she said. "We all need to recharge our batteries for a little while. But my decision is to only use manual resuscitation if something happens."

"All right. I understand, and I'll make a standing order. After we review the tests, maybe we'll have to revisit that decision. For now—go home."

*****

The Spare Room at Kim and Mike's House

"The guy is just being an asshole," Peter said as he sat on the edge of the bed next to Laura.

"Pete, aren't you being a little too harsh?"

"If you'd been there, you'd think so too," Peter growled.

"I'm not so sure of that. He has a right to an opinion."

"Yes, of course he does. But no matter what we say, he still insists on not letting them try to bring Dad back. Just let him die. I mean, what the hell?"

"You two haven't been communicating since I've known you. Are you sure it just isn't spilling over from that?"

"I don't know. True, we don't see eye to eye. Maybe it's spilling over. You know he's all—" he searched for words "—well, for lack of a more politically correct word, weird. If you know what I mean. Maybe it is spilling over, but I can't speak for him."

Laura smiled and rubbed his back. "I wasn't talking about him." She paused to give him time for that comment to sink in. "Maybe you're the one not listening to him."

"You're kidding. You're taking his side now?" He sounded almost betrayed.

"No, of course not. There's no sides to take except Dad's. Maybe you're just too close to the situation. Maybe Steve just doesn't want Dad to suffer," she said. "This 'communication' issue you two are having. Did you try to work it out?"

"Yes, just tonight. Or was it this morning? I don't know."

"Okay, good. How did it go?"

"Not so good. We basically decided to keep out of each other's way. As a matter of fact, it got pretty nasty."

"So what happened?"

"Basically he's just been mad at me since we were kids, and he can't let it go."

"What happened when you were kids? I know you don't want to talk about it or I'd know already, but maybe now's the time."

Peter stared at the floor.

Laura leaned in. "It's okay. You can tell me, honey." She hugged him around his waist.

He took a deep breath. "I couldn't support his queer… gayness and he won't forgive me and I can't help it. It still creeps me out. Maybe Dad didn't like it either. Maybe he just wants out of the family."

"Pete, that's absurd! Your father knows."

"I know, but maybe Dad didn't take it well. Maybe Steve just can't face him anymore."

"I can't believe you even said that. Not everybody hates the

117

gay lifestyle like you do. Sure, it's a different thing for your father to accept, but I'm also sure he wouldn't let that stand between him and his son. Maybe you should learn a lesson from him."

Peter hung his head again. "I know. I must be freaking crazy, but I can't help it."

She reached for his chin and turned his head toward her. "I would think you of all people could see beyond that stereotypical prejudice. When we got engaged, my parents didn't like you, but I told them that I loved you and they got over it. Right?"

He smiled. "What's not to love?" She pushed him away playfully. "Where's Sarah?" he asked.

"Sleeping in Bennie's room. I might have to go shopping today to get some dino PJs for her."

"That's good. I'm glad they're getting to know each other. There could be worse things."

"Like what?"

"Like going back to the hospital. I have a bad feeling about today."

"Well then, get showered and take your nap. How long?"

"Don't let me sleep past eight thirty. Okay?"

"You got it. I'll hang the do not disturb sign on the door."

"You've got a do not disturb sign?"

"No, silly. Boy, you really do need a nap. Maybe it will help you think more clearly about everything." She kissed him and left the room.

*****

The Rock

I was thrilled when Steve said he wanted to go fishing again. So the next Saturday, we went. He said he could only fish in the morning because he wanted to study for the final test in his English literature class. He didn't want to mess it up.

I was proud of him for making it through two years of college so far. I was sure he'd be graduating without any trouble. I even told him so when he called about going fishing. But I also understood that he wanted to ace the exam. So I said we'd go in the

118

early morning. It was best fishing then anyway.

It was a crisp May morning. We needed light jackets at first. But when the sun came up, it warmed us and the rock, and we were in our shirtsleeves by nine.

He seemed quiet, but I just figured he was thinking about the test. A little time at the reel end of a fishing rod can help a man clear his mind. I broke out a couple of peanut butter sandwiches I'd brought and handed him one. Then I took the top off the thermos, filled it with coffee, and gave it to him. I already had it mixed because we liked it the same way—extra light with sugar. I took a coffee cup out of my fishing creel, wiped a few flecks of dirt or whatever it was out of it, and filled it for me.

It was quiet and peaceful on the rock on that early morning. The spring water flowing over the rocks made an especially soothing sound. I felt relaxed and like I had come home again. It had been years since I last fished with Steve. Sure, Pete and I fished often, or at least as often as his schedule had allowed before he moved. Steve was who made this trip so special.

Things hadn't been the same between Steve and Pete for some time now. We all knew that. It seemed that Steve had taken a quieter path in his life, preferring to spend more time at home during his high school years, immersed in his painting.

We sat quietly for some time until he spoke. "Dad, I need to tell you something."

He seemed a little nervous. I tried to relax him a bit by bringing back our old-time nicknames. "Shoot. I'm all ears, Daniel." Sitting on the rock always brought back fond memories of our Daniel Boone and Davy Crockett days, but this time I noticed it seemed to make him sad. "What's wrong, Steve?"

He was looking down the fishing line into the pool of water at the base of the rock. He shook it off and looked at me. "Nothing's really wrong, Dad. I just want... need to tell you something."

My heart sank so deeply I thought I'd never recover. I knew this was going to be about him and Peter or maybe about the secret I had kept for so long. I didn't want to be right about that. Maybe that's why I'd kept my suspicions to myself and never told Jan.

I prayed it'd be about him and Peter. That would be easier to understand. Boys will be boys, and most times brothers argue.

Maybe if he told me what had happened between him and Peter, I could straighten it all out and things could get back to normal. My heart quickened.

But they say you can never go home again. I was afraid that even if he did tell me what was wrong, and even if I could straighten it out, things would never be the same. I could never go back to my Daniel Boone and Davy Crockett days again.

I steeled myself. "What is it, Steve? You can tell me anything."

*****

Kim and Mike's House

Kim was drying her hair as Mike finished shaving. "Bad night, huh?" he said.

"Horrible. It's bad enough Dad's so sick, but to have those two idiots fighting like cats and dogs has made it unbearable. I bet they'll never speak again if Dad dies. Each one will blame the other." She put the hair dryer in the vanity drawer and headed for the bed. "Where's Bennie?"

"I saw both kids get up while you were in the shower. The last I saw, they were planted in front of the TV."

"Have you been watching his screen time?"

Mike did a double take. "Really? With everything going on around here, you're concerned with screen time?"

"I know. Don't listen to me. God, I'm tired." She rolled her eyes at her own comment. She knew Mike was a good husband and father. He always made good decisions. But sometimes her mothering instinct was too strong to resist.

"Get some rest. I'll keep Bennie occupied till it's time to wake you up," he said, following her to the bed.

"Thanks, hon," she said contentedly as she slipped under the covers. He bent down and kissed her just as the door swung open and a little dinosaur charged through it.

"Rooooar!" Bennie growled as he ran across the room and jumped into Mike's waiting arms. "How's Grampa?" he asked his mother, looking over his father's shoulder. "Did he wake up from his nap yet?"

Kim's contented look quickly fell away. "No, not yet, Bennie."

"Wow, Grampa sure can sleep. Can you make Sarah and me dino pancakes this morning? Will you, Mommy? I already told Sarah. Will you? Please!"

"Tell you what, champ," Mike said. "Why don't you let Mommy take a power nap, and when she gets up, I'll make the dino pancakes."

Bennie frowned. "Mommy makes them better, Daddy. Yours always look like dogs, not dinos."

Kim and Mike each stifled a laugh. Kim said, "Let's have Daddy get all the pancake stuff ready so when I get up, all I'll have to do is pour them on the griddle. Then I have to go right back to the hospital. How's that work for you?" Raising Bennie was always exercise of give and take. Probably raising any kid was like that, she thought.

"Yep, that sounds great," Bennie agreed.

"Come on, buddy, let's let Mommy get some sleep." Mike said as they began to leave the room. Then he turned toward Kim. "Now get some sleep," he ordered.

"All right. Don't let me sleep past eight thirty. Okay? Oh, and no dino wake-up calls. Let me wake up gently, please. Deal?"

"Okay, Mommy, deal. Promise. No dinos." Bennie wiggled out of Mike's arms and ran to his mother. He jumped on the bed, kissed her, and raised his hand for a high five. With the high fives done and goodnight kisses over Mike grabbed him up again and walked to the door, clicking off the lights before he left.

Bennie said, "Sarah and I were watching TV. Can we play my Xbox?"

"Sure, buddy, as long as Aunt Laura thinks it's okay."

"She does. We already asked her."

"Of course you did," Mike muttered.

He released Bennie when he reached the kitchen. Laura was already sipping away at a cup of coffee. Bennie scampered into the next room. "Sarah! We can play Xbox now!"

Mike slipped an extra bold coffee pod into the coffee maker and hit the start button. As he waited, he turned to Laura. "Have any good news to report?"

"Well, the sun is coming up as planned, but that's about all. How about you?"

"Nope. The way it sounds, if you asked Pete and Steve the same question, you'd get conflicting answers."

"Yeah, it appears so. Crazy, isn't it?" She quickly looked over her shoulder toward the TV room. Little ears weren't listening. "Those two guys bring out the worst in each other."

"I know. They're driving Kim up the wall too," Mike said. "What did Pete tell you?"

She looked again over her shoulder to check on the kids. "He told me he and Steve tried to talk it out, but it just made things worse."

*****

The Rock

"Dad, I'm gay. I'm sorry to just blurt it out, but there's no easy way to say it," he told me. Then he looked down into the pool of cold water again as if he were ashamed.

Shit, I thought. It wasn't about him and Pete. It was about just what I didn't want to hear. Something I couldn't change or fix.

Of course, in the nineties, things weren't as open as they are today. But I think, no matter when or where you hear something like that, it's a shock. At least it was for me.

Well, it wasn't really a shock. I'd had my suspicions. Maybe it was disappointment I felt. No, not in him. I could never be disappointed in him. Maybe a disappointment in the plans I had made for him. Family… babies…grandkids for me and Jan. I realized this wasn't about me. It was about him and he needed me more now than ever before.

I don't know how much time passed while I sat there and thought. I was kicking myself for not broaching the subject back when I started to have my suspicions. Now I had found those suspicions were right.

I had thought it was wrong to have that sort of suspicions about your own son, especially if they were unfounded. But there had been clues.

I knew he was waiting for some sort of reply, and I thought about what to say. Should I ask him, "Are you sure?" No, that'd be stupid. Of course he was sure. Should I tell him that it was okay? That too seemed stupid. He didn't need my approval to be who he was.

I felt horrible that in telling me, he had to feel ashamed. Imagine that. Ashamed. Ashamed of who he was? I'd never felt that way about myself in my lifetime. In all seventy-two years of it, not once did I have to feel ashamed of who I was. Ashamed of a few things I'd done, maybe, but that was beside the point. It broke my heart to know he felt this way.

I cursed myself for letting my suspicions go on this long without acting on them. Was I a coward? What parent wouldn't cross the heavens to save their child this kind of pain? Instinctively I knew he didn't want my sympathy, but I did know what he needed to hear.

I love you, Steve, was what came to mind, so I told him just that. It wasn't a cop-out. It was how I felt and what he needed to hear. I wondered if he had already berated himself for years while coming to grips with his reality. He didn't need sympathy; he needed love and support, and that's what I could give him. My love and support and the feeling that nothing would ever come between us.

He moved a little closer to me after I said it, but not too close. Was he afraid that I wouldn't want to hug him? That I wouldn't want to hug a gay guy? Oh my God, I hoped not. So I moved next to him and held him tight.

He held me tight then too, and I could feel his chest begin to heave. Mine did too. "Don't cry, Steve," I consoled him. "It'll all be okay. I love you, and this doesn't change a thing."

In a minute or so he composed himself enough to say, "I know it will, Dad. I'm not crying about what I told you. I'm crying about what you said."

I sat back and took him by his shoulder so I could look him in the eyes. "You should have known that I'd love you no matter what."

"I was afraid you'd be ashamed of me," he said. I could almost feel the painful lump growing in his throat as it tried to cut off his last few words.

"Never, Steven. I would never be ashamed of you. Why would you think that?"

He looked down the fishing line again at the cold, dark pool. I wondered if he wanted that pool to swallow him up and end his misery.

"Just something someone once told me. Never mind. It was a long time ago. I shouldn't have even brought it up." He glanced at me. Not a full face-on look, but his pain crossed the distance between us and it broke my heart once again.

"Never ever worry about that, son. I believe in you. That's all that counts. Family doesn't desert family, no matter what."

"I know that's what you taught us, Dad, and you taught us well. It's just that some of us have forgotten the important part of being a family."

*****

The Connor Home

When Jan got home, she stopped at the door. The house was dark and empty. When she left with the ambulance, it had been a bright, sunny day, and there was no reason to have the lights on.

How could things have gone so badly in such a short time? One second she'd been watching him mow the lawn like he did every Saturday morning, thinking he was a stubborn old fool. The next second she'd been at his side, wondering if she'd ever be with him again.

She checked the kitchen door. No, it wasn't locked. Of course she hadn't taken the time to lock it. Still, she hadn't been sure. Nothing was clear about those minutes between Ed's fall and leaving for the hospital. It was a mass of disjointed memories stitched together by anxious moments: running to Ed, screaming for help, watching them load him into the ambulance, rushing him through the emergency room doors. The best she could do was keep up with the momentum as those events flew by. She felt like a rag doll being tossed around from moment to moment by the sheer chaos of the event.

She entered the kitchen and flicked on the lights. Everything seemed normal. Just like any other time she and Ed had come home to a dark house. It had never been threatening then, but now it was like sad monsters hid behind every fond memory of every event they had shared there over the years. Even behind Ed's newspaper he had left on the kitchen island, where he dropped it every day after finishing his coffee and leaving to start his daily routine. She felt guilty for having scolded him so often about not putting it away, and vowed never to do it again—if she was lucky enough to have him leave it there once again.

She folded it and tossed it in the recycle bin under the sink. She stared at in at the bottom of the container, pondering her possible future. When she closed the kitchen cabinet door, she straightened and saw the shattered coffee cup, dropped when she saw him fall. "Shattered," she said quietly. "That's my life right now."

She looked out that same kitchen window. The eerie image of the mower, silently parked in the middle of the backyard, began to appear in the gray twilight of the early summer's dawn. She tried to shake it off and headed for the bedroom, leaving the broken shards of the coffee cup… and her life there.

Jan removed the pillow sham but not the bedspread. She lay on the bed, flat out on her back. She folded her hands on her stomach and looked up at the fan turning lazily above her. The breeze it caused would normally have been welcome, but today it felt cold and unpleasant.

She had considered this moment before. Not this exact moment, but a moment when she or Ed would be forced to lie down in this bed without the other. She had hoped it would be her here all alone rather than him, for his sake, not hers. She didn't want Ed to go through the heartbreak of her dying and him being left alone. Ironic thing, she thought. She hadn't had a wish come true before.

"Oh, Jesus, Ed. What am I going to do?" she said aloud, but Ed wasn't there to help her through this dilemma. He'd always been there for her and she for him. They were a team—but not today. Today she was alone and about to make the most important decision of her life.

How could she choose between letting him die or going

against his wishes? How could she condemn him to a life he expressly wanted to avoid, telling the nurses and doctors to do whatever they could to save him? How could she live without her better half?

He was her better half because without him she would be nothing. Just an empty shell of what had been them.

"I don't want to do this alone," she forced out in angry tones. "I can't do this alone," she declared loudly. Her hands broke their hold on each other and slammed violently against the bed on either side of her. "Damn it, Ed! How could you leave me in such a mess?"

Chapter Fourteen

Hospital Room 321
8 *AM*

Jan was the first to make it back to the hospital room. She hadn't gotten any sleep. She was tired as hell, mad as hell, and frightened as hell. "Damn," she muttered as she walked up to the bed and smoothed Ed's hair. She looked down at his placid face. If only he were sleeping, she thought. She kissed him on the forehead. "Good morning," she said quietly, hoping he would wake up just like every Sunday morning when he'd overslept and she had to wake him up for church. She pushed a chair back from next to Ed's bed.

She thought she could still smell his cologne. Was it coming from the bag of his belongings resting against the small locker door, or just a melancholy memory? She'd forgotten to put the bag in the bedside locker in the crazy hours of yesterday. She decided to do it later.

She sat down with a thump and stretched her legs out, resting her head against the back of the chair.

"Mom," Steve said softly. "Mom…"

Jan became aware of the monitor beeping and Steve's voice and woke with a start. She became aware of where she was and saw Steve looking down at her. "What? Is Dad okay?" she asked in sudden panic.

"Yes, sure. There's no change. Sorry I startled you."

"Oh, God, I don't even remember falling asleep. The last thing I remember is sitting back in the chair to rest, and then you were calling my name."

"I'm happy you got a little rest. Greg and I were outside getting some air and saw you come in. By the time we got up here, you were already out like a light, so we waited in the hallway until everyone else got here."

"Thank you. I needed it. What time is it?"

"It's nine o'clock. We didn't want to wake you, but the nurses just told us the doctors are on their way."

"Where is everyone?"

"They're all just outside the door. Take a few minutes to wake up and I'll go bring them in. Okay?"

"Yes, sure. Tell them to come in."

Kim, Peter, and Greg had barely entered the room when the nurse came in. "The doctors would like to meet with you in the conference room down the hall."

"Okay, thank you," Jan replied.

"Do you want me to show you the way?"

Jan smiled. "No, thank you. We were there yesterday afternoon." She looked around the room. "Well, let's get going and face the music."

"I'll stay with Ed. You three go," Greg said. He moved Steve next to Jan with a discreet push on his back.

"Thank you, Greg," she said. "That's very kind of you. I'm sure we won't be long."

Jan and Kim led the way with Steve and Peter just steps behind. Jan hoped they would hear good news so a showdown between Peter and Steve could be avoided. She knew from experience how pigheaded Peter could be. Right now their personalities were clashing so much, it was making everything even more tense. She knew they both were trying to put that all aside for Ed's sake, but trying and doing were two separate things.

When they entered the room, Dr. Mehra and Dr. Chang were already there. They stood up. Dr. Mehra motioned to the chairs on the opposite side of the oval table. Jan seated herself in the middle with Steve on one side and Peter and Kim on the other.

Jan spoke up immediately. "Okay, what's the verdict, Karash?"

"Unfortunately, I'm afraid the jury, so to speak, is still out, but I'll let Dr. Chang tell you what he knows." He nodded to Chang.

"Mrs. Connor, we ran several tests on Mr. Connor, and the results are inconclusive."

"Inconclusive?" Peter repeated before Jan could get a word out. She shot Peter a look: *Not now, Peter*. He sat back in his chair quietly and folded his arms across his chest.

"The initial MRI in the ER showed a clot, or a shadow that seemed to be a clot. We have to assume that is was indeed a clot. It isn't visible anymore, so it appears the TPA—the clot-buster drug he received did its job. We're still hoping we caught things in time."

"So that's good news, right?" Jan asked quickly.

"Yes and no. Without any further evidence of a clot, we're hoping there wasn't any major damage. But given the location and the time that section of the brain was without blood, it is likely there has been some sort of damage. It could be minor and manageable, or it could be major and life-altering. There's just no way to tell until he regains consciousness—if he does."

Jan sank back in her chair, as did Kim and Steve. Peter leaned in toward Chang. "I'm still confused. What exactly are you saying? We're just left here to wonder?" he asked, sounding a little annoyed.

Chang drew in a deep breath. "We're still not sure what brought about the original seizure. Nor do we know if whatever caused the first attack is continuing to cause these mini-seizures I read about on his chart. Nor do we know what caused his heart to stop."

"That doesn't sound very good to me in any sense. So what is the good news?" Jan said, sitting forward again. She hoped to signal to Peter that she was still capable of leading the family in this discussion. After all, that was her role at this moment, just as it would have been Ed's if the tables were turned.

"In the brain scan, we also focused on a new area of interest called the posterior cingulate cortex or the PCC. We are finding the PCC is associated with consciousness. In a recent study of thirty-two people, the five who recovered from a coma had activity between the PCC and the frontal cortex. Ed has this activity, but—"

Jan cut him off quickly. "That's wonderful news then, right?"

Dr. Chang grimaced. "I hesitated to tell you this as I thought it might give you false hope. And I see it has. What I was about to say is that this activity seems to be only one of the criteria for recovery. It isn't a guarantee. Others who showed activity in the PCC never recovered, but no one without the PCC activity recovered. So it is at least essential to recovery. I think the hopeful thing you can get out of this is that Ed is in the group that *can* recover."

"So if he wakes up, he'll be as good as he was?" Jan asked.

"I can't promise or predict his recovery. As I said, we believe there was a clot, and part of his brain was without oxygen for some time because of that."

Peter broke in. "Then is it your considered opinion that we take all measures to resuscitate him if necessary because he has this PCC activity and he can recover?"

It was a well-crafted sentence, and Jan was sure it'd get a quick response from Steve. She glanced over at him.

Steve shook his head. "That's not what he said at all, Pete. You're trying to misuse this information to support your opinion. Please tell us, Dr. Chang, what is your opinion? Is my father a candidate to be resuscitated at any cost?"

Chang looked at the four of them, one at a time, before he spoke. "I don't have an answer. What I've told you is that the brain was without blood for some time, and there could be, at the least, minor damage and possibly major damage. If he continues to have more seizures and if his heart stops again, then his brain might be even more deprived of oxygen, which could cause more damage.

"But this is all speculative. He has PCC activity, which is essential for his recovery, but I can't tell you the outcome or what to do. Unfortunately, that will be your decision. Do any of you have any further questions?"

When no one spoke, he pushed himself back from the table and stood up, as did everyone else. "Dr. Mehra can answer any other questions you may have as they come up. For now I must leave as I have other patients to see. Good luck to you all."

"Thank you, Doctor," Jan said. She reached over to shake his hand. Peter and Steve also reached across the table to shake his hand. "Karash, will you stay?" Jan asked.

Karash checked his watch and nodded. "Yes, for a moment or two." They all took their seats again.

Jan said, "It seems to me that with the evidence of brain activity, we should all be hopeful for a good recovery. Do you agree?"

"Yes, in a way. At least we now have hope that he can

recover from this. But that doesn't mean he will recover fully."

"I understand," Jan said, "but in the same sense, doesn't this mean that we should discontinue the DNR order?"

"Not necessarily," Karash responded.

"Not necessarily?" Pete's response was quick and harsh.

Karash ignored the harshness. "Yes, not necessarily," he repeated looking directly to Jan, ignoring Pete's interruption. "If he has an arrest and his heart stops, or some other near-fatal event occurs, it could mean there isn't enough of him left to keep living. We could bring him back only to have him live with severe limitations in what he can do. He could be just living but not responsive. The prognosis Dr. Chang gave us isn't a glowing report. It just gives us hope that if he recovers on his own, he'll have the best chance to be himself again."

Jan fell silent. Kim slid her chair closer to hers and grasped her hand tightly.

Steve said, "Dr. Mehra, in the context of your discussions with my father, what would you do?"

"That's a hard question even for me as a doctor, Steven."

"But as a friend. What would you do?"

"You're putting me in a difficult position. As a doctor, it's not my place to make this kind of decision. As a friend, I would put the DNR in effect again. As things currently stand, in the event that no one is here to advocate for him, the staff will use all means to bring him back, no matter what. Let's face it, you all can't be here every minute of every day until something happens. It's just not reasonable. If a family member happens to be here when an event presents itself, you'll be able to get medical feedback at the time and make the appropriate decision."

"No offense, Doctor," Peter said in a very offensive tone, "but we're here, then we'll ask them to try and save him. But if *Steve* is here, my father a dead man."

Steve flared, "You cold-hearted bas—"

"Boys!" Jan had had enough. "Stop it!"

She turned to Pete. "Do you really think your brother is that cold? What's wrong with you?"

"I'm just stating the fact. He's been advocating for the DNR since he got here."

"Yes, but his intentions have always been in your father's best interest and never against him. Can't you see that? Really?"

Peter couldn't hold his mother's gaze. He let his chin drop and he stared at the floor. He finally looked up—not to Jan but to Steve. "She's right, Steve. I am so sorry. That wasn't called for. Putting all else aside I know you love Dad. I'm sure you're doing what you think is best for him. I'm not used to not being in control of every decision, and I think it's clouded my judgment and my remarks. For that, at least, forgive me."

It was apparent to everyone that Peter's apology was sincere, but a long silence hung over them as Steve considered his words.

"Okay. Let's agree to disagree—again," Steve said.

"Good. I'm glad that's settled," Karash said. "So you'll all have to come to some sort of decision soon. Why don't we break for now? You can go back to the room and think it over. What do you say?"

"That's a good idea. I think we all need some air," Jan said. She pushed her chair back, stood up, and walked toward the door. As she did, so did the others.

When she reached the door, Karash said, "Jan, why don't you go ahead? The rest of us will be there shortly."

She gave him a tired but hopeful glance. "Thank you, Karash. Ed picked his friends well." She left the room.

Karash turned toward the three siblings, who had never before been at such odds as they were today. "I've known you all for years now, and it breaks my heart to witness this bickering. It's common in families in situations like this, but I had hoped you'd be spared. I guess not."

He traded glances with Peter and Steve. "You two have to realize that this decision probably won't fall on either of you to make. You all, Kim included, have your own lives waiting for you to go back to. You have jobs, and the children have to get back to school. You'll all have to think about getting back to a life that's as normal as you can. Your father may be here for days, weeks, even months, and that will leave your mother here to make that call alone. Let's not make this harder than it already is."

Kim surveyed her brothers. "I think I can speak for all of us when I tell you that we won't put any more stress on our mother.

Will we, guys?"

*****

The Rock

"Looks like a storm is brewin'," my father said as he looked at the dark clouds rolling in across the sky. The vibrations from a roll of threatening thunder shook my very insides and brought about the anxiety I dreaded from time to time. "Maybe we should reel in our lines and get out of harm's way. What do you think?"

"Oh, I don't know. Maybe we should. That's probably the safest thing to do," I replied, looking him squarely in those all-knowing, comforting eyes.

But hadn't I already taken the safe road for years? Hadn't I taken refuge in silence, not wanting or maybe not willing to upset the cart? Things weren't that bad. Our holidays and birthdays were always fun, albeit a bit reserved when it came to Steve and Pete interacting. Or was it the lack of Steve and Pete interacting?

Oh, our family would gather around the Christmas dinner table and exchange stories and memories of the good old days. There was lots of laughter and heartwarming times still to be shared, and still to be made, but it was like the guitarist was just a half beat behind the band. I would tease the kids and Jan about something that happened in the past, and she would do the same. Kim would joke with Steve and Pete and they would carry on with her, but Pete and Steve never razzed each other directly.

We grew to accept it. It seemed like a small price to pay to have the good times we were enjoying. Yes, they spoke to each other when required and didn't make a scene. "Pass the mashed potatoes, Pete." "New car, Steve?" That was about all we could expect. Somehow it seemed to be contrived or obligatory conversation for the sake of the family's good times.

I knew it but let it slide. Why should I upset our family gatherings if they were happy with how things were going or how they interacted?

"So what do you think, Ed?" My father interrupted my thoughts.

"About what?" I had totally lost track of him and what we

133

were even talking about.

He gave me an inquisitive look, "Should we get in out of the rain before it starts? Seems like the smart thing to do. Doesn't it?"

"I suppose so. Better safe than sorry."

I guess that had been my mantra for every single family gathering we'd had since the boys were in high school. I suppose I could have spoken to them before or after those gatherings—but what if I opened up a chasm that could never be closed? Would I then be left with a family that could never enjoy being together again? The thought frightened me. Better safe than sorry, I thought.

I tried to talk to each boy separately back in their high school days. They just shrugged it off without a real answer, and I let it go. *Boys will be boys*, I thought.

Now they were adults. I should have demanded an answer before, but it had been so much easier to look the other way. I figured their issue was some of that sibling rivalry I had heard about. That's how it stayed: getting along on the surface with a storm brewing underneath.

That damned anxiety grabbed me by the throat every time I thought of forcing those two idiots to come clean with me and get whatever was ailing them off their chests. I was afraid to take the chance that it could possibly destroy what we had. Maybe it wasn't the best way to handle it, but at least we were together in some sense.

"Maybe we'll just wait out the storm," my father said. "Sometimes these things look worse than they really are. Besides, they say the best fishing is just after a storm. Maybe if it does storm, things will change. We'll catch ourselves a fish or two to bring home and have one of our favorite cookouts. Don't worry. Things will be all right."

Now what the hell did that mean, I asked myself. There was certainly a subtext going on there. "Thanks, Dad," I said. He gave me that all-knowing smile of his.

Oh God, he was good. He never handed me anything on a silver platter. Never wrapped everything up with a big bow and hand it to me. Nope, that wasn't his way. He was an old old-fashioned sort of guy. I think he always believed that we learn things best when we learn them on our own. Whether it's done the hard way or not.

Chapter Fifteen

Hospital Room 321
9:30 *AM*

When Jan got back to the room, the nurses and Greg were just coming out. "Is there anything wrong?" she asked the charge nurse.

"No. Not as far as we can tell. His heart rate began to rise for a minute or two, and then it settled back down. Probably just one of his dreams again. We'll page Dr. Mehra."

"Thank you," Jan said. The nurses walked away, and she turned to Greg.

He told her, "I was on my way to get you all when he started to settle down and they called me back. He seems to be resting quietly again."

"Thank you for being there for him and us, Greg. I really appreciate it," she said, leaning in to give him a little hug.

"Sure thing. I'm happy I could be worth something around here while you're all going through this."

She hugged him tighter. "If you make my Steve happy, you're worth the world to me and always will be, Greg."

"Thank you," he whispered before they broke the hug. He let his eyes drop and then looked up again. "Are you back for a while? I think I'd like to get a little fresh air, if you don't mind?"

"By all means, get some air. They'll all be back in a moment or two. Thank you again for being here for us."

"You're welcome, Mrs. Connor. I'll be back shortly."

Jan entered the room and sat next to the bed and held Ed's hand. The steady beep, beep, beep of the monitor filled the air.

"Dear Lord, please don't take him from me—from us now. We aren't ready," she whispered. "He's not ready. We have so much yet to do, to see. Bennie is just a little boy. It will break his heart if

135

his papa is taken away from him. He's too young to understand. And Sarah hasn't even had a chance to know him yet. She deserves to know him and have the fun times Bennie has had too."

"How's it going, Mom?" Kim's soft voice seemed to drift across the room.

Jan looked up. "I… I was just asking for a favor," she said quietly.

"I know. I think we've all asked for the same favor lately."

Her brothers followed Kim and sat in the chairs surrounding the bed. Jan waited until they all got situated. "Your father had another spell while we were having the meeting."

"What? What kind of spell? What did they do?" Peter spit out the rapid-fire questions before Jan had a chance to answer any of them.

"Okay. Slow down. Dad is all right now. They said his heart rate began to race a little, but then it settled back down to normal. They thought that maybe he was having another one of those dreams."

"Jan, may we speak?" Karash asked from the doorway.

"Absolutely," Jan replied and immediately went to his side. He hooked his arm around hers, and they disappeared down the hallway.

"I thought this Greg of yours was supposed to be here with him, Steven. To help us. Is he really so flighty that he would just walk off like that?"

Steve's body tightened, and he glared at Peter. "I'm sure there's a good explanation. He wouldn't just walk off."

Peter gave him a disgusted frown. "I'm sorry. I just don't get it. What do you see in him?"

"Well, if you took some time, I'm sure you'd like him."

"I doubt it. All that gay crap. It creeps me out. Makes my skin crawl. How can you profess to love him?"

Steve stood and so did Peter, but Kim stepped between them. "Stop this craziness," Kim demanded. "Guys, we can't go down that road again. It's killing Mom."

"Mom's not here right now, and I wouldn't have said that if she were," Peter said. "It just pisses me off to no extent that he just walked off like that."

"We can't go there now." She stole a look at Steve. "I'm sure there's a good reason Greg left."

"Thank you, Kim," Steve said. "I've tried, but Pete just won't let it go."

"And why should I? It's just not right. You know we are all thinking it. I'm just the only one with balls enough to say it out loud."

"Don't presume to be speaking for me, Pete," Kim admonished him.

"Sure, maybe you think you honestly love him. I just want you to fully consider the consequences."

Steve's face wrinkled with confusion. "The consequences? What the hell does that mean?"

"Don't play dumb, Steve!" Pete threw back at him. "The stigma of all this will follow you forever. Do you really want the whole town thinking about you, about us as a family with the queer-guy marriage?"

Steve looked at him with contempt. "That's what it's really about, isn't it, Pete? You're afraid you'll lose some of your local accounts."

"Bullshit!" Peter yelled. "It's not about me. It's about you and the way people look at you when I'm around—back then and now!"

"Right, right, right," Steve droned. "High school. You're still holding that bag of shit over my head."

"And why shouldn't I?"

"You had a choice!" Steve blasted. "Pick all your cool friends and girlfriends or me. You chose them and left me hanging. Alone." Steve could hardly contain his anger.

"Guys, stop it, please," Kim pleaded. They ignored her.

"Yeah, I chose the normal life. It's not such a hard thing to do," Peter chided him.

"I suppose so. At least for you." Steve threw back.

"What is that supposed to mean?"

"It means when you brought home Laura, nobody busted your balls like you're busting me."

"Of course not. She's a beautiful woman."

"Well, Greg's a handsome guy. But we're not talking beauty

here, are we, Steve?"

"Okay. Out with it. What are you exactly saying?"

Steve took a deep breath. "Nobody, I mean *nobody* busted your balls. Not Mom, not Dad, not me, not Kim. Nobody. Laura's black, Pete, or didn't you notice that? She's not *our kind.*"

Peter's body seemed to almost rise off the floor in anger as he glared at Steve. "You son of a bitch. I ought to drive you into the floor so hard you'd never get up for saying that." He stepped even closer, but Steve held his ground. Kim pushed Peter back with both hands against his chest.

"You're right. Horrible words. Unthinkable prejudices," Steve conceded. "I'm trying to make a point. How can you love her, knowing people might talk? And your child is neither white nor black." It was obvious Steve was playing devil's advocate, but it didn't lessen the sting of his words.

"She's just a woman, Steve. Not black, not African American. I don't see her that way. She's just my wife, the person I love. I don't owe you or anyone else an explanation, nor do I have to justify my love for her."

"Exactly. Don't you hear yourself? 'Just a woman.' 'The person I love.' 'I don't have to justify my love for her.' And maybe that's true, and maybe in this house you don't, but that shit still goes on every day in the world."

"Not like it used to be." Peter said trying to rationalize the lessening of prejudice in the past few decades.

"Maybe or maybe not," Steve threw back. "But there are shootings and racially charged violence still today. It's in the headlines, but you're sheltered from it because we don't see her or your life like that. You're right, she's just a woman. Your wife, but what about Greg and me?"

"That's different. That's not how God intended things. It's unnatural."

"Unnatural? God? You're so full of shit. You never even go to church, and now you invoke God's name? You're such a freakin' hypocrite."

"Guys, shhh. Mom's coming in," Kim warned them.

Jan entered the room with Greg not far behind.

"Where have you been?" Peter demanded an answer from

Mark.

"I was with Dr. Mehra," Jan answered.

"Not you, Mom. I was talking to him." Peter's comment was directed toward Mark Greg. Greg gave Peter a hard glare.

Jan answered, "Greg was on his way to get us when Dad settled back down. Seeing I was back, he decided to get a little air. More importantly, Dr. Mehra wasn't encouraged by this last episode."

"Why?" Kim asked. "They said it was mild, and he seems to be the same as he was before it."

"That's just it, Kimmy." Even though Jan was speaking to Kim, she included everyone in the room with her eyes. "There isn't a change. Both he and Dr. Chang were hoping for some sort of improvement by now. It's getting close to the twenty-four-hour mark since this all started."

"Hmm," Kim muttered. "Only twenty-four hours. It seems like a lifetime that we've been trapped in our little piece of hell." She shook her head, glancing at Steve and Peter. "And you guys haven't helped."

"I know," Jan agreed, "and that's exactly why Karash said what he did about making a decision. We have to come to some sort of consensus about how we're going to proceed. We can't stay here forever, even though we'd like to. So I'm open to suggestions."

She closed her eyes and sat in her chair and waited. When no one spoke up, she finally said, "That's okay for now. Just think about it for a while. We shouldn't be talking about this in front of Dad anyway."

*****

The Rock

"Looks like a storm is brewin'," my father said as he looked up at the dark clouds rolling in across the sky. The vibrations from a roll of thunder shook my very insides and it brought about the anxiety I dreaded from time to time. "Maybe we should reel in our lines and get out of harm's way. What do you think?"

I looked at him but it seemed like we had done this before,

139

though it also seemed like I was just returning from that black space I had frequented so often lately. The rock and the words and the storm clouds seemed all too familiar. "I think we've done this before."

"Oh, so you're having déjà vu?"

"I'm not sure what that is, but I know we've already had this conversation."

"Ya know, some people believe that when you have déjà vu, you're just remembering similar events in your past life. The old memory circuits aren't clear if it's happened before or not, so you get that funny feeling like you've done it already."

"Yep, I guess that makes sense." I was willing to let it slide, just as I had so many times before in my real life. But now in this obscure existence I was participating in, he drew me in again. I sat back and waited for his words of wisdom that I somehow needed to decipher.

"But then again, some people believe that you're remembering actual events. You're looking back on your life. They say you're drawn to specific points in your life when you wish you could've done better. The closer the déjà-vu experiences get to each other, the closer you're getting to your own death. Those points or those memories are the last fleeting thoughts before death. They come quicker because they are the real things you cherish or hate about your life. They're the things you want to keep and hold on to forever or the things you wish you could change. Either way, they're the important things in your life."

"So that's what I'm doing? Dying?"

He smiled. "This is your journey, Eddie. I'm just a sounding board. Maybe the good cop-bad cop of your own design."

I remembered how he smiled, and it brought me back to my childhood. To when he would pose a question that would make me think of the answer to the dilemma I was in at the time. "So what difference does it make? If I'm dying, there's nothing I can do to change it," I told him. There were no answers I could see, not even just beyond my grasp—but somehow I knew there would be if he told me so.

"I only said some people believe déjà vu is about the moments before death. What do you think?" he said, and then smiled that damn smile again.

*****

Hospital Room 321

"It's me, Bennie! I'm back!"

No one really needed the introduction, but it was a welcome reprieve from the tone of the room for everyone at that point. The room had been essentially quiet since Jan posed her question about how to proceed.

Jan stood and then squatted down. "Come on over here, Bennie," she said as she held out her arms to him. Of course, he came running and latched his arms around her neck, almost pulling her to one knee in the process.

"Whoa there, buckaroo. Be careful," Kim cautioned him.

He immediately let go of Jan's neck and stood with his arms straight along his sides like a little soldier. "Sorry, Gramma. You okay?"

Jan smiled and ruffled his hair. It was her favorite thing to do when she first saw him. The expressions he made when she did it always conjured up shades of Ed in their younger years. "I'm fine, Bennie. I'm happy you're here."

By that time Mike, Laura, and Sarah had made it to the doorway.

Peter walked to Laura, and they stood in the doorway while Sarah and Mike continued in.

"No harm done, Kim," Jan said. "He's exactly the breath of fresh air we needed in this room." She held her hands out to Sarah. When Sarah started to charge her, Bennie spoke up. "Careful, Sarah. You don't want to knock Gramma over."

"He's such a little shit," Kim whispered in Mike's ear when he walked over and hugged her.

"Yes, he is." Mike chuckled quietly. "He and Sarah had a wonderful night and morning together. I wish we could do this more."

Kim stroked his cheek. "Me too," she said in a distant tone.

"Mommy, can me and Sarah talk to Papa? Or is he still too tired to wake up?"

"You can talk to him if you want, Bennie. He probably won't wake up, but if he does, that's okay too."

Bennie took Sarah by the hand, and together they walked to Ed's bedside. "Come on, Papa, when are you going to wake up? Sarah is getting dino pajamas like mine, and we're hoping you'll play dinosaur with us when you wake up. You can be the Papa dino and we'll be the baby dinos and when we need help crawling up the mountain, you'll have to help."

Bennie turned to Sarah. "Don't worry, Sarah. The mountain is really the sofa in the downstairs playroom and the floor is the ocean and the chairs are safe and... well, you'll find out. Papa makes it lots of fun."

As they looked on, Peter put his arm around Laura's waist and she turned to him. "I hope Ed recovers. I really want us to spend more time here with your parents so Sarah can get to know him better. He's practically a stranger to her now. Did the doctor come in yet today?"

Peter motioned toward the door and they moved through it into the hallway. "Yes. Earlier this morning."

"What did he say?"

"We spoke in the conference room while... Greg stayed with Dad. Karash said Dad was about the same and that it's all up to him now, but the DNR issue is still up in the air."

"What about you and Steve?"

"I'm afraid that's a lost cause, honey. There's nothing I can do about that." Peter tried to sound sincere, but the anger still echoed in his voice.

"Of course there's nothing you can do about that. You can't fix him. He's not broken," Laura said. "All you can do is love him as your brother. Did you two settle anything?"

"No. I think it's even worse now."

"Why?"

Peter searched for the words. "He practically called you the N word."

"The N word? I can't believe it. That does not sound like Steven."

"Well he didn't say that exactly. He just called you black."

"Steven…" She rolled her eyes. "I am black, you know," she teased. "But why did he say that?"

"He was trying to equate me marrying you to him sucking face with that Greg. So I told him the difference is that I'm a man and you're a woman and that's the way God intended it. Not some unnatural quee—" He made a face. "Okay, political correctness. Some *gay* thing." He still spit the word out like it was poison.

Laura smiled. "There, now, was that so hard? But do you think Steve can change who he is just because of your interpretation of what God intended?" She asked him softly.

"I suppose not," he said, breaking eye contact.

"Good start," she said with an encouraging smile. "Maybe in another couple of decades, you'll catch up with the rest of the world."

He shrugged it off. "Yeah, well, maybe. Me and a couple of million more people. But probably not. Right now, though, that's not even the worst part of it. He still wants to keep the DNR in place and let Dad die."

Laura fell silent for a moment. He snapped, "What? You agree with him?"

"I'm not agreeing or disagreeing. It's not my place to make that call. What does your mom think?"

"After Karash left us the last time, he told us to come to some sort of decision. Mom said she'd need our help making that decision."

"So did you make it?"

"Not yet."

"Okay then," she said, taking him by the hand. "Time for us to go in."

When they entered the room, Steve, Greg, Mike, and Kim were sitting beside Ed's bed. Bennie and Sarah played with a couple of rubber dinosaurs Mike had brought along to help keep them occupied.

"Okay, Mike, it's time you, Bennie, Sarah, and I go PJ shopping and give these folks time to discuss some important business. Greg, can you sit with Ed again while they're out?"

Greg looked at her and nodded thoughtfully. "Thank you,

143

Laura. I'd be more than happy to help in any way I can."

"Okay, you three. Let's hit the road and do a little Dino shopping. What do you say?" Laura asked.

"Yippee!" Bennie said, reaching for Sarah's hand. He grabbed it and pulled her toward the door. "You can be the baby sister, Sarah, and I'll be the big brother. When Papa wakes up, he'll be… well, of course, the Papa dino." He turned to Mike. "Ready, Daddy?"

Mike winked at Kim as he pushed himself out of his chair. "Ready as I'll ever be, kiddo." He said to Jan, "We'll do a little shopping and we'll be back around noon. Then maybe we can all grab a bite in the cafeteria for lunch."

"Sounds delicious," Jan groaned. She got up and gave the four shoppers a hug. "Have fun," she said. As they left, she sat back down and the room fell into an awkward silence.

Greg broke it. "Oh, Steve, we got an email from City Hospital. They'd like us to stop by. They need some upgrades and want to thank you for the painting you donated— Well, read it for yourself."

He fished his phone from his pocket and handed it to Steve. Steve took it as he got up from his chair. He walked to the far side of the room and stood facing out the window. He scrolled through the email and Greg joined him.

"They say they hung my portrait of Mr. Gates in the new Gates wing of the hospital," Steve said after he read the email.

"I know. I told you they'd love it," Greg said. "I think you captured him perfectly. You found that look of compassion that exudes from him."

"Well, I should have. We spent hours and hours with him projecting the hospital's equipment budget line and trying to fit within that budget. I knew he wasn't playing us for fools either, just to get our best price. I knew he really cared."

Greg put his arm over Steve's shoulder. "I think you care too. How many times did we let our margin slip just so they could afford the stuff they really needed?"

"It didn't kill us. Without that stuff, some people wouldn't have gotten the care they really needed in time. Like the new MRI. Not to mention the defibrillators and the updated computers with remote vital sign monitors, in each intensive care room just like they have here." Steve turned and surveyed the room's myriad of state-of-the-art medical wizardry.

"You're right," Greg said as he too looked about the room. "We did make a difference, and we could afford it. Gates made a few sizable donations himself. Between the three of us, we helped make that hospital a state-of-the-art hospital. But you're still missing the point."

"What point am I missing?"

"The point is that they hung your portrait of him in the new wing. When are you going to wake up and open that gallery I've been hounding you about?"

"What, and leave you holding the bag on this business we've both worked at so hard?"

"I suppose if I needed someone in a pinch, you'd be willing to help me out, wouldn't you?"

"Of course, but—"

"I know you would. And wasn't this my dream long before it was yours?"

"Well… I guess so. When we met, you were working at it," Steve said. "But it didn't take off until we pooled our resources and talents."

"You're right, and we worked our asses off getting to where we are. Now it's time for you to use your real talent. Please, Steve, chase your dream the way you helped me chase mine. Allow me to help you see your dreams come true too. I can see it in your eyes when we've been in galleries. It's your dream."

"I never said any such thing," Steve protested.

"Not in so many words, but I could tell when you had a show someplace, how you hated to take the pictures down and home again. You've got the talent. Don't waste it on selling bells and whistles to hospitals. I can do that."

Steve looked Greg squarely in the eyes. "I love you, Greg. Thank you. When this is over, maybe I will."

*****

"Kimmy, can I speak to you for a moment?" Jan said quietly.

Kim gave her an inquisitive look. "Sure, Mom. Is there something wrong?"

"Not really, but let's talk in the hallway."

"Okay," she said and turned to Peter. "Mom and I are going to take a walk. Do you mind?"

He shook his head lazily. "Not at all. Take your time. There's nothing exciting going on now anyway." He rolled his eyes and nodded toward Steve and Greg, embracing for a moment near the window. Kim gave him a stern look before she and Jan left the room.

"Okay, let's have it," Kim said.

"Oh, it's nothing special, but I haven't told you everything about when your father had his first spell."

That stopped Kim in her tracks. "What haven't you told us Mom?"

Jan's eyes fell to the floor and then came back to hers. "When I saw him fall from the mower, I ran to him. He was halfway off the mower, so I pulled him off and onto the ground. I begged him not to die. I know," she said, rolling her eyes, "like he had any control over the situation."

"I understand What more could you have done? Right?"

"I hate myself, Kimmy. I feel like I kind of yelled at him. I called him a stubborn old fart for mowing the lawn. I just panicked, I guess."

"Don't blame yourself for such nonsense. What else could you say? I mean, it was a scary time. Anyway, he is a stubborn old fart." Her smile caught Jan's eye.

Jan released a long sigh. "I should have told him I loved him instead of yelling at him. He probably heard me, and those might be my last words to him."

"Mom, he was already unconscious. He didn't hear anything."

"That's just it. He was conscious for a second or two. When I pulled him up into my lap, he opened his eyes and said 'broken' and then slipped away. I told the doctors all this when we came in with the ambulance, but I didn't tell you or Pete or Steve."

Kim considered what Jan had said for a few moments. "I can understand not wanting to share that with us. Not that it would have mattered, but 'broken'? What do you think he meant?"

146

"At first I thought he was worrying about the damn mower or something like that." Jan laughed softly. "Your father is such a guy. It'd be just like him to worry about the mower rather than himself. God forbid the lawn gets a quarter of an inch too high."

Kim giggled at that. "Yep, that's Dad."

"But now, Kimmy, I think he was talking about us."

"Us?"

Jan looked away for a second. "Yes, us. About the family. He worried a lot about Steve and Pete not being close like they used to be. A couple of times he said that our happy little family was all broken up." She looked away again when her eyes glazed over with tears. She looked back to Kim. "He meant our family was broken. I just know it. So yes. When I was busy yelling at him for being a stubborn old fart, he was only thinking about us. I should have been telling him how much I love him, because I don't think he's ever going to wake up."

Kim hugged her. "Mom, don't think like that. He knows how much you love him. He always will."

"I know. But that's why I think I'm fighting Dr. Mehra's and Dad's wishes about the DNR. I know Dad knows I love him, but I want to tell him again, one last time to his face, so he really knows it. But it's time for me to stop being selfish. This is about him, not me." Jan stood straight and took a deep breath. "Come on. We have to speak with your brothers." She took Kim by the hand, and they turned back to the room.

When they went in, the room was ungodly quiet except for the monitor singing out its constant beeps. Peter was still sitting at Ed's bedside, and Steve and Greg were still on the windowsill. "Come on, boys, we've got to talk. Do you mind, Greg?"

He stepped forward. "Not at all."

When they were in the hall, Jan asked the charge nurse if they could use the conference room again. The nurse told Jan to help herself and that it was unoccupied. "Okay, great. And if Dr. Mehra is still in the hospital, could you ask him to stop by?"

The nurse consulted her computer screen. "Yes. I see he's still here. I'll page him for you."

"Thank you," Jan said. She led her entourage toward the conference room. When they were all seated, she began, "We have a

147

lot to discuss because we need to come to some sort of decision about Dad's DNR. Any thoughts?"

Peter spoke up quickly. "I still think we've got to do whatever we can to keep him alive."

"I don't agree, Pete," Kim said. "We can't let them do everything they can. He could just as easily be kept alive in a vegetative state for years with assisted breathing and a feeding tube."

"I agree with that," Peter said. "What I really meant was anything they can do to resuscitate him."

"They could resuscitate him and then he could remain in a coma. So what are we going to do then? Let him starve to death?" Steve said.

"We have to try something. We have to show some sort of heart here. We just can't let him go," Peter argued.

"I don't see the heart in that," Steve said. "He's already had two major episodes, and Karash said each time there were moments his brain went without oxygen. I don't want him coming back brain dead. That's a fate worse than death."

Jan broke in. "Okay, boys, let's take a break for a minute. I have to tell you something. Just before your father went unconscious, he said one word: 'broken.' I didn't really think anything of it until the past few… several hours with you two bickering. He was concerned about you two not seeing eye to eye anymore, and it was breaking his heart. He even told me once or twice that his family… we were all broken up. So that's it. Even on death's door, he was thinking of us and not himself. So get over it, for his sake. This is my decision, and I'll be the one to make it."

She sat back quietly, waiting for someone to speak up.

Kim spoke first. "Whatever you decide, Mom, we'll support you. Won't we, guys?" It really wasn't a question.

A knock at the door put an end to the discussion. They all looked toward the door. It opened slowly, and Karash came into view. "Sorry to disturb. You wanted to see me, Jan?"

"Yes, I did. Thank you for coming." She took a long look at each of the children. "I've decided to keep the DNR intact. It's what Ed wanted, and I agree. I think we should keep the IV in just to keep him hydrated, in case he has any hope of recovery. I'm sure he wouldn't want a feeding tube. The DNR is what you thought was best and what I believe is best for him too. If anything at all, I think I must honor his request. It may be the last request he makes of me. It's really about him and we all know it. If he dies, I'll have to live with this decision for the rest of my life, but it's not about me now. It's all about him and the quality of life he deserves and wanted."

"Is that it then?" Karash asked the group. No one spoke. More importantly, no one objected. "Then I'll make the notation in the chart. They will have a paper for you to sign, Jan."

He walked to Jan and rested his hand on her shoulder. "It was a hard decision but the right one to make. Especially since this was his wish. Why don't you all go back to his room and try to relax a bit. You may be in this for the long haul. I think I saw a pair of flashing dino sneakers running toward the room when I got off the elevator."

Jan welcomed the break in tension. She could almost hear Bennie now: "It's me, Bennie. I'm back!"

"That's our Bennie!" Kim laughed. "We'd better get back."

Karash left the conference room first and stopped at the nurses' station. When Jan reached the desk, he motioned for her to come over. He slid a piece of paper to the edge of the desk and handed her a pen. Kim was quick to follow and put her arm around Jan's waist as she signed the DNR.

With a sigh Jan said, "Well, I'm glad that's over. Now it's in God's hands."

"That's right, Mom," Kim said. "You did the right thing."

When they reached the room, Laura, Mike, and Greg were talking. Sarah and Bennie were still playing with the dinosaurs on the windowsill.

"Why don't we all go down to the cafeteria and have some lunch?" Jan suggested.

"I'd love to, but I have to run over to Longview Hospital," Greg said. He turned to Steve. "They called and said they needed help placing an order. I won't be long. Sorry for the last-minute changes, but that's our biz."

"I know. Thanks for staying with Dad while we were away."

"No problem. Where will you be later? Here or the hotel?"

"I don't actually know. Text me."

"Okay," Greg said. He turned to the rest of the family. "I

hope this all turns out for the best," he told them, and then left the room.

Jan asked again. "Lunch?" They all agreed and started for the door.

Steve remained behind. "On second thought, I think I'm going to stay here a while. I'll be down in a bit. Just a little one-on-one time with old Boone here," he said.

Jan said, "Okay, but don't be long."

Chapter Sixteen

Hospital Room *321*

With a single lurch, all of Ed's muscles tensed at once. Then he settled back onto the bed, still and motionless. Not even the previous rise and fall of his chest was evident.

The monitor sang out its unnerving squeal of a flat-line heart in a steady, unwavering tone. It seemed almost to stop Steve's heart as well.

A flood of nurses came into the room and surrounded Ed's bed. In a flurry of action, they checked his pulse and listened to his chest with a stethoscope. They poked at the keypad of the computer, bringing up another screen. Then the action stopped. It was like someone had slammed on the brakes, bringing all hope of Ed's recovery to a screeching halt.

The nurses turned to Steve. "We're sorry," the charge nurse said, touching Steve on the shoulder. "Without us interceding, he can't come out of this by himself. The DNR prevents us from doing anything more. The monitor is telling me he's in ventricular fibrillation."

From his work in the medical field, and selling equipment like defibrillators Steve knew exactly what she meant. Ed was dead.

Steve's heart went from the devastated, slowed pace of sadness to racing as a crazy thought crossed his mind.

*****

The Rock

"Still with me, boy?"

It was different this time. It was more like Dad was asking from afar. It wasn't like he was right next to me on the rock. Had night fallen? I couldn't tell. It was dark and cold.

"Yeah, I'm here, Dad, but I can't see you. What's happened?"

"It's late, son. We should get going."

"Going? Where?" I was still confused.

"Well, your mom is waiting, and Grace. We talked about this, remember?"

"Yes, but why is it so dark now when it was so bright not long ago?"

"This is the end, son," he told me.

I heard the compassion in his voice. Then I remembered asking him if that was why I was here and if I was actually dying. "So this is it? Is that why it's so dark? Am I dead?"

From the other side of the dark void, I heard him chuckle. "No, not dead, just late. Here, maybe this will help."

I heard him strike a wooden match on the rock's rough surface. The tiny flame lit the area around us, and I could now see him as if through a light fog. In the glow of the match, I could see the crayon figures of the family drawn so long ago. Steve's image was even fainter than it had been before.

*****

Hospital Room 321

"Is there anything we can do for you, Mr. Connor?" the nurse asked Steve.

"No, but thank you for everything," Steve said in a cold monotone voice. "I'd like to be alone now with my father. If you could send someone to get my family or page them. They're in the cafeteria."

"Of course," the nurse said. They left him alone to mourn the passing of this man

"I'm sorry, Dad. I knew this DNR is what you wanted. You've always tried to make life painless for all of us," Steve said as he approached Ed's lifeless body. "Maybe it's because you've experienced too much pain in your life, but life isn't for the weak of

152

heart. Is it? You told me that once. You told me to be brave and stick with my convictions and go where my heart led me. And I did. It's because of you I found the strength to love Greg without worrying about what the rest of the world might think. Your love is unconditional, just as mine is for you. I held on to that when I was fighting for your right to die in the way you wanted to. Oh God, I wanted to agree with Peter so many times, but I just couldn't. You gave me freedom, and I wanted to free you in the way you wanted. I love you, Dad, and if you want to be mad at me you can, but I can't let you go without a fight."

With that, Steve pulled his father's gown open to expose his chest. He knew enough about the defibrillator to operate it, but chose to switch it to automatic mode rather than the manual mode the doctors might have chosen. He took the defibrillator paddles from the bedside compartment and pushed them hard against Ed's chest. "Love you, Dad," he said again and pushed the buttons.

Ed's body lurched upward once. Steve looked at the monitor for hope, but there was none. Again he pushed the buttons. Various bells and alarms sounded, and Ed's body once again jolted upward, but Steve saw the monitor was not offering any sign of life.

At that moment the nurses burst into the room. "Hey, stop that! You're not allowed to use the equipment."

Steve turned his attention quickly back to Ed, "This is it, Dad. Now or never." And he gave the buttons one last push.

$$*****$$

"What do you want, Bennie?" Kim asked her little dino boy while they were in line at the cafeteria.

"I don't know. Do they have dino chicken bites?"

"I very much doubt it, sweetie. That's something I get at the market. I see they have hamburgers, hot dogs, chicken soup, French fries. Hmmm. How about a burger and fries? And maybe a juice? We have to have something healthy." She smiled to herself.

"Okay, Mommy."

Kim grabbed a lukewarm burger wrapped in shiny foil, a box of French fries, and the juice. "Oh, what the hell," she muttered and grabbed one another of each for herself. Soon they were sitting with the rest of the family at a table in the dining hall.

"So how is everything?" Jan asked, and got everything from a simple "good" to "tastes like cardboard" from Mike.

"Mine won't be cardboard, will it, Mommy?" Bennie demanded.

Kim took a deep breath and shot a look at Mike. "No, of course not. Daddy was just being funny."

"That's right, Bennie," Mike said. "It's more like shoe—"

"Mike," Kim warned.

"Shoooooouper good. Yep, it's super good, Ben." He winked at Kim, seeming proud of his quick save.

"So what do we do now, Mom?" Peter asked.

"Sit and wait. I guess."

"I know, but for how long and where? Do we take shifts or what?" Peter was visibly shaken. It was a state the family rarely had an opportunity to see him in. He was always so damned sure of himself.

"Sometime soon we're all going to have to go home. It's inevitable," Kim said.

"She's right," Jan added. "You'll have to go back to your own lives soon—unless, of course, we see a definite change in Dad's condition. But there may not be a change for days or weeks. I'll be here daily and I'll give you updates. The nursing staff will call me, day or night, if there is any change."

"I think we should all be here, at least on weekends, to help take the pressure off Mom," Peter said.

Kim looked at him with confusion. "What? Who are you and what did you do with my 'it's all business' brother?"

Laura spoke up for Peter. "He's not always all business. I think you only see that side of him when he's home visiting on holidays and stuff like that. His issue with Steve and Greg has made our visits home few and awkward. Would you say that's a fair appraisal, Pete?"

"I guess so. Has it been that obvious?"

"No. We all liked having an elephant in the room for all of our gatherings," Mike taunted him lightheartedly.

"Really?" Peter returned.

"Well, it was a smallish elephant," Jan observed.

At that moment Jan's cell phone went off. She looked at the screen. "It's the nursing station." She answered it instantly. "Hello... He has? Okay, we'll be right up." She immediately stood. "Dad's had another attack."

"What else did they say?" Kim asked.

"All they said was that Dad had an attack, and they left Steve with him."

Peter lifted Sarah from her chair as Mike did with Bennie. In a flash they were at the elevators, waiting for the eternity to pass until a chime sounded.

"Oh my God," Peter complained. "Should we take the stairs?"

"It's probably like all the other episodes, not an emergency. Try to relax," Laura said.

"Okay," he said.

Laura rubbed his shoulder. "It'll just be a minute or two. We'll get there."

When the door opened, Peter had to pull back to avoid colliding with the exiting passengers.

*****

The Rock

I saw my father looking at me through the slight, foggy light of the match, and I knew I was leaving this world. I was dying. I also knew I'd be leaving behind my family. It saddened me to know I never had a chance to say goodbye to them.

"What's wrong, son?" he asked.

"I'm leaving them without a word. Without being able to be there for them any longer. That's what I lived for. Since they were my little babies, I've been there for them and for Jan too. Now I won't be. I never had a chance to say goodbye."

"But didn't you?" she asked, and I looked up to see Gracie there instead of my father. That was okay. I was used to having people or memories of people pop in and out of my mind lately.

"You're back," I said with a certain amount of calmness. I

felt like all things would be better now.

"Of course I'm back. I never really left you. You know that."

I was confused. I was sure it was lack of oxygen to my brain causing my last dying thoughts to be confused. "Why did you say that?" I asked her.

"What? That you didn't have time to say goodbye?"

"Yes."

She smiled thoughtfully. "Remember when I collapsed and you wondered if our eyes touched and if I knew you were there and if that was our final goodbye?"

"Yes. It's bothered me forever, not knowing if you knew I was there and if we had our last goodbye."

"I knew," she said. "I felt our eyes touch, and it said more than words could have ever spoken. Our eyes embraced that day, just like yours and Jan's did the day you collapsed on the mower."

"I remember now," I told Gracie. "I wanted to tell Jan everything that was in my heart. That I'd miss her and I loved her. I also wanted to tell her that our family was broken and I wanted her to bring them back together again, but I couldn't get the words out."

"I think she heard you too."

"She's right, boy," my father said as the light from the match began to fade. "It's time to go."

"Go where?"

"That's up to you, son."

*****

Hospital Room *321*

When they stormed into the room, Steve was standing at the foot of the bed, looking at his father. Ed's eyes were still closed. The monitor sang its monotone song, as it had since Ed's arrival.

"What's happened, Steve?" Jan cried out as soon as she came through the doorway.

"He had another attack and I…" Steve paused, knowing he had a lot of explaining to do. He also knew Peter was not going to understand.

"He used the defibrillator on Ed. In doing so, he's broken hospital rules and put us all, myself included, in a very difficult situation," Karash said from the doorway.

"He what?" Jan said, looking at Dr. Mehra and then at Steve.

Mehra continued, "Now that he's brought Ed back, so to speak, we have no assurance that Ed won't remain in a vegetative state for years."

"Why is that, Karash? He's had seizures like this before." Jan asked.

"Well, because this was different. The steps we've taken with the past seizures didn't work. This seizure was much longer in duration. The only reason Ed survived is because of the defibrillation."

Peter scowled at Steve as he stepped forward. "Ya know, that's what I just don't get. You fight me tooth and nail against using all that stuff. Convince me, Mom, and Kimmy that we shouldn't use it. That Dad wouldn't want it. And then you go and do it yourself?"

Steve approached his brother calmly. "Pete, let me explain-"

Pete cut him off, "I don't give a crap what you've got to say and all your touchy-feely queer bullshit. That's the trouble with you people—you're all too flighty. You gave us this 'do what Dad wants' crap and now you go and—"

"Pete." Kim touched his arm, but he shrugged her off and continued with his tirade.

"And now you pull the rug out from under all of us and do your own thing and make Dad worse!"

"But what if he came out of it after I shocked him? What would you say then?"

Peter scowled. "But he didn't. Did he?"

"That's enough!" Jan shouted loudly enough to be heard well into the hallway. "I won't have this. Everybody out. I want some peace and quiet with your father." She glared at Steve and Peter. "After you two are long gone, this is where I'll be. With your father, here and all alone. And that's the way it's supposed to be. So please, go back and finish your lunch or take a walk or just go home for a while. I'll be fine. Please remember, the next time we all get together as a family, with or without your father, I don't want to see any more of this arguing. Understood?"

Steve spoke up first. "You're right. I'm sorry. I think we all need some peace and quiet. I'm going to go back to the hotel and taking a nap until Greg comes back. Don't worry, Mom; there won't be any more arguing, at least not from me."

When he turned toward the door he gave Peter a look that could only mean "we're through." Peter returned a "like I could give a shit" smirk.

"Oh, I'll be here with you, all right." It was Ed's voice, weak but undeniably his. "What the heck is going on here?"

The voice startled them. When they turned, they saw him awake—barely awake. His eyes were only slightly open, and his pale complexion was a testament to the ordeal he had gone through. But yes, he was awake.

Jan was the first to move. The others weren't far behind. He stopped them all in their tracks by managing to hold up his hand. He sounded stronger when he spoke again. "Let's hold up on all the mushy stuff until you tell me what the hell is going on."

Jan said, "Honey, you've had some sort of seizure and have been… well, asleep for more than a day."

He stopped her again with his hand. "I kinda got that feeling while I was in that place I was in. There seemed to be a storm brewing there. I think now that the storm was here and not really there. Pete, I think I just heard you disrespecting your brother. What was that all about?"

"Sorry you had to hear that, Dad. Let's just forget it. You're awake now, and that's all that counts."

Steve was quick to agree. "Yeah, forget it, Dad. Our prayers have been answered and you're back with us now. Pete and I are fine. Just the stress, I think."

"No. Not so easy this time. It appears I've been given a second chance. I'm not going to sidestep it for my own convenience or sweep this argument under the rug like we have for years, just hoping it'd go away. No. Not this time."

"What do you mean, honey?" Jan said as she approached him.

He tried to stop her again. "I want to know what's going on!" he demanded once again.

"No, you stubborn old donkey. A team of wild horses

couldn't keep me from you." She pushed by his hand and wrapped her arms around him. As she hugged him, she began to weep. "Oh my God, Ed. I thought I'd lost you."

"And I was lost, I think," he muttered in a far-off voice.

"Where were you?"

He looked away for a few seconds before he spoke. "Merry Moose Park, the fishing rock, at home when the kids were little, watching them build that silly soap box… Watching them grow apart… Watching me do nothing about it… Taking the safe road." He paused again. "And nowhere. In a black void that threatened to swallow me up whole and never let me see my family again."

"Oh, Ed, you were just dreaming."

"Maybe so. I remember being with my dad. It was like I was a kid and under his wing again. Learning my lessons the hard way, just like when I was a kid."

"Well, that's a good thing, isn't it?"

"Yes, I guess so. He helped me understand some things. But there is something else…"

His voice trailed off weakly and he looked away again. In a moment he looked back at her and searched her eyes for forgiveness. Jan took a deep breath. "What is it, Ed? You can tell me anything. You know that."

"I'm sorry to tell you this, but Grace was there too," he said in a monotone.

"Grace?" Jan's question was controlled. Measured.

He took her hand. "Yes, Grace was there. It wasn't like an 'I missed her so much that I can't go on' sort of thing. The last thing I remember was looking into your eyes when I fell from the mower. I tried to tell you to fix our family. Do you remember?"

"Of course I remember. I've been trying so hard to do it, but they just don't want to listen. I'm sorry."

He smiled. "Don't worry about that. We will… together. I think that's why Grace was there with me. In the moments before she died, I wasn't sure if our eyes had touched the way yours and mine did when you were holding me there on the lawn. I always wondered if Grace and I said our goodbyes. I think she was there to tell me we did."

Jan rubbed his hand. "That's good, honey. I'm happy for you.

Really. I think you needed that closure."

"Yeah, it was a good way to say our final goodbye. But there was more."

"More?" Again Jan's voice was measured.

"Not really about her, but about why I didn't tell you about the DNR. For some reason I kept coming back to that."

"Well, we did have a lot of discussions about that while you were sleeping. Maybe you sensed it or even heard us." She looked him squarely in the eyes and with a smile said, "And, yes, you did piss us all off."

"Karash told me it would, but I didn't care. I had to pick the best of the two evils. I'd rather have you mad at me than put you through the decision of pulling the plug on me. I had to pull the plug on Grace, and it haunted me for years afterward. I didn't want that for you."

"Well, it's still going to haunt you. Maybe not for years, but we're going to have a long talk about that."

Ed faked a hard swallow. "I think I'm going to be sorry."

"You bet your life you will." She said as she kissed him long and tenderly. Then she pushed the emergency call button, and quickly the room was flooded by the nursing staff.

Chapter Seventeen

Hospital Room *321*

"So, Karash, what really did happen?" Jan pressed. Ed sat forward in the bed, also waiting for Karash's response.

"We're still not sure," Dr. Mehra said almost despondently. "We're leaning toward an extreme reaction to an electrolyte imbalance, called hyperkalemia, instead of what we thought was a stroke. Parts of the brain are still a mystery to us. I've never seen a case as extreme as this, but it's possible." He looked directly at Ed. "It's possible that when you were mowing the lawn, you became dehydrated—or more likely you were already dehydrated before you started. Most of the time it would only make you dizzy or maybe faint, but in extreme cases it can cause a coma-like event. It's likely the IV fluids we were pumping into you brought you out of it when your system became balanced."

"Well, that's a relief," Ed responded with a sigh.

"No problem, buddy. We'll be back on the golf course before you know it. Don't worry. Things like this often happen to old folks. They forget to drink." Karash sat back and folded his arms across his chest, waiting for Ed's response, which didn't take long.

"Don't be pulling that old man card on me, fella. If my old memory serves me right, you've got six months on me."

"True, but I take care of myself. I realize I'm not Superman anymore." It sounded like a half-tease and half-truth that needed to be said.

"Amen to that, Karash," Jan added. "Then no tumor or anything like that?"

"No, not at all. He seems in perfect health again for an old-"

"Don't say it," Ed growled.

Karash smiled. "All right, then. I won't. But don't let me find you back in here. I don't want to ever face this angry mob again."

"Angry mob?"

"Sure. Your family loves you and only want the best for you, and they are all adults now. You can trust their judgment and feel assured they're capable of handling the hard choices as well as the easy ones." He raised an eyebrow at Ed. "Got it?"

"Yep, got it," Ed said sheepishly.

"Okay then," Karash said. "I'm going to sign you out tomorrow as long as you take it easy. No physical labor until I give you the go-ahead. Call the office and make an appointment for next week. We'll discuss if I can lift the no-work ban at that time. Understood?"

"Absolutely," Ed replied.

Jan said, "His definition of 'absolutely' isn't quite the same as mine, Karash. As you might know." Karash nodded. "If he tries anything stupid, I'll superglue his butt to his recliner."

Karash grinned. "You might have to." He turned again to Ed. "But all kidding aside, no work. Clear?"

Ed raised his hands in surrender. "Okay, okay. I know when I'm outgunned. I surrender."

Karash stood up. "Okay. See you in a week." He turned toward the door, but quickly turned back. "Oh, and Jan, please come along." Without waiting for an argument from Ed, he turned back toward the door and left.

Ed looked at Jan with a troubled expression. "I don't like to be treated like a kid."

She smiled. "Well then, don't— Do I need to finish?"

"No," he said in a resigned tone.

"Honey, look at me."

He looked up at her.

"I'm not saying we're fossils, but we are older now. I know we still think and feel like we're kids, but the truth is we're not. We have to slow down a little bit."

"I know. I just don't like it."

"I understand, but you try to work too hard. I see you lifting and tugging at things you could have done easily twenty or thirty years ago, but you have to let some of that go in favor of enjoying our golden years for as long as we can. Isn't that what it's really about?"

He fell silent for a while before he spoke. "You're right, of course. But it's hard for a man to give up being the man he knows he was. Remember how you cried when we decided not to have any more kids? You said you loved being a mommy and it was like you were giving up a part of you."

A tear trickled down her cheek, and she looked at him with glassy eyes. "You're right, but my life is filled now with everything we do with the kids and grandbabies. There's just one thing missing."

"Missing?"

"Yes. Steven."

"I know," Ed said. "I've thought a lot about that too. We're gonna fix that."

She smiled and moved closer to him. He moved toward the other side of the bed so she would have room to lie down.

*****

Jan and Ed turned toward a tap at the hospital door. "Steve! Greg! Come on in, guys," Ed said. The back of the bed was now pulled up as far as it could go. Ed was in a full sitting position, while Jan was sitting on the edge of the bed next to him.

"We wanted to say goodbye before we hit the road," Steve said almost apologetically.

"Of course. I know you both have to get back to your lives. It's not about me anymore. I appreciate everything you've done… you too, Greg. Jan told me you were a great help. Kind of a hard way to get introduced to the family, but I'm happy you were here to help out and support Steve."

"Well, I did what I could. I'd do anything for Steve."

Ed looked long and hard at him before he spoke. "I can see that. I'm happy he had you to lean on. Thank you." He smiled at Greg, and then his eyes finally drifted to Steve's. "I mean that, Steve. I am happy for you both."

Steve crossed the floor to his father and hugged him. "Thanks, Dad. I'm so happy everything worked out the way it did. Are you still scheduled to get kicked out of this joint tomorrow?"

"Yep, they say so. I already filled out my menu for tomorrow, and they're having open-face turkey with gravy, so I'll probably wait till after lunch." He gave Steve a sly wink and shifted his eyes quickly toward Jan.

"The heck you will," Jan protested. "As soon as Karash signs you out, we're gone, outta here, and no looking back. If it's turkey you want, I'll put one in the oven as soon as I get home and you can have the whole damn—"

"Jan…" Ed warned.

"Okay. All the *darned* turkey sandwiches you can eat. But we are not staying here for one second longer than absolutely necessary."

"Well, if you say so, honey." He gave Steve another little wink. "You'll make the gravy too, won't you, hon?"

"Yes, gravy too," she conceded.

"And cranberries on the side?"

She frowned at his teasing. "Don't push your luck, buddy. You'll have to wait for Thanksgiving for the cranberries."

"Yes! The cranberry relish with oranges with the rind minced up and mixed together. Greg, you haven't had cranberry relish till you've had Mom's."

Greg grinned. "I'd be honored," he said sincerely.

"Well then, you can have my share," Peter said from the doorway. Sarah came running into the room. Steve scooped her up and brought her over to Ed and Jan to let her give them both a kiss. Peter and Laura weren't far behind.

"So you're getting sprung? That's great," Peter said.

"Yep," Ed said. "Probably before lunch."

Jan added, "Yes, before lunch. Dr. Mehra gave him a clean bill of health, but he's on light duty."

"Good luck with that!" Peter said.

"No, she's right, Pete. I'm on light duty until further notice and"—he glanced at Jan—"actually, Karash said I've got to slow down a little bit all around, and I'm going to. I don't want to find myself back here anytime soon."

"That's great to hear, Pop. Now I won't have to hear an argument when I tell you I've set up with a lawn care guy to do the mowing and raking and yard work from now on."

"Now hold on for just one minute," Ed protested.

"Just be gracious, Ed," Jan coaxed.

"Pop, you've got plenty else to do. You've got the garden, and maybe you can find some time now to get back into your woodworking. I never understood why you ever stopped."

Ed glanced at Steve. His mind flew back to that day when Steve tried to tell him he was gay, and how he had missed what Steve was trying to tell him. He'd realized he'd totally blown the opportunity to be there for Steve shortly afterward. Yes, they'd finally straightened it out later, and when he was in that faraway place during his coma, he had spoken with his dad about it. Only now he was beginning to understand that no man is invincible or without faults and mistakes.

Steve came back into focus, and Ed saw him looking at him with a wondering look. Ed pursed his lips a bit and smiled with an approving nod to Steve. He could actually see the tension slip away from his son. Steve smiled back. Ed caught Peter looking at them with his own questioning look.

"I'm sorry, Pete. I drifted away for a moment, back to my woodworking days. You're right. I don't know why I stopped now myself." Ed felt a relaxed feeling cover him, and he realized that he wasn't feeling the anxiety and guilt he had so often felt when he relived that episode in his mind. No 'what ifs' or 'could have beens' were haunting him. He could almost feel his father's hand on his back, and he swallowed hard to fight back the knot building in his throat.

"Maybe Sarah and Bennie can help me with a couple of projects when I get out of here."

Sarah wiggled out of Steve's arms and crawled up on the bed next to Ed. "I'd like that, Papa. Can we make a crib for my baby dolls?"

Ed exhaled. "Yes, we can, sweetie. That sounds like a great project. It'll give your mom and dad an excuse to come and visit more often, because it might take a while for us to finish it."

"One that rocks?"

"Yes, one that rocks to help you put those babies to sleep."

Peter crossed to Ed. "It's good to have you back, Dad. I think that's an offer we can't refuse." He kissed his father on the cheek.

"Hail, hail, the gang's all here," they heard Kim say as she, Mike, and Bennie walked into the room. They all turned and offered their own personal version of hello.

"My, aren't we a cheerful little crowd? We're happy we caught everyone still here."

"Me too," Steve said. "We were about to shove off."

"Hey, Bennie," Sarah squealed. "Did you hear? We're going to do woodworking with Papa, and we're going to make a baby crib."

Bennie stopped dead in his tracks and his face froze.

"Well," Ed jumped in, "I was thinking that Bennie could make a fishing rod rack and I could help you both at the same time. After all, he doesn't have any babies to put to sleep. How's that sound?"

"I guess that's okay," Sarah said, sounding a little disappointed.

"Don't worry, Sarah. If you and Papa get stuck, I'll come over and help," Bennie said. The adults exchanged glances, and Sarah perked back up.

"Okay, Bennie. As long as we can help each other. And maybe we can have another dino sleepover too."

Kim grabbed Bennie and walked him to the bed, where he gave Ed and Jan a kiss. Then she sat him next to Sarah. "I think we can manage as many sleepovers as possible." She looked at Laura and Peter, who nodded.

"That sounds like fun," Laura said. "And it will be a little easier now that Peter has asked for a transfer to an office less than an hour away."

Ed was stunned. Maybe they all were, since no one spoke until Ed finally did. "Really, Pete? Really?"

With a wide grin, Peter confirmed Laura's announcement. "Yep. It'll kick in soon, and then the kids will play together and visit you guys all the time. I…" He looked at Laura. "We decided Sarah was missing too much. Time waits for no man—or kid, I guess."

Jan stood and wrapped her arms around Peter and then pulled Laura in. "This is so wonderful. I can't believe it's happening." She turned and looked at Ed. "You should have had this episode years ago."

At first Ed was confused. Then a slight smile crept across his face. "A last-ditch effort, I guess." He then got serious. "I'm so happy too. It's about time you came home."

Steve spoke up. "Yep, great news, Pete, Laura. That's great. Especially for the kids." He paused. "Hate to break up the festivities, but we're going to get going." He gave Sarah, Bennie, Ed, Jan, and Kim a kiss.

Before he had a chance to turn toward the door, Ed spoke up. "Hey, don't forget our annual Labor Day picnic is just around the corner."

"Not for a minute, Pop." He first shook Mike's hand, and then walked to Pete. He extended his hand and Peter readily took it. "Congrats," Steve said. As he did, the smile on Steve's face disappeared—as did Pete's.

The exchange wasn't lost on either Ed or Jan.

Chapter Eighteen

"What are you going to do, Steve?" Greg asked.

"I don't know. I just don't feel up to playing this game with Pete anymore. It's way too stressful for me, you, and really everybody, as far as that goes."

"I know, but this is your first family gathering since your dad got out of the hospital. Don't you think he'll want you there?"

"Of course he will, but isn't it better for me not to be there than to be there talking to Pete? Dad would be expecting that. Sure, we'll talk and be all friendly, but I just can't do it. Pete really went too far this time. Before I thought he was just outright rude, but now I know he really is appalled by us, as a couple. We repulse him."

"I don't think it's that bad."

"Please don't try to put a positive spin on it. You heard him, and you only heard a small part of it. Pete and I are done. It's no use pretending. Mom and Dad aren't stupid. I think it's best if we just break it off with him without causing a scene. At least his way, they'll think it's just like it used to be, not the way it really is between us."

"I know I can't change your mind, and if that's the way you want it, I can't stop you. But try to keep an open mind. Maybe time will help heal all of this."

"The eternal optimist. That's why I love you. But it won't change."

"I'm sorry if I was the catalyst to all of this. I should have just stayed home," Greg apologized.

"Don't go there, Greg. You didn't cause this. He disowned me years ago in high school. I never told you about it, but I guess now's the time."

"Okay, slow down and tell me. First, let's sit down." He

motioned to the kitchen table, and they sat facing each other. Greg slid his can of cola to the side, and Steve looked at him.

"You know that shit isn't good for you."

Greg shook his head. "This isn't about me. Stop stalling and let me have it."

Steve bit his lip in deep thought. He studied his hands folded on the table. "Okay. Here goes. Some guy ratted me out to the baseball team, and they told Pete they didn't want me around because I was gay. They made it so hard on him, he was practically an outcast. Finally they told him to choose between me and the team, and if he picked them, things could go back to the way they were."

"And he did," Greg filled in the blank.

"How'd you guess?" Steve fell silent.

"Steve, back in the day, we were much less accepted than we are today, and still today there's a stigma. I can understand... in a way... that he wanted to be accepted by the team again."

"Well, yeah, I suppose so. But it wasn't just for show. He hated me for it. He told me he wanted me out of his life forever. We haven't spoken unless absolutely necessary since that time."

"What'd your parents think?"

"I think they thought it was just some boyhood squabble. I'm sure they didn't know how deep this whole thing went."

"So you let things fester for years?"

"I didn't *let* things fester," Steve said defensively.

"I'm sorry, that was a rhetorical 'you.' I meant *both* of you let things fester."

"Sorry. Yeah, we did. I hoped that as times changed, so would he, but he didn't. I don't know what to do now. One thing I do know is that I can't go back to what it was."

*****

Laura's cell phone jiggled on the granite kitchen countertop as it rang and vibrated. She put down the knife she was slicing cucumber with for the salad, and wiped her hands quickly. She picked up the phone and looked at the screen. "Steve," she said aloud. "Hi, Steve," she said after she touched the screen.

"Hi, Laura. How are things?"

"Great. Is everything okay? Is your dad okay?" she asked nervously.

"Sure, he's fine."

"Whew, that's good. I was concerned when I saw your name pop up on the phone."

"Are you all moved in yet?"

"Yes, just about there," she replied.

Silence. "How's Sarah?" he finally asked.

"She's good."

"Oh, great." Silence.

Finally Laura spoke. "I'm sorry, Pete's not here. Did you try his cell?"

"Oh yeah, I must have hit the wrong number."

Laura's forehead wrinkled a bit. *P* and *L* weren't that close on the contact list, she thought. She was also sure they weren't on his speed dial list, and he hadn't dialed the landline that would reach them both. She knew Steve had called her intentionally.

"So what's up?" she said, trying to keep her suspicious thoughts from her voice.

"Not much. I just wanted to tell you that Greg and I won't be able to make the Labor Day picnic."

Not surprised, she thought. "Shouldn't you be telling your mom and dad instead of me?"

"Well… that's just it. I didn't want to get them all riled up in advance. I thought I'd call that day and tell them we have an equipment problem with one of our hospital clients, and we can't make the picnic. So I thought I'd tell you and Pete."

"Why are you telling me?"

"I just thought you should know. I will, however, be able to make Thanksgiving."

The furrows on her forehead deepened. "Oh, I see," she said. "So you'll be around for Thanksgiving but not for Labor Day."

He paused. "It looks like that, I guess."

"I don't like it, Steve." She didn't want to be part of this facade.

"I know, but it's got to be. Sorry, Laura."

She knew from his tone that he really was sorry, but where

did that leave the kids? They were too young to even try to understand. "So where in all this does Sarah fall? You know she fell in love with you this last visit. Is it fair to her?"

"Probably not," he admitted. "Maybe when there's one of those sleepovers and woodworking weekends, I can pop over to help with the woodworking. Ya know, if I happen to hear about it. I did a bit of woodworking myself with Dad when I was a kid."

"She and Bennie will miss you, so don't forget to 'pop over.'"

"I won't. I wouldn't… I never could."

"Okay, I'll take you on your word. I hope to see you soon if we can. Say hello to Greg for us," she said.

"Okay. I'll tell him you said hello," he said, stressing the word *you*. "Oh, and Laura. We'll probably be visiting Greg's family for Christmas."

She didn't respond.

"Sorry, Laura. Bye."

The phone's screen announced that the call had ended.

*****

"So he said he won't be able to make Labor Day or Christmas?" Peter questioned as he took a bottle of wine from the wine cooler shortly after Sarah had gone to bed. He poured them each a glass and sat on one of the stools at the kitchen island. Laura took hers and sat opposite him.

Peter stared into the wine before he took a sip. "I guess that's a good thing. I was wondering how we were going to manage that," he finally said. "That leaves us Labor Day and Christmas. The kids will want to play at Mom and Dad's house with their Christmas stuff from 'Santa's second drop-off,'" he added with a little smirk.

"Oh, your parents don't give them that much." She knew she didn't sound convincing.

He gave her a look. "You do know who you're talking to, right?"

She laughed, "Well… not *that* much," she answered coyly.

"No more than your parents," Peter said. "Between Santa, your parents, and my parents, Mommy and Daddy come in a distant fourth!"

"Your parents and mine are in the 'grandparents get to spoil the grandkids' club, so just get used to it."

"I have no complaints, especially now that he's not going to be around."

Laura exhaled a deep breath, "God, I hate it when you talk like that."

"What? About him?"

"Yes."

"Better get used to it. It will never change. If you don't like it, just don't mention his name. Simple as that. Problem solved."

"I hate having to say it, but you're the only one under my reign of influence, so I have to try to help you see the light."

"I think it's time to give that up, don't you?"

"I suppose so, but not until you tell me what the heck this is all about."

He frowned and looked back into his wineglass. "He ruined everything," Peter said. "Practically ruined my whole life."

Laura raised an eyebrow. "Ruined your whole life? Hello! Now, do you know who you're talking to? I just happen to know you're married to a beautiful woman who simply adores you, except at this particular moment. You have a precious little daughter who thinks the world revolves around you. A to-die-for house and job. Ruined? Please explain ruined for me."

"I said practically."

"You're a long ways from 'practically ruined my whole life,' my friend," she corrected him.

"Okay, not my whole life. Just my teenage years."

"Well, that's a start. Go on." She was hoping this would be the moment he finally shared with her what had really happened so many years ago, and why he just couldn't let this war against his brother and every other gay person in the world go.

Peter took a sip of the wine and caught her glance for an instant. But let his eyes follow the wineglass back to the granite countertop. "All I want to say is he deserted me long before I deserted him, and I'll never forgive him or that gay crap because of it." He looked up, and she knew he had shut down his emotions and wasn't going to say anything more. But she had to try.

"Okay. He deserted you. How?"

He swirled the wine in his glass and then downed it. "Doesn't really matter. It's done. Over. Kaput. The game's on. I'm going to relax for a while before bed." He stood up and started for the media room.

"What about Labor Day?"

"What about it?" he said, turning back to her.

"Don't you think you two should at least try to fake it for Mom and Dad's sake?"

His expression softened. "I know you're trying your best to make everything right for us again, and I love you for that. But no, we're not going to be faking it anymore. What did he say about telling them?"

"He said he would call the day of the picnic and tell them something had come up with one of their hospital clients and they wouldn't be able to make it."

"Typical coward's approach. Works for me." He turned and left the room, leaving her heartbroken and confused.

*****

The call came around two in the afternoon. Ed was watching Bennie and Sarah enjoy what would likely be their last time in the little wading pool he had set up in the backyard this summer. Usually by Labor Day, the nights were cool and the afternoon sun was lower in the sky. Ed knew if he relied on Mother Nature to heat the water, it would be still cold by the time the kids got there. So he'd been hauling buckets of warm water from the house to the pool, tempering it to a nice eighty-some-odd degrees. He'd had to make a few extra trips because Jan had warned him not to carry full buckets and give himself a heart attack or something, so he complied. Ed wondered if the extra trips weren't as bad or worse than the full buckets, but nevertheless he'd be damned if the kids didn't have a warm pool to play in. Luckily the weather had cooperated, and it was a warm and sunny afternoon for the picnic.

He often resented the Labor Day picnic. For him it was more of a signal of the end of the summer and all of the fun they'd had during those days of school vacation when Peter, Steve, and Kim

173

were little. It had been precious and not time to be wasted. He felt the same way now that his kids had grown up and had kids of their own.

"Dad," Kim called him. He turned and saw her walking toward him with his cell in her hand. "Your cell was going off at the picnic table." It rang again. "It's Steve."

"It's okay, answer it," Ed called to her.

She swiped the screen and said hello, then stopped for a minute to listen. She nodded and walked on to Ed and handed him the phone.

"Hey, buddy boy," he said in an enthusiastic voice. "Where are you? I'm about to put the burgers on." He listened for a moment and his smile dropped. "Oh, that's too bad. Are you coming later?" Again he listened and made a frown for Kim's benefit. "Okay, I'm sorry. We'll miss you. Yep, I'll tell everyone. Take care, Steve, and say hello to Greg for us all." He listened again. "Okay, you too. See you soon. Bye." He hit the end-call button with a single thrust of his finger that could have been a little gentler and looked up to Kim.

"He's not coming, is he, Dad?"

Ed shook his head slowly. "No, I'm afraid not. Something about a new piece of equipment they just installed that isn't working right. The hospital asked them to take a look at it."

"Aw, that's too bad. The kids will be disappointed… well, everybody, but especially the kids."

"Yeah, I know. Put my phone back on the table. I've had my one call for the day," he said with a sarcastic grin. "Oh, and tell the rest." When he handed her the phone, he glanced back toward the family gathered around the picnic table. He saw Laura watching them. "Maybe you should tell Laura first. She seems concerned."

"Okay, I will. We'd better get the kids out of the water first. It's getting cooler."

"I'll get them dried off in a minute. You go and spread the bad news. Maybe Laura will want to tell Sarah herself."

"Okay, I will," Kim said as she turned and left.

"Okay, kids. Just a couple more minutes and we've got to get dried off and get dressed because we're having dinner soon."

They replied in unison, without stopping what they were doing, "Okay, Papa."

He smiled and turned to see Kim and Laura walking away from the rest of the family with their heads together.

In a few minutes the kids were out of the pool and off with their mothers to get dressed. By the time they were back out, Ed ad the burgers ready and was announcing, "Come and get 'em."

He turned to Kim as she, Mike, and Bennie walked toward the grill with their plates in hand. "I think we should get you one of those wagon train triangles you can ring when the grub is ready," Mike yelled.

"I know you're joking, but he probably would like it," Kim said cheerfully. She shepherded Bennie toward the grill with his bun opened on his plate.

"You want four or five burgers, Bennie?" Ed asked with a serious face.

"Just one, Papa," Bennie said quietly.

Ed immediately noticed it. "What's wrong, buckaroo?" he asked as he slid a burger onto the bun.

"It's not good, Papa."

Ed shot a glance toward Kim and Mike. "What'd you mean, buddy?"

Bennie pouted and finally said, "Uncle Steve's not coming."

"I know, but he'll be here next time."

"But it won't be the same," he squeezed out, almost in tears. "He always draws a dino on my burger with the squirt mustard."

"Oh… that's too bad. But your daddy can do that."

Bennie looked up. "It's not the same, Papa. Uncle Steve does it best."

"Well, can I try, Ben?" Mike pleaded.

Not sounding very confident, Bennie replied, "If you want, Daddy."

"Okay, let's give it a whirl," Mike said, raising an eyebrow to Ed as he ushered Bennie away from the grill.

Ed looked at Kim. "That didn't sound too promising."

"No, it didn't. He looks forward to these family times, especially with Steve and Sarah."

"Well, then, there's always Thanksgiving. We'll all be together then," Ed rationalized.

"We'll hope so," Kim said.

175

"What's that supposed to mean?"

"Laura just told me they might not be able to be here for Thanksgiving. Something about they might be spending the day with her family."

"They always spend some time with both families. What's different now?"

"Something about some family from California might be in town, and they might spend the whole day with them this year."

"I can understand that, I suppose," Ed said.

"It's all up in the air for now. Laura said she likes to be here too, and she's going to try hard to make it happen."

"That's why I like that kid. She's got a heart of gold and has always been right here with us as part of the family through thick and thin."

"Yeah, I know. She told me she's going to try as hard as she can to get Pete, Sarah, and herself here for the holiday. I think we're as important to her as her own family. I think of her as a sister, and she's told me she feels the same way for me."

"She's a good wife and mother. I'm proud to have her as one of us. I just hope she can pull something off. It'd be a shame to miss them entirely on Thanksgiving."

"Yeah, I know. Fingers crossed," Kim said. She kissed Ed on the cheek and started toward Mike and Bennie.

Chapter Nineteen

"Hey, what's going on in here?" Steve said as he came through the shed door where Bennie, Sarah, and Ed were working on a couple of woodworking projects.

Bennie and Sarah jumped down from their stools, which were pulled up close to the workbench, and ran to him. Bennie was first to reach him, and he jumped up into Steve's waiting arms. "Hi, Uncle Steve. How did you know we were here?"

Steve smiled. " A little birdie told me," he said coyly. He squatted and took Bennie with one arm and scooped up Sarah with the other. He rested each of them on one of his knees. He looked at Ed. "Sorry I missed the picnic, Dad."

"That's life, kiddo. We all missed you."

"I'm sure," Steve said with a little edge to his voice. "So what are the three of you up to?"

Bennie wiggled off Steve's knee and grabbed his hand. "Come on over here, Uncle Steve," he said as he pulled Steve toward the workbench. Steve stood and walked toward the bench with Sarah still in his arms.

As they approached the bench, Steve could see a wooden cutout of a vintage Chevy Corvette and another cutout of a dolly with lacing holes already drilled through it. He glanced at his father but spoke to the kids. "Wow, you three have been busy."

"Papa cut them out for us, but we sanded them and—"

"And now we're painting them," Sarah announced proudly.

"I can see that. Very nice work indeed. So now are you going to make wooden clothes for the dolly to be laced on?" He sat Sarah on the stool in front of her dolls.

"I've been thinking about that. She can cut out some cardboard ones with your mom and color them too. You mom loves projects as much as we do." Ed winked at Steve and then turned toward Bennie. "He saw the 'Vette on the car calendar as the October picture, and when I changed the month to November last week, he saw the Model T Ford and thought he'd want to make one of those too. So if things go as planned, Ben and I have ten more cars to make from this calendar. That'll give Sarah and I plenty of time to make some dolly clothes. Either way, Mom will have to be the fashion designer."

"Sounds great, guys," Steve said, lifting Sarah from her stool and ruffling Bennie's hair. "Reminds me of the good old days, Dad." He noticed his father's expression change to something a little introspective.

Finally Ed spoke. "Yep, the good old days. Ever wonder how quickly things can change?"

Now it was Steve's turn to do a little soul searching. "Sure do. All the time. But what do you mean?"

"You know. You guys grew up and apart. Our woodworking didn't last as long as I really wanted it to. What happened?"

Steve knew what his father was asking but didn't want to go there. "You said it yourself, Dad. We grew up. Different interests, different people. That's all. But," he said, quickly changing the subject, "I think I can still handle that jigsaw. Why don't I draw up a Model T for Bennie and cut it out while you help Sarah with the painting?"

Ed scrunched up his face. "Not too sure about that. You're the painter in the family."

Steve laughed. "You can paint more than houses, Dad. I've seen some of your finished work. Tell ya what. I'll work the saw for a bit and then we can switch. Fair?"

"Okay, but don't go cut out all ten. I want this job to last as long as I can."

"Got ya," Steve replied and turned toward the stack of wood in the corner.

Bennie crawled down from the stool once again and tagged along behind Steve. With a quick look over his shoulder, he said, "Papa, I'll be right back. Me and Uncle Steve are gonna find a good piece of wood. Maybe even one with a knot in it for character."

Steve looked questioningly at his father.

"Just something my dad once told me. I guess it stuck.

Thought I'd pass it down to the boy." Ed winked.

"I don't remember you passing it down to me or Pete."

Ed nodded. "Just kinda remembered it, I guess. Can't waste good advice."

"True," Steve said. "Come on, Bennie. Let's get us a piece of wood with character."

*****

Later that afternoon, Laura came to pick up Sarah. When she entered the workshop, she beamed to see Steve there with the kids.

"Well, well. Look what the cat dragged in!" Steve said with a smile.

Bennie spun around and then asked, "What cat, Uncle Steve?"

Steve ruffled his hair and explained it was only a saying.

"Okay, I knew that, Uncle Steve," Bennie said, pretending to be all grown up and in the know. "Sometimes my daddy has to 'splain things like that to me too." He ran off to greet Aunt Laura, who was already being pulled toward the workbench by Sarah.

"My oh my," Laura said. Steve thought she was overacting a little bit, but the kids didn't catch it at all. They smiled proudly as they both tried to catch her attention first.

"Mommy, come see my dolly Papa cut out. I'm painting it and—"

"Aunt Laura, look at the car I made. Its—"

This time it was Ed's turn to interrupt. "Ben," he said with authority but not harshly, "remember, ladies always before gentlemen."

Bennie stood straight. "You're right, Papa. You first, Sarah."

Laura patted him on the top of his head. "That's very considerate, Bennie. Thank you." She turned to Sarah. "Go on, honey."

Sarah pointed to the doll cutout. "This is the dolly Papa cut out. I sanded it all smooth and now I'm painting it. See the holes?"

"Yes," Laura said, leaning in for a close inspection.

"Nana is going to draw some dresses, and Papa is going to cut them out. Then I'm going to paint them all pretty and tie them on the doll with shoelaces."

"Wow, that's a lot of work to do. I'm happy we moved here so you can work on your dollies whenever you want," Laura said with a little adult sarcasm as she shot Ed a wink.

"Not a problem at all for Jan and me. You know that. Anytime."

When the door squeaked open, they saw Kim. "Hail, hail, the gang's all here. Steve, I thought that was your car in the driveway."

"Yep, came to check in on the woodworkers," Steve said.

"Well, how are they doing?"

"Not bad at all. They've got a good teacher."

"Great. How did you end up here today?"

"Laura called and told me that since I missed the party, they have been missing me, so I thought I'd drop by."

"I thought a birdie told you, Uncle Steve." Bennie was confused again with all this adult secret-meaning stuff.

"It's just—" Steve began.

"I know, Uncle Steve. It's just a saying. Sometimes you grown-ups don't make any sense with your sayings," Bennie said, a little annoyed.

"Any luck with Thanksgiving, Laura?" Kim asked.

"Not yet," Laura said, sounding disappointed. "I'm trying, but I can't seem to work it out."

"Thanksgiving?" Steve asked.

Ed dove into the conversation. "Yep. Haven't you heard? Pete, Laura, and Sarah might not be able to be here for Thanksgiving."

"Not again," Bennie moaned. He buried his face in his hands. "I'm going to miss Sarah too much."

"Mommy, we won't be here for the parade on TV this year?"

"No, we might not be able to, honey."

"But we're always here!" Sarah was almost in tears.

"I know, honey. I'll try to fix it, but no promises." Laura stole a look at Steve.

"That's too bad, Laura. No chance at all?"

"Not that I can see."

"I wish there could be a way. But if there isn't, then that's the way is has to be, I guess," Steve said. He gave Laura a look that conveyed his sadness over the kids being disappointed, and also his resolve to stick with his decision of not playing the loving brother game any longer.

"Hopefully, things will change and we'll be able to see you after all," Kim suggested.

"That would be nice. I wish we could, but I don't give it much of a chance…" Laura's voice trailed off to nothingness.

*****

Thanksgiving came without Pete, Laura, and Sarah making an appearance. Despite their absence, everyone was having a good time, even Bennie. There was, of course, the Macy's parade, complete with the season's first appearance of Santa, and then a trip to the woodworking shop with Ed, Mike, Bennie, Steve, and Greg. "Ben picked out his next car," Ed explained to Greg and Steve. With a roll of his eyes, he continued, "He skipped over the December picture of a 1956 DeSoto, which he described as being lame, in favor of the 1966 Ford Mustang, which was last January's car."

"Lame? Where did you hear that, Bennie?" Steve asked.

"The bus. Where else?" Mike answered for Bennie. "He doesn't miss a trick, especially with the things we don't want him to remember. He's like a sponge."

"Yep, the bus. All the big kids say stuff like that," Bennie informed them all.

"I can imagine," Steve groaned, glancing at Mike.

"I wish Sarah was here to show you the doll stuff she made," Bennie said with a glance toward the cradle on the other workbench. "Want me to show you?"

"Maybe we should wait for her to show us. I think she'd want to," Ed suggested.

"Okay," Bennie said. "I think you're right."

Steve's cell binged and he dug it out of his pocket. He swiped the screen and tapped the "new text" message. "Looks like dinner's ready," he announced.

"Well all right then. 'Bout time those womenfolk got the grub out."

Mike shot him a warning look. "Sponge," was all he said, nodding toward Bennie.

"Sorry," Ed returned.

When they approached the house, they could smell the aroma of turkey in the air. When they entered, they could see the dining room table set with all the makings of a grand holiday feast.

"Is the grub ready?" Bennie asked.

Jan and Kim gave each other a little smirk. "Sure is, fellas," Jan said. "Just mosey on over to the sink and wash up and sit on down." It was the best cowboy talk she could come up with.

Bennie looked at Ed. "Mosey?"

"Yep. It means just walk on over and get cleaned up for dinner," Ed told him.

Mike turned to Greg and with a wink he said, "Mosey just isn't in his dino world vocabulary, I'm afraid."

"Yeah, I was thinking that was probably the case," Greg said. "You're a lucky man, Mike. He's a wonderful kid."

"Thanks. He's a handful, but I don't think we'd want it any other way."

"You're absolutely right. Enjoy him for who he is. That's all he needs."

Mike studied Greg after that remark but didn't pursue it any further.

When everyone was sitting at the table, Ed surveyed each one of them before he took Steve's hand, who sat on his right, and Kim's hand, who was at his left. In turn, each person took the hand of the person next to them. When all hands were joined, Ed bowed his head, "Dear Lord, thank you for this wonderful meal before us and for allowing us all to be together today. Please bless all of us seated here to enjoy this meal of Thanksgiving, and also bless those who are not with us today—Pete, Laura, and Sarah. Amen."

After they all said amen, Jan spoke out. "I can't help but remember when we sat around your hospital bed." She found Ed's eyes with hers before she continued. "We all sat at your bedside, Ed, and joined hands much like this. We held you until the circle was complete. I think we all prayed silently for you and your recovery every time we made the circle. Thank God you came back to us." She choked back her tears by tightening her grip on Mike's and

Greg's hands. "We were terrified we'd lose you, but we tried to keep our spirits up by telling stories of our favorite family moments, just like when we sat around the campfires. I think those stories are what made our wait bearable."

Ed smiled warmly. "I only wish I had been awake to enjoy those stories. Too bad Pete, Laura, and Sarah aren't here so we could do it all again. I think I have a few stories to tell myself. Maybe at Christmas we can do it. I'm sure we'll all be here then. I don't think there's been a Christmas ever that we haven't all been together."

Kim shot a glance toward Steve and then Greg, and neither could hold her gaze.

"That would be nice, Daddy," Kim said, "but we should eat before everything gets cold?"

"You're absolutely right. Let's dig in. Pass the turkey," Ed said as he took a scoop of mashed potatoes.

When dinner was over, Kim and Steve went into the kitchen to help Jan clean the dishes, as they had ever since the two of them were kids. Meanwhile, Ed, Mike, and Greg gathered around the television to watch the game. The crackling and slight scent of burning wood from the fireplace added that special holiday feeling to the evening. Mike, closest to the fire in an overstuffed recliner, slowly drifted off into a turkey-induced Thanksgiving nap.

Ed grabbed the controller and lowered the sound a bit and turned to Greg. "That boy works like a dog, and that Bennie gives him a run for his money. If anybody deserves a nap, it's him. How about some fresh air before we pass out like him?"

"No thanks. I'm fine, but don't let me stop you."

Ed stood and looked down at Greg sitting in his chair. "Yeah, I think we need some air." He extended his hand. Greg looked at it for a split second before he took it. Ed hoisted him from the chair and turned him toward the door with a gentle arm around his shoulder. "If we were real men, we'd be going outside to smoke a stogie, I guess, but we'll have to settle for fresh air."

A little confused, Greg could only nod in agreement. *Oh shit. What's this all about?* Greg asked himself.

"We're going out for some air," Ed announced as he opened the front door. Before he closed it, he looked toward the kitchen and saw Jan give him a little wave. He pointed to Mike passed out in the recliner. She nodded an acknowledgment. He closed the door and stepped onto the porch with Greg.

"So what's up?" Greg asked quickly.

"Oh, nothing special. I just thought we could get to know each other a little better. We didn't really have much time at the hospital, and you and Steve weren't at the Labor Day picnic."

Greg reached for his chin and stroked the dark stubble that grew back each day much too quickly for his liking. "Yeah, I'm sorry about that. Business, you know."

"I get it. I understand. A lot of people depend on you and Steve and the equipment you sell," Ed said as he leaned back against the porch railing.

"Good, thanks for that," Greg replied, "but somehow I don't think that's all that's on your mind."

Ed grinned a sheepish grin. "You're right. That's not what's on my mind. You and Steve seem to be hitting it off quite well, but he's had a rough road, you know. I just don't want to see him getting hurt again."

Greg looked Ed straight in the eyes before he spoke. "You know…" he paused. "I mean, thank you," he finally said. "That means a lot coming from you."

"It means a lot that I'm questioning your intentions?" It was Ed's turn for confusion.

"No, not that. It's just nice that you think enough about Steve to be straight with me, no pun intended." Greg smiled and he could feel the tension lift from the conversation.

Ed agreed with a nod and slight laugh. "Ya know, I'm not too old to get that," he teased.

"I had no doubt that you would. It's usually the first word to take on a different meaning. You know, most men would rather walk on glass than ask a gay guy about his lover. Even in this new era of gay rights and everyone being out, a lot of people would like nothing better than to sweep it under the rug again. A don't ask, don't tell sort of thing. So it's a big compliment."

"Thanks for saying that," Ed said. "I did want to know your intentions. But more than that, I wanted to get to know you better."

There was a silence, but Greg didn't see it as an awkward silence. It was more like a moment to reflect on the past few

184

minutes. He suspected they both needed it after the awkward start to the conversation.

minutes. He suspected they both needed it after the awkward start to the conversation.

"Well, to answer your question. We're in it for the long haul," Greg said quietly. "We're making a life for ourselves and we're doing okay. It's all good."

"Great. That's all I needed to hear. Earlier, when you were speaking to Mike, you said that all Bennie needed was understanding, and I got the feeling that maybe you didn't get that when you were young."

"No, I didn't. School was hard enough to deal with, but my parents never really did accept me being gay. My mother kept suggesting it was a phase or a fad and maybe I'd grow out of it. She even asked several times if I was sure. Things between my father and I never really seemed the same after I told him. I mean, he didn't hate me or anything, but we were never really comfortable together after that. I was always a little envious of Steve. He said you always understood and accepted him."

Ed looked away. "Well, not always," he said.

Greg's face took on a puzzled look. "Hmm. That's not the way I heard it."

"There was a time when he tried to tell me but I was too pigheaded to actually listen to him. I always felt that hurt us—our relationship," Ed confessed.

"Ha!" Greg laughed. "You mean the crash-and-burn talk?"

"Crash-and-burn talk?"

"Yep. Steve always refers to the first time he tried to tell you he was gay as his crash-and-burn talk."

"I was that bad? I've regretted that day ever since." Again Ed couldn't hold Mike's gaze.

"Not you!" Mike laughed again. "He always said he wanted to tell you but was afraid he'd hurt you somehow. He says he was ashamed to say the word *gay*, so he kept beating around the bush and getting you more and more confused until he finally gave up. He felt bad that you were trying so hard to fix things. Fix him up with a girl. Get him to go the dance. All those things Pete had done that he wasn't interested in. He is"—Mark stressed the word *is*—"so thankful that you loved him so much that you were racking your brain to help him."

"I never knew that. I didn't realize what he was trying to tell me until a few years later, and I've felt bad about it since then. I felt like I let him down just when he needed me most," Ed lamented.

"And he never knew you felt this way. I think it's time to clear the air about the crash-and-burn episode. Don't you?"

"I'd love to."

When they went back into the house, Greg simply announced, "Hey, Steve. I told your father about crash and burn."

Steve spun around and walked from the kitchen toward them. "Why?"

"Because he needed to know."

"That's right, son. I needed to know, and thank God Greg told me. I've been kicking myself for years thinking I hadn't listened to you that day, and you've been kicking yourself for that same number of years for not being clear enough for me to understand you. It's funny what we do to ourselves, isn't it?" Ed pulled Steve closer and hugged him.

"Yes, it is," Jan interjected. "Now how about a little eggnog to celebrate this monumental lessening of the guilt?"

Most everybody had some eggnog, some with a splash of whiskey or rum. But not Greg, who announced he was driving. "And speaking of driving, we should hit the road, Steve," he suggested.

"You're right. It's a long drive back," Steve said.

After the eggnog was gone, Jan brought Steve and Greg their coats from the hall closet. "Okay, boys. Have a safe trip."

"Yes, and you don't have to wait for Christmas to visit, you know," Ed said, giving Steve another hug.

"Sure, Pop. We'll try to get back soon."

"Well, if not, then we'll see you on Christmas," Ed said.

But Steve's eyes diverted from his. "Sure thing. I'll call when we get home. Okay?"

"That'd be great, honey," Jan said, also giving Steve a hug and then Greg. "You know we're always up late. Bye."

Kim walked up to Steve and Greg. "Please don't be strangers."

Steve gave her a big hug and whispered in her ear, "We won't, sis." In a moment Steve and Greg were out the door.

Kim closed the door and leaned heavily against it. "We've

got to talk," she said.

"What is it, honey?" Jan asked quickly.

"I've got to call Laura first," she said, taking her cell from her purse resting on the hallway table.

"I thought they were busy all day," Jan said.

Kim just made a frown and waited for Laura to answer. "Hello, Laura. Can you talk, without Pete hearing, I mean?"

Ed shot a look at Jan, then back to Kim.

"Okay. I'm putting you on speaker."

Chapter Twenty

It was about five o'clock in the morning when Bennie came charging out of his mother and father's bedroom and into the living room. He was wearing his footed Rudolf PJs and almost slid under the Christmas tree with excitement. When he stopped, he saw Ed and Jan sitting on the sofa, waiting patiently for his arrival. They had quietly let themselves in after they got a four-thirty text from Kim telling them she couldn't hold him back much longer. It was expected, and they had been waiting for it.

"Okay, Bennie. Why don't you see what's in your stocking while Mommy and I get a cup of coffee?" It sounded like Mike was pleading with Bennie rather than telling.

"I put the pot on," Jan said. "I thought it'd be quicker and easier than us all waiting in line with those little pods in our hands. It should be ready. I'm right behind you."

"Me too," Ed chimed in.

"But Santa came," Bennie pleaded.

"I know, buddy. Be patient for just a few more minutes and then you can rip into those presents as fast as you like. Okay?"

"Okay." He sounded a little dejected, but the adults knew he would be just fine very soon.

As they stirred in their cream and sugar, Mike yawned.

"Long night?" Ed asked with a grin.

"You don't know. Santa had a hell of a time getting Dino Mountain put together."

"I don't know? Me? You do know who you're talking to, don't you? Father of a certain little lady named Kimmy who wanted every Barbie house, cottage, and castle ever made, as well as an almost life-size play kitchen with the worst assembly instructions ever written by man? Me? I don't know?" Ed tipped his coffee cup as if it were a glass of wine and took a sip.

"Okay, so you do know, but that doesn't make my three

hours of sleep feel any better."

"No, I bet not. But maybe you can get a power nap in before you come over for dinner," Ed said as he turned. They all made their way back to the living room and the tree.

It was a real tree in true Connor fashion. Mike had suggested a fake one when they were first married, and Kim had let him know in no uncertain terms that nothing but a real tree would do in her house. It was the way she'd grown up knowing Christmas, and a few needles on the floor wouldn't dissuade her from having one.

When they were all situated, Bennie turned to them. "Now?"

They all laughed and Kim responded, "Absolutely. Have at it, Bennie. It looks like Santa thinks you were a very good boy this year."

"And I was. Wasn't I, Mommy?"

The look of contentment that blanketed Kim's face told the story of their happy family Christmases over the years. It was a tradition she had brought forward to her own family. "Very, very good, Bennie," she told him.

He beamed a wider smile and went to the largest item first. It was in the corner next to the tree, and the wrapping paper was covered with pictures of Santa and his reindeer. They were dashing through the snow, flying through the air, and landing on housetops all over it. An eerie red glow lit the paper from within. With a few tears and a couple of rips, Dino Mountain was born, complete with caves for dinos to live in and a volcano at the top that appeared to be ready to send forth its hot lava from far within its depths.

"Dino Mountain!" he yelled. "Santa, I love you."

Mike smiled at Kim, who was sitting next to him on the sofa, and she took his hand. "That old man gets all the credit," Mike moaned. She gave him a playful poke in the ribs.

"Hey, Bennie," Ed called out. "Stand next to the mountain. I want to get a good picture of it with you."

As Bennie rearranged himself to be next to the mountain, Kim looked at Ed with his video camera and sighed. "Dad, there's such a thing as digital now, you know," she teased him.

"I know, Miss Smarty Pants, but all of our family stuff is still on these things, so I might as well keep using it until I can figure out how to transfer them over to DVDs."

"You know, you have a son who is not only artistic but also a computer genius. Between Steve and Greg, I'm sure we could get every one of your VHS tapes transferred to DVD without any trouble at all."

Bennie looked up. "Uncle Steve and Greg are coming today too. Right?"

They all traded glances. Mike said, "No, Ben, they won't be able to make it."

Disappointment played heavily on Bennie's face. "Again? Why not?"

"They have to visit Greg's family this year."

Bennie pouted for a second or two. "What about Sarah and Uncle Steve and Aunt Laura?"

Jan took over. "Yes, of course, they'll all be here. You and Sarah will be able to play with some presents that you'll find under our tree this afternoon."

"Well, okay. But I'm going to miss Uncle Steve and Greg. I hope they don't forget me."

Another round of glances were exchanged.

"They never will, Ben. Don't worry about that. It's okay to miss them. Anyway, maybe you and Sarah will just happen to find a present or two under our tree that Uncle Steve dropped off yesterday," Jan said, trying to help him through his disappointment.

Bennie's face lightened. "I knew Uncle Steve wouldn't forget me."

"What about Greg? I think his name is on those presents too."

Bennie thought for a moment. "If Uncle Steve likes him, then so do I."

One last round of glances were exchanged. This time they told the tale of proud parents and grandparents who saw a truth in the eyes of unfettered youth.

*****

After they arrived at Jan and Ed's house, Mike and Kim got Bennie settled in with one of new Christmas toys. The four adults gathered in the kitchen. "I hope this works," Jan said.

"It can't hurt," Mike offered.

"You don't know Peter as well as I do. He might just go back to burying himself in his work and being a stranger again," Jan replied.

Ed chimed in, "I don't care. We've got to try something. My father once told me, 'You can lead two jackasses to water, but you can't make them drink. Sometimes they need to be pushed in chin deep before they give it a try.' And so that's what we're going to do. I'm not about to let my boys be broken apart like this any longer."

When the doorbell rang, they all took a collective deep breath and went to greet the guests. "Here goes," Ed said quietly.

When the door opened, Sarah ran to Jan and Jan snatched her up easily. "Hi, honey. Merry Christmas!"

"Merry Christmas, Gramma Jan. Is Bennie here yet?"

"He sure is, sweetheart. He's in the media room playing with some Christmas toys."

Jan set her down, and on her way past Ed, Sarah yelled over her shoulder, "Merry Christmas, Papa!"

"Merry Christ…" Ed's voice faded as she ran out of sight. He tilted his head. "Oh well. Merry Christmas, kids," he said as he hugged both Laura and Peter.

"Merry Christmas, Dad," Laura said.

"Did you hear that Steve can't make it?" he asked.

"Yes, that's too bad," Laura said. "I spoke to Greg about it the other day. It's a shame, but there's nothing we can do about it other than carry on."

"Come on in. Let's get those coats off and warm up by the fire while the kids open some presents."

"Sounds great," Peter agreed.

"Oh no. I left my slippers in the car. I'll be right back," Laura said.

"Nonsense. I'll get them," Peter offered.

"No!" Laura said tensely. "I mean, no. I'll get them. See, I've already got my keys out," she added, fumbling through her purse and withdrawing her keys. "You've had a long week. Relax with your dad and I'll be right back."

"That's right, Peter. Relax by the fire and I'll get you and Dad a beer. Maybe there's a game on?"

"You suggesting a game and a beer—on Christmas? That's the first time I've ever heard that in, well, forever. You feeling all right, Mom?" Peter asked.

"Don't be silly. Daddy's been watching a lot of games lately, and I thought you two would enjoy it. Right, Ed?"

"Huh? Yeah. Right. Sure. Fun. Beer. Come on, Pete."

As they walked toward the fireplace and television, Kim rolled her eyes at Jan and Laura. "Go on out and get your slippers, Laura," she said with a half-smile. Laura shook her head with a grin and went out to get her slippers.

Jan put her arm around Kim's shoulder and turned her toward the kitchen. "Now you know why I turned gray at forty. Let's go and get those two a beer." She giggled. "I can't believe I invited them to watch a game on Christmas Day."

"Desperate times call for desperate measures, Mom," Kim teased her.

Laura came back in after a few minutes. "What took you so long?" Peter asked from the recliner in front of the television.

"Umm… I couldn't find them. They got stuck under the passenger's seat." She dangled them in front of her. "Got 'em. See?"

Kim took another deep breath and whispered to her mother, "These people. They just can't act, can they?"

Jan covered her mouth, stifling a laugh.

*****

"This is really fortunate," Steve said to Greg as he turned the corner leading to his old homestead.

"Fortunate?" Greg repeated.

"Yeah, that Pete and his family decided to go to Disney for the holidays."

"Fortunate for us, but I'm afraid it's going to be really crowded down there on Christmas break."

"I'm sure it was Pete's decision. You know he always gets his own way."

"No, when Laura called me to tell me they were going, she said they've been talking about it a lot and wanted to get Sarah there when she could really enjoy the magic of it all."

"Why'd she call you?"

"Well, luckily Pete told her about the crazy agreement you and he cooked up. She thought it'd be silly for us to pretend to be away when they wouldn't even be there."

Steve nodded. "She's a good kid. Too bad she's married to such an idiot."

"You gotta let it go, Steve. It's poisoning you. If you want to be done with him, then be done, but then let it go."

"Does it not hurt you when you think of your father and mother not fully accepting you?"

"Sure it does. How couldn't it? It hurts, but it's not hate."

"It's different for me. I can't forgive him."

"He was under a lot of stress in the hospital. Just like the rest of your family."

"The only difference is they didn't turn on me like he did, as usual."

"Are you ever going to tell me everything?"

Steve looked out the window. "Yes, but not today. Tomorrow maybe. I don't want to spoil the day."

"We can always hope that today is a good one, I guess."

"What's that supposed to mean?"

Greg stared out the windshield before he spoke. "I guess it's just because your parents would rather have the whole family together. They're not stupid, Steve. They're going to catch on someday. Especially now that we're flip-flopping our excuse not to be there. Someday you both will have to look at each other in the face again."

"I'll deal with that when that time comes, but not before."

"Okay, but remember it's your choice, and it'll probably be sooner than later," Greg countered.

"So be it." Steve quickly changed the subject as they drove passed a bottle recycling return site. He read the sign over the door aloud, "We CAN Recycle It." The word *can* was inside a picture of a tipsy can. "Boy, things have changed over the years."

"How so?" Greg asked.

"That used to be a little corner store we shopped at when I was a kid."

"That place isn't new to you, is it?"

193

"No, but this is only your second time through my old neighborhood, and I thought I'd share some neighborhood history. Besides, I was feeling a little nostalgic too."

"The way you've been acting lately, I didn't think feeling nostalgic about the old days would be someplace you'd want to go," Greg said.

"Thinking about him and what happened always brings me down, but those days weren't all bad."

"That's a start, I guess," Greg said and gave Steve an encouraging smile.

"Don't bank on it, Greg. But that's why I love you. You'll never let me down or let me stay where I shouldn't be in my mind for too long."

"Like I told your dad: the long haul. Nothing less. Here we are." Greg pulled the car into the driveway next to Kim and Mike's car.

"Ah, good. Kim, Mike, and Bennie are already here," Steve said. "That kid always brightens my day."

"Okay, let's go in. Remember, I love you too."

Steve looked at him inquisitively before he got out.

"What?" Greg said. "You're the only one who can get sentimental?"

"No, no problem at all. Get as Christmassy as you want," Steve said. They got out of the car and walked toward the door. "It's lucky we already dropped off our gifts."

*****

Jan and Kim each set a tray of hors d'oeuvres down on the coffee table in front of the television. "Why don't we turn the TV off for a while, guys?"

"But you're the one who told us to put it on," Peter complained halfheartedly.

"I know, but I guess I reconsidered that idea. Here, we've got some chips and dips and eggnog and—"

"Not the fruitcake again, Mom!" Peter protested playfully.

"Your father likes it," she said with a tip of her chin, acting unflustered by his comment. "Go ahead. Take a piece. It won't kill

194

you."

"No, but it might break my toe if I drop it." Peter caught Jan's eye.

"Oh, go on, Pete. Try some. Maybe you'll like it this year," she coaxed him.

He laughed. "Unlikely, but I bet I know a couple of kids who'd like some." He nodded toward the media room, where Bennie and Sarah were playing. "Kids, come on out and have a piece of Gramma Jan's fruitcake."

There wasn't much of a lag between the invitation and their response as Bennie and Sarah came stampeding toward them.

"Mmm, fruitcake. I love the cherries Gramma Jan puts around the top," Bennie said.

"Is there some sweet eggnog in those fancy glasses with Christmas trees painted on them?" Sarah squealed, running alongside Bennie.

"Yes, there is," Jan said, slipping Peter a victorious smile. She slid two glasses to the edge of the coffee table and then placed a slice of fruitcake on a Christmas paper napkin for each of them. "Now try not to make a mess," Jan said.

Bennie answered for the both of them, "We won't, Gramma." With that, they knelt next to the coffee table. Bennie reached for his fruitcake, plucking the candied cherry from the top and gobbling it down. Sarah carefully picked up the eggnog glass.

"Hey, we're here. Merry Christmas," Steve called from the doorway.

Bennie dropped his fruitcake. "Uncle Steve's here!" he said and ran toward the door. It took Sarah a moment longer to set her glass down, but she followed him quickly out of the room.

Peter turned quickly toward Laura and then his parents. "Steve?"

Steve scooped up Bennie. "Merry Christmas, kiddo," he said, and then saw Sarah running toward him. He squatted. "Sarah? I didn't think you'd be here. I thought you were going to Disney."

"I don't think so," she said as she ran into his open arms.

"I didn't think you'd be here either." It was Peter's voice and he didn't sound happy.

Steve looked up to Greg, who only gave him a sheepish

smile. "Likewise," Steve growled.

"Well, isn't this a nice surprise," Jan said. "Now we're all home for Christmas," she added nervously.

"Not for long," Steve grumbled. He set Bennie down and stood, all the while staring at Greg. "You set me up." If looks could kill, Greg would have been toast.

"Not just him," Ed said. "We all did and it was my idea." He turned to the kids. "Bennie, Sarah, get your fruitcake and eggnog and go to the media room and play a little. We have some grown-up stuff to talk about."

"Okay, Papa," they both agreed. But the way their smiles dropped, it was apparent that even they knew something was wrong.

As they wandered off to the media room, cake and eggnog in hand, Jan lashed out at both Steve and Peter. "You two should be ashamed of yourselves. You're breaking those two kids' hearts."

"We wouldn't be if you hadn't meddled where you don't belong," Peter said accusingly. "Grab Sarah, Laura. We're leaving. What'd you do? Put the car out back so he wouldn't see it?"

"That's right, and if that's what it takes to get you two in the same room together to work this crap out, I'd do it all over again. We're not leaving." There was no doubting that Laura was serious—dead serious.

"Get Sarah dressed. We're leaving," Peter demanded.

Laura didn't budge. "No," was all she said, folding her arms across her chest as Ed stepped up.

"We'll all do it over again if need be," Ed added.

"You won't have the opportunity." Peter's voice was cold as ice. "Grab Sarah and meet me in back. I said we're leaving." He started for the kitchen and the back door, but Laura beat him to it. She stood in his way with her arms pressed against the door frame.

"Don't bother, Laura. We'll leave. It's not fair to Ben and Sarah," Steve flared. He turned to leave but bumped directly into Greg, who stood his ground like a sentry at the castle gate.

"Afraid not, Steve," Greg said. "I told you sooner or later. It's sooner. You're going to talk to your brother."

"He's not my brother anymore. He hasn't been since he chose between me and the baseball and football team. His status as big man on campus was more important to him than his own brother." He turned to Mark, "There. Satisfied?"

"Not really, but I'll take the heat if it means getting you and Peter back together again."

"Well, it won't. You wasted your time and broke our trust. You've screwed up everything."

"Now stop. One crisis at a time," Jan said as the voice of reason. "Talk to your brother, Steven," she insisted. "What could possibly be so bad?"

"Okay, but you won't like what you hear. In high school, a kid told the baseball team that I was gay. Not because I came on to him, but because he was trying to stop a rumor that was going around about him. So he threw me under the bus to save his own reputation." Steve scowled at Peter. "Stop me whenever you want if you think I'm not telling the truth."

Peter nodded. "Go on."

"So the team stopped talking to Peter, and when he approached them about it, they told him to keep his queer brother out of the locker room. So he did. He told me I was an embarrassment to him and I was ruining his life. He told me to quit the JV baseball team and stay out of his life forever, and I did just that. He deserted me. Dumped me like some used garbage just to be accepted by his friends."

Ed turned to Peter. "Is this true, Pete?"

"That's about it," he said defensively.

"And you can't let this go?" Ed asked them both.

"You'd think so, but that's not all of it."

"Well, then, by all means. Tell us, Peter," Steve taunted him.

"You deserted me too," Peter said solemnly.

"Me? Deserted you? You've got to be kidding me. You've got a strange definition of desertion, I guess."

Peter shook off the comment and continued, "Things never really got better for me, Steve. Even though I gave you the heave-ho, they never let me back in. Even with that, I could have gotten over it, but it was this whole que—" He stopped and rephrased, "Gay thing, and all your artsy stuff that took everything from me." He seemed to spit the word *gay* from his mouth as if it were poison.

"Pete, don't you hear yourself? You're thinking in stereotypes," Steve countered. "It wasn't the so-called 'gay thing' that made me take my path, no more than being straight made you an aggressive stockbroker. It's just who we are. That's our core. Not every gay man is artistic, any more than every sports star is straight. We're all just people. People who have different paths."

"It didn't look that way to me," Peter shot back angrily. "Remember, I was just a kid then too. It changed… ruined my whole life. It got so I couldn't even hear or read about it without getting angry."

Laura came up behind Peter and wrapped her arm around his waist and then took his hand. He was looking at her when his first tear fell. "I had nothing until I found Laura."

"Why do you say you had nothing, Peter?" she asked. "You always had Mom, Dad, Kim, *and* me, even if you weren't talking to Steve."

"That's just it. I lost Steve, my best friend, years before the baseball thing."

Steve took a half step forward, "What?"

Peter looked Steve straight in the eyes. "You were my only friend. I didn't really like fishing that much. What I liked was exploring with you. I was Davy Crockett and you were Daniel Boone. I was the driver and you were my pit man. We did everything together. Even though we walked up and down that creek a hundred times, it was like the first time each time we did it. We were explorers at every turn. Then all of a sudden you weren't there. Even when you were there, you really weren't. You had your paints and your world of art, and all I had was the damn fishing pole. The last time I asked you to come with me, you told me to grow up. That you'd grown past all that. All I had left was Kimmy trailing behind me…" He looked at Kim. "I'm sorry, Kimmy. No offense."

She frowned a little and then said, "None taken."

Steve looked deeply into his brother's eyes and knew Peter was telling the truth from his heart. "Pete, I was just a kid too. I don't remember saying that. I don't even remember that discussion ever happening."

"Sure, why would you? You were just fine and I was alone. Later on at Merry Moose, when you and Kim were late and Dad blamed me, he said the same thing. 'Grow up.'"

Ed interrupted, "I didn't know, Pete. I was so worried that

198

your brother was being reclusive that I didn't see you. That you were hurting too."

"I know, Dad. And how could you? I was putting up a pretty good act. Then that guy told me Steve was being… gay with his brother, and it suddenly all made sense." Peter turned to Steve. "This gay crap took you away. You deserted me. So when the team told me to keep you out, it didn't seem much different. You hadn't spent any time with me for years, and I figured what the hell. I needed a life and you'd let me go long ago and it was all about this gay stuff. It took my best friend away, and I hated it. I was mad at you because of it."

"Well, what the hell was I supposed to do? We were kids, and you stopped being my brother!" Steve yelled.

"You deserted me first!" Peter didn't hold anything back either.

"That sounds like an awful long time ago to still be mad at each other about it. Doesn't it?"

The sound of Bennie's voice turned them all toward the media room, where he and Sarah were standing.

"Ben, how long have you been listening?" Mike asked.

"Long enough to know Uncle Steve and Uncle Pete are mad at each other."

"It's okay, kids. It's just grown-up talk. Go back and play with your toys," Mike told them calmly.

"We can't. Sarah broke it and it was brand new, but I can't be mad at her like Uncle Pete and Uncle Steve are at each other. She said she was sorry. Why don't they say they're sorry and stop being mad?"

"It's not that simple, Bennie," Steve tried to explain.

"Why not? Don't you love each other anymore?"

It was straight and to the point, and something no one had ever thought to ask them before.

Steve knew he really wasn't ready to say that. "It's not that, Ben. It's just that…"

Peter spoke up when Steve got lost for words. "We just don't see eye to eye anymore."

"That's okay, Uncle Steve. Sarah likes dolls and I like cars, but we still love each other."

"It's not that simple, Ben," Steve said again.

"I think it could be if you wanted it to be," was Bennie's simple answer, but it was so full of truth.

A long silence fell over the room. Finally Ed spoke. "He's right, boys. Rarely do things in life go as planned. As hard as we may try, it seems like something comes up. When you plan on a big project and the grain in the wood isn't just right—or worse yet, there's a big old ugly knot right in the middle of it—you've just got to make the best out of it. When you plan on lots of grandkids and something comes up, you might not have as many grandkids as you planned, but instead you get another son." He reached over and rubbed Greg's back. "We're blessed with a beautiful family, and I want us to enjoy our family for as long as we can. God almost took me away, but at the last moment I think he gave me a choice. A choice to give up or fight for my family, and I chose to fight. This family is my heart. Can't we all put this behind us?" He surveyed each and every one of them.

Steve broke the silence. "Pete, I know it wasn't easy for you in high school. I know I was the cause of your falling out with the teams and, well, just about everybody in your class. But please believe me when I say I didn't come on to Jimmy. It happened just like I told you. I didn't want to cause that sort of trouble for you. I knew the school… the world wasn't ready yet. He came on to me and I shut him down to keep us safe from that stigma. Unfortunately, it wasn't safe, so you and I paid the price for it. I understand your anger at the time, and I'm sorry we never got past it. Bennie is right. Now is the time. Don't you think?"

Peter stepped closer. "I'm such an ass. You were right at the hospital. I've been able to accept and get past every other prejudice, but still I wasn't able to accept you, my own flesh and blood. I let the past cloud my judgment and poison my heart. I blamed you and the rest of the gays for all of my troubles. The worst part of it is I don't even have any troubles anymore. I have a beautiful wife, a wonderful daughter, a good job, and everything I could possibly want. I never let the past go. I let my anger over all those years become a judgment against you and Greg and every other gay couple I'd ever seen.

"Truth be known, with my attitude about women then and

how easy I found it jumping from one to another, I'd probably be on my third wife by now, because I had no respect for them. After that episode, my dates in high school were few and far between. I learned to appreciate each girl I dated for who she was, and that continued right on through college until I met Laura. Those days became a life-changing event for me, whether I like to admit it or not. I thought they were horrible, but really, they saved me.

"I'm sorry I never took time to look at it like this. In an ironic way, all this crap has helped make me a better man, and I owe it all to you. Those days in high school were hard for us both, but it's time I grew up. I'm ready to be your brother again, Steve. If you'll have me."

Steve walked toward Peter. "More than you know. Of course I will."

The men hugged. It was real, affectionate, and long overdue.

The End

Made in the USA
Middletown, DE
19 July 2018